ORCA AND BIRD

ORCA AND BIRD

a novel by Anna Chilvers

Bluemoose

This book is dedicated to the memory of my sister,
Sarah Joy, 1971–2017.

First published in 2025 by
Bluemoose Books Ltd
25 Sackville Street
Hebden Bridge
West Yorkshire
HX7 7DJ

www.bluemoosebooks.com

British Library Cataloguing-in-Publication data
A catalogue record for this book is available from the British Library

ISBN 978-1-91-569337-2

Printed and bound in the UK by Short Run Press

As you journey through this tale of forests you will encounter species of tree which are marked by small leaves in the margin which relate to a collection of poems and prose pieces at the end of the book. If you choose you might pause to read them, in the way you might pause to admire specimen trees on a walk in the woods. These pieces aren't part of the main story, so if you prefer, continue with the novel and read them when you get to the end.

Trying to photograph an ancient yew

the robin flies away
sunlight banishes the dark spaces
the years don't show up
on the screen
there's no smell

turn the phone off
touch the bark
inhale

Prologue

She isn't supposed to dream. She isn't even supposed to sleep. She shuts down at night so that she can be rebooted, updates loaded, files cleaned and tidied. For this she is meant to go to a safe place. If they knew that she sometimes lay down on moss beneath a tree, that she called it sleep and that she dreamed things which were not connected to her hard drive, they would say she was malfunctioning. They would call her in for a wipe and reload.

She dreamed of Bird. She saw him, full on. He stood on a low branch of a tree and dropped his head to one side, looking at her quizzically – yes, quizzically was the word that came up in her memory – meaning curious, with interest, maybe slightly mocking. He showed off the left side of his body and then the right, all the time maintaining eye contact with her. But now she can't remember what he looked like, what colour of bird he was, or his size.

Yesterday when clear light was falling through the branches of the trees and landing on the path in splats and pools, she'd seen two butterflies circling each other in the middle of the ride. They were brown, patterned, fluttering fast as their wings absorbed the sun's warmth. Speckled Wood. It came up straight away. The pattern, the colour, the way of flying, all came together and the name popped up.

Why couldn't she do that with Bird?

It wouldn't do of course, in the report. There's a bird, but he never shows himself, he's always just out of sight. A flash across the sky, a call from the depths of a thicket. *What call?* Dorcas will say. *Have you recorded it? All bird calls are stored in your drive, you should be able to find it.* She can't recall the sound.

She just knows that she has heard it. The same way she knows she saw Bird in her dreams.

Chapter One

A rustle of leaves, the beeping of the dustbin lorry from the estate on the far side of the wood, the first birds. This is the way the morning always begins. Before the lines of grey appear between the birches, before the sky turns from black to navy blue, these noises mark the start of the new day. Orca can smell the severed trunks of felled trees. She knows some are larch and some are red oak, but she hasn't yet learned to distinguish them by smell. She closes her eyes. A dog is barking, but it's far away. Her limbs creak as she unbends them. She wonders if it's the damp air getting in. She will talk to Dorcas. There may be something they can do – a lubricant in her joints perhaps, or an extra layer of waterproofing on the outside.

Now another bird has begun, a different sort. She could look up their names, but for now she just listens. The two of them seem to be having a conversation. One chirps a few notes, then it stops and the other twitters back at a higher pitch. Perhaps she is intruding on their morning ritual. Every night she finishes in a different place and folds her body into resting mode. This time here, beneath this tree, where these two birds are greeting the new day.

The sudden crunch of feet on gravel. A person. No animal would be so heavy footed. She can't see them. The stars have faded, and there's no real light in the sky. It will be an hour or more before the sun makes its entrance in the east, and the dog walkers don't usually appear until then. She's not seen a human in the woods at night.

The birds are still conversing, unbothered at the approach. Orca stays still, in the black space between the canopy and the ground.

The person has a light, a beam that is coming her way. Narrow at one end, spreading out in a long thin cone. White light, moving erratically, left then right, then upwards at the sky, creating a line of illuminated foliage, as though they were brandishing a sword.

The beam moves across her. What is this person looking for? If it's her, how should she behave? Dorcas didn't say anything about this sort of thing. She said, rest through the hours of darkness, start moving again when the light returns. In the daylight hours you will meet people, and some of them may speak to you. Use the phrases you have been taught. *Good morning. What a lovely day. Do you think it looks like rain?* Be polite, but move on as soon as you can. She didn't say there would be people in the dark with light beaming from their hands.

The beam comes back, slower this time. It finds Orca's feet, then her folded legs. She wants to close down, but she can't. Whatever is going to happen next, she will be present for it.

The light travels slowly up her body until it rests on her face.

The birds have stopped singing. She can hear the dustbin lorry reversing again. The dog is quiet now. The only other sound is the movement of leaves above her.

"Hey," the person says.

Orca hasn't turned on her voice yet. She parts her lips but can't speak. She moistens them with her tongue. The systems are booting up. She closes her eyes, opens them again.

"I am Orca."

"What are you doing here?"

The voice is light, in the higher end of the human register. Female then. She feels some of the tension leaving her body.

"I am resting," she says. "I am the surveyor."

"Can you help me?"

Orca can only see bright light. She narrows her eyes.

"Sorry, I blind you."

The light vanishes and silence fills up the space between them. In the aftermath of the glare Orca can see red circles on black, but her eyes adjust until she sees a figure in a hooded coat.

"What sort of help?"

"I need to get away. The baby – he is in the van – I have to get him ..."

"I don't understand."

The person takes a deep breath that shakes her body. She breathes it out again. She makes a noise, and then she clears her throat. "I am staying in a van, we are at the carpark. My boyfriend, he looks for beetles."

"The khaki van with the yin and yang symbols?"

"Tak." She pauses. "You have seen us?"

"I heard people in that van, they were shouting. A baby was crying."

The person takes another of those shaky breaths. "Yes, that was us. That is why ..."

There are a series of sniffs. Orca notices the birds have started singing again since the torch was turned off. It's getting lighter. She can now see a clear outline of the person from the van. The trees behind are long ribbons of black on dark grey.

"That is why what?"

"We fight. I need to get away, but the baby is with him. He won't let me have him."

"What can I do?"

"You could distract him. So I can open the side door and get Eli."

"Eli is the baby?"

"Tak."

"I would need to distract your boyfriend for many minutes to give you time to get away."

"I think yes."

"What if Eli cries. He has a very loud cry."

"He won't cry. He will be asleep. He loves me, he will be quiet for me."

"I would need to get your boyfriend away from the van."

"Oh thank you, thank you bardzo."

The person leans towards Orca as though she is going to hug her. Orca steps back. The tree is behind, she can't go further.

"I haven't said I will do this."

"Oh."

"Why should I do this thing for you?"

"Please. Please help us. We need to get away. Look!" She turns the bright light on again and shines it at her own face. Her cheeks are wet and shine white in the glare. Around her eye the skin is much darker. Her lower lip on one side is swollen. "He did this to me. We aren't safe. Please help us, there is no one else."

"Your lives are in danger?"

Another pause. "I don't think ... We are in danger. It is not safe."

Orca closes her eyes. This is not included in the training. There is nothing in the surveying programme about helping people in danger. She could say *no*, she could say *I hope you have a nice day*, she could say, *this is not within my capabilities, you should call the authoritie*s. But this would be a lie, she would be pretending to be less complex than she actually is.

The uploads from Dorcas are at a surface level. There are deeper levels of programming, older than the surveying instructions, as old as Orca herself. This person is in danger. If she can help, without endangering herself or her mission, then she should do so.

"Let's go."

The person is crying now. The signs have come together, the strange noises and shaking, the wet skin on her face. These things together make crying. Orca tries to bend her mouth into a smile, searches the banks for something appropriate to say.

"It will be OK."

In the car park all is quiet. Orca stands with the woman in the edge of the trees. Early daylight lies damp and heavy on everything, the new leaves on trees, the picnic benches by the café, the children's play equipment. The grey van is the only vehicle parked on the wide expanse of tarmac. It's covered with a layer of condensation.

"You wait here," Orca says in her lowest register. "I will go to the road on the other side. I will get the man from the van ..."

"His name is ..."

"No, don't tell me. It is better that I don't know that." On the far side of the carpark a fox runs diagonally across tarmac, through the hedge into the lane. "When he is out of sight, you get Eli and run. Go through the woods, not along the road. There are many paths and he will not know which you have taken. He will not be able to drive the van in pursuit. Turn often, and keep moving"

"Thank you ..."

Orca shakes her head. She doesn't look at the woman. She walks down to where the forest drive meets the lane, then back along on the other side of the hedge, until she is beside the gap the fox had shown her.

She could use her knife, but it would be too neat. Instead she searches the hedge until she finds a piece of blackthorn with spikes half the length of her thumb. She rolls up her left trouser leg, grits her teeth, then pushes a spike into her shin, dragging it to the right so it carves through flesh. Blood wells immediately, and it is not hard to begin to scream.

Once she starts it fills her, becomes a thing in itself. She can see the blood, can feel heat and pain in her flesh, but it's the noise that takes her over. It wells up through her throat and she pushes it out with her larynx, a single long arrghh that winds around her head and into her ears before spinning out through the morning air. The leaves in the hedge tremble, a bird flies up.

p.270

Orca runs out of breath, but it wasn't enough. It might have woken him, but he'll be lying in the darkness wondering what the hell was that.

She takes another deep breath and starts again, this time differently.

"Help! Help! I need help.'

Down the lane the Grange has been turned into an old people's home, added to with red-brick extensions. There could be people already awake there. Hopefully the band of trees between should muffle the noise.

"Help! Help!"

The blood is running down her leg in a thin sheet, like water over a weir. She hears the door of the van open. She puts her hand in the blood and wipes it across her face.

"Hello? Is someone there?"

"Help me!"

The van door closes, then there are footsteps. He follows the same route as the fox, but he's bigger than the fox. He has to get down on his belly and wriggle through the gap. His head appears first, topped with sandy curls, then blue eyes moving left and right. He sees her.

"Oh my god! Are you OK?"

She holds out her bloody hands, then her leg.

"Please help me."

He walks his elbows until he's far enough through to draw his knees into a crawl, then he's on his feet, crouching next to her.

"What's happened? Show me."

"I feel faint."

"You need sugar. I've got chocolate in the van. I'll go ..."

"Don't leave me."

"I have a phone there. I can call for help."

She sits on the verge, puts her head in her hands and cries. The blood flow from the wound is slowing, but she has managed to spread it. It's hard to tell the source.

"I can't move."

He pulls his t-shirt over his head. He's wearing grey jersey shorts, sleeping clothes. The t-shirt is orange. He uses it to dab at the blood, sees the seepage on her shin.

"I'll tie this around your leg above the wound. It will slow down the blood flow. Then we must get you off the road, get some proper help."

Orca hears a click, the smallest sound, from back in the carpark. She wails again. He hasn't noticed the sound, he is concentrating on tying the t-shirt round her leg. He ties it so tightly she gasps.

Then he's standing in front of her holding out his hands. He has flipflops on his feet; his chest glistens with blond hairs. She allows him to pull her to standing.

"Lean on me. It's not far, just along to the entrance and round to the carpark. My van's parked there."

She manages to make the walk last ten minutes, hobbling slowly, stopping every few steps to cry again. She's surprised how easy it is. When Sylva disappeared she hadn't cried, but obviously the function is enabled. She just hadn't thought to use it before.

He's becoming agitated. It's a long time to leave a sleeping infant in a van, and she is pulling heavily on his shoulder.

They round the corner into the carpark and he gasps. The door of the van is wide open. Orca curses the woman inwardly. If she'd closed the door behind her it would have given them another couple of minutes. Probably she didn't want to risk the noise.

The man lets go of Orca and runs to the van. He leaps inside and gives a shout. There is some crashing and banging. Is he looking for the child? Does he think it has hidden itself? Or rolled off the bed and underneath?

He appears in the doorway and thrusts a phone into Orca's hand.

"Here phone the police – and an ambulance if you need one. That woman has stolen my child."

"Your child?"

"Yes. My little boy was asleep in the van. While I've been helping you, she's kidnapped him."

"She?"

"My girlfriend. We'd had an argument?"

"His mother?"

"No, she's not his mother. Look, I'm going to look for them, they can't have got far. Please – phone the police."

He runs across the car park and vanishes between the trees. Those at the edge of the forest stand still in the morning sunshine, the branches on one side reflecting the glowing sky. The birds are singing loudly now. The forest has swallowed the man completely, she can't hear him.

She examines her leg. The bleeding has stopped. It's a nasty wound, but it will heal. It produced a lot of blood, which was the intention, but it's clean, and not even as deep as the thorn she'd used. She looks inside the van. It's pretty tidy. There's a travel cot filling the floor space – empty of course – next to it some nappy changing items. She takes the wipes and uses some to clean her leg, her face, her hands. She walks over to the café and throws the bloody wipes in a bin by the kiosk, then looks at the phone in her hand.

She really doesn't want to be involved.

She dials 999 and asks for the police. She tells them there has been a fight involving a child, possibly violence, possibly kidnapping. When the police ask for her name she hangs up. She wipes the phone clean and leaves it in the van, then goes back into the woods.

It's darker here. The trees are keeping the sun to themselves, up above in the canopy. She walks fast. She doesn't want to be anywhere near when the police arrive. Dorcas explicitly said, don't get involved. Be polite, answer as necessary. Dorcas will be angry if she finds out what she's done.

She does a body check. Heart rate up. Perspiration. Over-production of saliva. Tingling feelings in her legs and along the inner edges of her upper arms. Her body is behaving like a human's. The trees around her are still. She can feel their presence, but they are unmoving, unmoved by what has happened.

She turns onto a narrow path. Barely a path, a gap between trees. She will move into a denser part of the wood, hide herself, try to turn off the images flashing across her mind, the livid bruised eye, the panic-stricken face of a father, the empty cot. She puts her hand on the bark of a young oak. It is neither warm nor cold.

Chapter Two

Up to now Orca has mostly followed orders. During daylight she has walked, recorded, moved. At the fall of darkness she has found a place to close down. But this day is not like the others. Every time she blinks it is there, the baby blanket pushed to one side, the small indentation where a head had been.

When she's deep enough into the wood she stops. The trees here are young. Looking at their thin trunks she thinks fifty years, perhaps seventy. They are birch and larch, crowding closely together. Too close. She leaves the narrow path by a bloom of holly shrub. Behind its darkness she closes down all systems, allows her legs to bend, closes her eyes, switches off.

Let everything that will happen, happen. When she resurfaces it will all be done. The man, the girl, the baby, the police – they will all have gone. The woods will have returned to a state of sanctuary. She will be able to carry on.

Four hours later when she wakes the sun is high in the sky. She can feel its warmth even before she starts reactivation.

She does a quick scan. Throbbing in her leg. Brain surface blank, no images. Holly leaves pricking against her skin. She opens her eyes and looks at their dark shine, the depth of green.

She closes her eyes again, and an image flashes. It's not the man or the woman though. A child is running along a path. She's wearing a red coat made of plasticky material. The hem and hood of the coat are rimmed with fake fur. She's wearing brown shoes and white socks, and the soles flash as she runs. On either side of the path holly bushes loom. There is frost on the ground and the girl is laughing. As the girl reaches the bend, the clip returns to the beginning. Five seconds. It loops.

Orca stands quickly and opens her eyes. She has wasted enough time. She must start work.

She makes her way back between birch and larch to the main ride. People are about. It's the weekend and the sun is out. They have brought dogs, children, grandchildren. They are shouting and running, chasing sticks.

Orca nods in greeting, passes by quickly. She realises she's returning to the visitor centre. She examines her motives and finds curiosity. Will there be any signs of the events of the early hours? Will the van still be there?

The children's play area is crawling with children. The café is open and all the picnic benches are full. Orca stands in the edge of the trees where she had stood with the woman at break of day.

At the nearest picnic table are a couple with a baby. The woman is wearing sunglasses. The man has reddish curls and is bouncing a baby on his knee. All three of them are smiling and laughing.

The man glances in her direction and sees her. He waves.

"Hey," he calls. "Come and join us."

Slowly Orca walks over to the table and sits down.

"This is the woman I met earlier," he says to his partner. "The one who'd cut her leg."

Orca and the woman look at each other.

"This is my girlfriend, Nadia." He joggles his knee up and down and the baby grins.

Nadia holds out her hand in greeting. Orca can't see her eyes behind the sunglasses. They shake hands and Nadia's is dry and light.

"It is nice to meet you. I hope your leg is healing."

"Thank you. It wasn't as bad as I thought. There was a lot of blood."

The man introduces himself as Nick, and the baby Eli. Nadia offers Orca some water. Nobody says anything about the police. The baby is saying words, which all sound much the same to

Orca, but Nick says they are *car, bird, drink, Nadia*. Orca sips her water. An aeroplane is flying high overhead, a distant hum, joining this place to all the others it will fly over. She is disorientated. She's not used to sleeping in the day. She's not used to chatting with strangers.

"Are you on a journey?" she asks.

The van has been here for a couple of days. It was two nights ago that she heard them arguing.

"I'm an ecologist," says Nick. "And an entomologist. I'm surveying the woods for beetles."

"And you too Nadia?"

The woman shrugs. 'I am just coming along. I like the forest, but I am not a specialist."

"This is our last day here. We're heading east."

"What about you?" asks Nadia. "What are you doing in the forest?"

"I am also a surveyor. I'm studying the forest holistically, building a complete picture of every aspect – mapping all types of plants and animals across the woods, recording the pathways, and the effect of the forest on the human body. For example, heart rate, blood pressure – but also the deeper physical systems – digestive enzymes, salivary amylase, the lymphatic system. When changes occur, I monitor what has changed in the environment. Over time we hope to build up enough data to discover if there are correlations."

The baby burps and Nick lifts him to his shoulder, rubs his back in a circular motion.

Nadia frowns. "How do you know what is going on in your body. Don't you need a lot of equipment."

"I am the equipment."

Nick waves a milky tissue at them. "I'll throw this in the bin." He walks away, singing softly under his breath to the baby.

Nadia is still staring at Orca. "What do you mean?" Orca shrugs. She glances at Nick who has thrown the tissue away and is returning. Before he reaches the table she asks "Are you OK?"

"Thank you for your help." Nadia's voice is low, and then Nick is back.

"Hey, we're getting the barbeque out tonight. Do you want to join us?"

Orca looks from one to the other. Nick is large and exuberant, his curls glowing in the sun, reflected in the golden fluff on the baby's head. He's wearing a yellow t-shirt with a panda on it, brown camouflage shorts. He's smiling and friendly. Nadia's eyes are invisible behind the dark sunglasses. She wears black jeans and a black t-shirt and is as skinny as the shadow of a young birch.

"OK, what time?" Orca replies.

The day continues sunny and by the time Orca returns to the top of the woods the shadows are long, the grass on the top field dry. Nick has set up the barbeque on a concrete platform near the picnic tables. He calls out in welcome and hands Orca a beer. She hadn't realised there would be other people as well as Nick and Nadia. Nick introduces her to the forest ranger, a couple who run the food kitchen in the village pub, the daughter of the man who runs the post office, another girl and two men whom Nick had met in the pub. A party. She hasn't uploaded the socialising programme.

Soon she finds it doesn't matter. Beer is flowing and the voices get louder. No one seems to mind that she is sitting on her own on the grass. Nick is in his element, handing out burgers and beer and jokes, everyone is laughing. He is the centre of energy and the others circle around him, chatting in ones and twos. Even Nadia is animated, beer in one hand, baby on the other arm, her bruises hidden by make-up. When someone starts strumming a guitar Nadia moves her feet, tentatively at first, then her hips sway and she is dancing, swinging the baby so it giggles.

When the sun disappears over the horizon Orca decides to slip away. She'd tipped the beer in the grass, and she hasn't eaten anything – it isn't her sort of food. She doesn't think anyone will notice if she's there or not. Since his initial welcome, Nick's been busy being the genial host, and Nadia is dancing with the girl from the post office.

Orca walks quickly down the hill. The woods are waiting, the entrance as dark as a hole. But when she steps through it isn't completely dark. She can see the black trunks and the shine of the path winding between them. She walks quickly down the main ride, then turns and turns again, aiming for the centre of the woods. When she finds the place where a tall larch has fallen across the path, she heads into the undergrowth to shut down for the night. Darkness falls and she hears owls calling. Somewhere a muntjac barks.

The next morning begins in the normal way, with songbirds, the wood pigeon's soft call, the last owls of the night. The sun is glinting off trunks making them glow like fire. Orca slides her hand into her pocket and finds a piece of paper which wasn't there before the party.

It's a takeaway food menu, folded into four. She opens it up and finds a message written in black felt pen – *Please help me, Nadia.*

Orca walks up to the field at the top of the woods. The barbecue has been tidied away. They haven't left any rubbish, there is just some flattened grass. The car park is empty.

She has choices. Or maybe she doesn't. Maybe all she has are orders and choices are for others. She returns to the woods and takes the top path that runs along the edge near the road. It's a wide gravelled path, signed to show that it's suitable for wheelchairs. The trees in this part of the wood are American red oak. The oldest are a hundred years old.

She leaves the path, places her hands on the bark of an oak and stretches out her back which is still stiff from the night's folding.

She must gather data from the forest.

She must keep interaction with humans to a minimum.

She must not leave the forest to search for random individuals who have requested her help.

At the party she'd noticed Nadia chatting to the girl from the post office. The post office is at the end of the road. She can see the road through the trees. She'd only have to leave the wood for ten minutes.

It's too early. The post office won't be open for hours.

She goes back to the path and sits down in the middle, her legs crossed. The gravel is sharp, digging into her thighs through the fabric of her trousers. She places her hands on the ground. Underneath the imported gravel the earth is red. Red earth, red oaks. The gravel is light grey. The red oaks were planted because people wanted their wood packed in close for maximum productivity, then culled because they weren't native.

She closes her eyes.

Sap rises, sap leaks, tears well, blood seeps.

Behind her lids she sees the path before the gravel was laid, a red path that is narrow and winds between closely planted trees. Young trees, their roots still making friends with the soil. They crowd the path, keeping out the light. She's running after the girl in the red coat. She can feel the impact of hard soles on packed mud as she runs fast, one foot, the other. She can see the legs of the girl in front, the flash of white socks, the red plastic, the black fur. The path winds – the girl vanishes, then comes back into view.

Orca's feet stop short at the edge of a huge hole.

The girl has disappeared.

She knows from the data that American soldiers were sent here during the war to live in the old manor house which was then bombed out of existence. The wood still bears the marks.

The bomb hole has brambles growing in the bottom, and there is litter caught in it – a crisp packet, a piece of tissue, a plastic drink bottle half hidden by grass. There is not meant to be any litter in these woods. How have these pieces been missed? Where is the girl?

Orca opens her eyes. She is still sitting in the middle of the wide gravel path. The trees have backed off leaving a wide verge. Light fills the space they have left behind. The red clay is hidden by grey gravel and the path is accessible.

She gets to her feet. For the next two hours she walks, registering what she sees. She notes the plants growing at the sides of the path, the shrubs and trees which are further back. She lists their names, and when she is unsure, she refers to the database. She is getting good at this now. She recognises most of the plants that grow in these woods. She knows some of the mosses and liverworts, but not so many of these.

Orca is making a map of the wood, which includes all the plants she finds, and the type of paths they grow near – wide accessible paths, signposted walks of varying length, denoted by different coloured marks on wooden poles, small paths known only to locals and dogwalkers, animal paths, stream beds. She is also taking soil samples and noting the day to day weather conditions. The wood isn't huge – not even a hundred and fifty acres – but that makes it possible to map it in intricate detail. She started with the trees, then she moved on to the higher plants. Later she will attempt the lower plants, before moving on to mammals, invertebrates, fungus. In the past these surveys would be done by many different experts, but Dorcas is hoping that in time Orca will be able to collect all that they need.

She doesn't usually keep track of the time – not clock time. She wakes when it gets light, and shuts down when it's too dark to see any more. The passing of minutes and hours are less important than the position of the sun in the sky or the extent of cloud cover.

At ten minutes to nine she changes direction and walks swiftly up through the woods to the road. She arrives at the post office at five past the hour. There is a small queue of people holding parcels or clutching pieces of card or brown envelopes. The post office is also a shop selling basic groceries and stationery items. The post office man's daughter is behind the shop counter. She looks tired. A cup of tea is steaming on the counter in front of her.

She looks up when she senses Orca waiting. "Hello, can I help you?"

"You're a friend of Nadia's?"

The girl frowns and squints at her. She is sweating slightly although it isn't particularly warm. She smells faintly of alcohol.

"Were you ...?"

"I was at the barbeque last night. I left early. I need to find Nadia."

"Their van – her and Nick – it's up at the country park. They won't be awake yet. I wouldn't be if ..." she glances around the shop. "I'm working for my dad for a bit. We all had a skinful last night."

"Their van is gone."

The girl sits back and creases her forehead. "You sure? Did you look in both sections of the carpark?"

"They aren't there. Do you know where they were going?"

"That's really weird. I can't see either of them being fit to drive – and they've got the baby as well."

"They were planning to leave today. Do you know where they were going?"

"Sussex. No Suffolk. Somewhere like that."

"Did they name the place? The forest?"

The girl picks up her tea and cradles it in both hands. She lifts it to her lips and looks at Orca through the steam. People in the post office queue are watching them, listening to their conversation.

"If they did I don't remember. What do you want them for?"

Dorcas told her always to be honest, never lie. Orca can feel the throb of blood behind the cut in her leg. It’s healing well, but there is heat in it. Dorcas also said she didn’t have to offer information if she wasn’t asked.

“Nadia asked me for something.”

“I could text her, ask her if she’d like you to send it to her.”

“No, that wouldn’t work.” If Nadia wanted her to contact her by phone she would have written the number on the takeaway menu. “I need to find her.”

“Maybe they’ve just driven somewhere to get breakfast. They might be back by now. I can’t see them setting off until after lunch.”

“Thank you for your help.” Orca walks to the door, then turns back. “If you contact Nadia, please don’t tell her I was asking for her. I want to surprise her.”

The girl shrugs. It will have to do.

Orca is walking back up the road when the girl shouts after her.

“Hey, you!”

Orca turns. The girl is standing on the pavement, still holding the mug in two hands.

“They said there were really old holly trees. Like, the oldest.’

Orca nods. “Thank you.”

She returns to the carpark. She knows the girl is wrong – Nick and Nadia had gone hours ago, while it was still dark. They won’t be back. But she has to start somewhere.

There’s a lot of holly in this wood. It fills up spaces between other trees, bursting with dark, shiny life. Sometimes the narrower paths pass between holly shrubs and Orca has to squeeze through, her limbs protected by clothing, her face scraped by the sharp points – never enough to break the skin. She has tried to smell holly, sure something so green must be aromatic, but the holly holds its secrets, presents a hard surface, protects what it knows.

p.271

Orca has mapped the trees in this wood, and she included holly although it mostly grows as a shrub here. Now she is meant to be mapping the flowering plants. But her mind walks the paths through red oaks, through limes, through larch, wild service trees, ash, alder, birch. And always holly.

There is a flourish of it at the back of the children's playground. But she would be seen there, she wants some privacy for this conversation. Right, left, twist this way, turn that. She knows she can't get lost anymore. She has walked all the paths and their grooves are imprinted on her. They have become part of her. Even when she leaves the path she is held in their web.

An animal path skirts around a number of bushes which crowd together in a shape that might once have been a circle. She puts her hood up and fastens it beneath her chin, then, head down, pushes between the branches. The spikes press against her clothing, she can feel them running across gortex like the light scrape of fingernails.

Shrubby growth has nearly filled the centre of the circle, but there is space for her to stand without leaves in her face. When she turns forty-five degrees she can crouch. She feels the bushes pressing against the back of her head, but they are curious enough to leave her space to breathe.

She searches the database. The oldest holly trees.

"OK," she says. "Where have they gone? Nick, Nadia, the child? Where are the oldest of your tribe?"

The database gives various options so she narrows the search, remembering the girl in the post office had said Sussex or Suffolk. These counties aren't next to each other. Why was the girl not sure? Orca says the words out loud. The words begin with the same sound, perhaps that's why she mixed them up.

"Suffex, Sussolk, Suffolk, Sussex."

The hollies shiver in a breeze. The database has some entries, but many of them are not relevant. Pub names, arboretums, garden centres. An ancient oak wood in Suffolk with some of the tallest hollies in the country.

"Is this the place?" she asks. "Is this where Nadia has gone?"

The breeze has passed on and the branches are still. She will wait. She has learned patience since she came to the woods. Some things can be learned with a touch on a screen, by logging in to the information networks. In the woods knowledge comes more slowly. She closes the database, shuts off the communication networks. The last thing she wants now is a message from Dorcas, asking how she's getting on, wanting a progress report.

One of the shrubs has a thick stem – not yet a trunk but sturdy enough to lean against – if you don't mind the spikes. Orca parts the branches to make room for herself. They bristle, but she ignores them. What can they do to her? Scratch at her clothes? Prick her skin? She leans against the stem. The branches close again, sealing her in.

"Where is Nadia?" she asks.

Chapter Three

The words from Nadia are enigmatic. *Please help me.* What might she need help with? Why did she not speak to Orca about it? Orca thinks this through. If Nadia's need was something she could speak about she would have spoken to her at the barbecue, or earlier in the country park with Nick and the baby. The only other time Nadia said she needed help was in the woods in the dark. Orca thinks about that moment. Did it really happen? She slides her fingers to her shin. There is the wound. If she presses the flesh next to it there is a warm glow of pain. The cut has dried to a line, a crust is forming. The moment in the woods was soon after shut-down and the memory is grainy, but what else could it be? Words come into her mind – *dream, imagination* – these words are not attached to her mission. She is to collect data, information, facts. She pulls the takeaway menu from her pocket and looks at the message. *Please help me.* It is real. It is marked in black ink across the names of pizzas and burgers. Nadia's need is a fact.

Is the need urgent? Is there a time factor? The note does not say. The way that Nadia delivered the note suggests danger. In the morning dark she had said the danger was Nick. Later Orca had met Nick and he didn't seem dangerous. He seemed to carry sunshine within him. He smiled and everyone around him smiled too, except Nadia. Nadia was thin and dark and her light was like the light of the moon. Could Orca believe that Nick was a danger?

The sun can burn.

The sun can scorch and dessicate.

Is this wood in Suffolk the right place?

The hollies are silent.

Then something alights on the outer branches causing the whole of the bush to shudder. Orca can't see it, but she knows immediately who it is.

"Bird."

She listens. Is there a song that wasn't there before? She can hear woodpigeon, blackbird, wren.

The branches shake as Bird hops about. She slides forward, out of her hiding place. The holly parts to let her through. She wants to be silent but her clothing crackles. If she stands very slowly, if she makes no sound, she might see him.

She unfolds. There is a flurry of wings and the branches bounce with the take off. The dark leaves impede her sight, and Bird has flown off. She will follow. The holly has answered. Bird will take her to Nadia.

Her instructions are to stay in these woods, to map and log these woods, to gather all the information that is needed. When she is finished Dorcas will send someone to collect her. It might take many months.

There are no facts to collect about Bird. She has not been able to see him or hear him. She leaves her systems on standby and squeezes through the shrubs back onto the path.

The post office door is ajar. She could speak to the girl, ask her advice. Would this be a good idea?

Nadia could have asked the girl for help – they were friends after all. But she asked Orca.

Orca walks on. Further down the road there is a bus stop. She checks the databanks.

She could catch a bus from here to the nearest town. She could pay electronically. If she did that, Dorcas would trace her immediately. The town is three miles away. She looks at the map and memorises the route before returning her systems to standby. She may not be able to hide from Dorcas completely, but she'd like to get a head start without giving off warning signals.

After the woods it's strange to walk along streets with pavements. There are trees in gardens, but they're alone, and not as friendly as those in the woods. They hold their pores closed. The tarmac is hard under her feet. The sunshine is unimpeded, as rain would be if that were to fall.

The route is easy though. Wide roads, signposted. In an hour she is at the railway station looking at the departure boards. There are no barriers, nothing to stop her stepping onto a train. She doesn't want to turn the data on, so she looks at a map on the wall. It's made of lines, joining one station to another, and it vaguely resembles the shape of the country. She finds the town she is at which is called Nuneaton. She follows the lines eastwards. Peterborough. Ely. Ipswich. Woodbridge. The nearest station to the hollies. The next train to Peterborough is in ten minutes from platform seven.

The steps up to the enclosed bridge are lined with roofing felt. The space echoes as she walks above the tracks. Platform seven is on the far side of the station, beyond the toilets and coffee stop. A fast train shoots through, leaving a wind that blows through her clothes. She thinks of the woods, of the dark places, the smell of wet earth, leaves brushing flesh. She is uneasy in this hard, open place.

She could still return.

The black ink on the note is sharp like Nadia herself. She hid the bruising on her face with makeup and sunglasses, but Orca saw it clearly enough in the dawn light.

The train glides into the station and the doors slide open. Orca steps in, and her journey begins.

She has no ticket. This would not be a problem if she were willing to buy one. But if she buys a ticket she will be traceable. She sits in a seat and waits.

When the guard eventually passes through the carriage, he isn't really interested in checking tickets. "Anyone need to buy

p.272

a ticket?" he calls. Orca looks out of the window, doesn't make eye contact.

She changes train at Peterborough, then again at Ipswich. The scenery has changed. There are fewer trees, there's less greenery, but also stretches of open water, mudflats, the sky fills more of the train window.

At Woodbridge there is no one to check if she has a ticket. She walks over a small bridge and out of the station. It's well into the afternoon now. She doesn't know the way, but she still doesn't want to alert Dorcas by logging in.

There are paper maps. If she is willing to walk into the town, if she is willing to make interactions with strangers, she might find one.

Behind her there are boats, and she can hear the bell sound of their masts in the breeze. There are other sounds, birds which are different from the birds in the woods. Not the soft cooing of the woodpigeon from treetop to treetop, or the trilling of blackbirds and wrens through foliage. These birds are flying on salt air and their calls are like blades, long and sharp, bending against the wind. She hasn't spoken to anyone yet, but she has travelled from Nuneaton to Woodbridge, she has made unauthorised decisions, she is standing in a new place.

The station clock says half past three. Orca walks away from the river, she crosses a road and follows a sign which says Town Centre. She walks along a small road of cottages with roses round the doors, across a carpark, through a precinct and into the high street. There is another sign. Toilets, Library, Town Hall. The library will have maps.

It's in an old building that used to be a school. Orca goes in and looks around. She can rule out the children's area, decked out with colourful soft furniture. They won't keep maps on the shelves with the novels, or in the computer suite.

"Can I help you?"

She's been standing too still. She has shown signs of disorientation and attracted attention.

"Do you have a local map?"

"Yes. What sort of map are you looking for? A street map of the town or an OS map?"

She can't check the data, she needs to remember. OS? What is that? Ordnance Survey. It's something she has heard before, but she can't attach meaning to the words. She definitely doesn't want a street map.

"OS I think."

"Do you need to take it away?"

"Can I copy the bit I need?"

The woman frowns, then smiles. "Yes, if it's not more than ten percent."

Five minutes later Orca is back in the high street clutching an A4 photocopy. She knows where to go now and doesn't need to hang about in the town. She walks fast, avoiding the shoppers, keeping her gaze on the ground.

She almost misses him. A glimpse of golden hair in her peripheral vision and she looks quickly. He isn't looking her way. He has just come out of the supermarket with a bag of shopping in each hand. She ducks into an alley between two shops.

There is Nadia. She has the baby in a sling on the front of her body. She's wearing sunglasses even though it's a cloudy afternoon. Orca thinks she looks different. She's talking to Nick. She's not smiling and she doesn't look happy. Her bottom lip is more swollen, giving her a lopsided appearance. The two of them walk off, and Orca follows, keeping her distance.

They go through the precinct and across the carpark. Their yin and yang van is parked on the far side. Orca keeps to the edge.

Nick opens the back door of the van and puts the shopping inside. Nadia climbs into the front with the baby. Orca gets closer, bends low so she can't be seen above the cars.

Nick walks round to the driver's side and is momentarily out of sight. Orca stands up and waves her arms in the air to attract

Nadia's attention. Nadia becomes very still. Then the door opens and Nick climbs in. Orca crouches again behind the parked car.

She waits for the sound of the engine, for the van to back out of its bay, but that doesn't happen. After a couple of minutes there is the sound of doors opening again. Orca crouches low, her belly against her thighs, her chin on her knees. She has her eyes closed.

Footsteps are coming her way, and then a voice.

"I sent him back for bananas."

Nadia's feet in black boots.

She stands and tension tightens her joints, pain flames through her thigh then extinguishes itself.

"I was heading for Tangham, for the campsite."

"Get in the back of the van. Keep your head down. I'll tell him you're a hiker."

Orca sits behind the driver's seat out of Nick's sightline. She keeps her hood up. Nadia can see her if she turns around, but the only one looking her way is the baby, strapped into its baby seat. It waves its arms at her.

The enclosed space smells of baby – milk and talcum powder. Her elbow juts against a pack of nappies. She can feel her cells calcifying. She stays as still as rock, as chalk, as diamond. Her surface programming is closing down. Dorcas has given her nothing for this.

The baby makes a noise.

"He said Dad," says Nick.

"He burped," says Nadia. She rubs the baby's tummy and he burps again.

They leave the town and cross the river and drive out to where fields give way to heathland. The baby is gurgling at Orca and she is immobilised.

"What are you doing at Tangham?" asks Nick. "You meeting people there?"

She doesn't like lying. It's not part of her programming, and it feels as though small connections are being broken. The cut on her leg is healing, but she knows that the damage isn't only on the surface. She doesn't want to make it worse. But if she tells him she is a surveyor it may jog his memory.

"I'm studying the recreational use of forestry plantations," she says. She keeps her voice calm and low, hopes he doesn't connect her to the distressed woman he met in the Hayes.

This study is not her remit, but she will do it anyway. It will not be a lie if she makes it her intention.

"Cool, what like cycling and running and stuff?"

"There's husky racing here. And extraterrestial hotspots." She saw posters for both of these in the library.

"What, like aliens?"

"Yes, it's one of the best places for UFOs. I'm interested in the people that come looking for aliens."

"Hey, it would be cool wouldn't it. Maybe we'll see an alien Nads."

The baby starts to cry. Nadia murmurs to it and strokes it. It grabs her finger and puts it to its mouth. Orca can imagine the feel of the hard gums on the fingerpad. She curls her hands into fists.

"You're a natural," says Nick, glancing over. "You wouldn't know she's not his real mum would you?" he says to Orca.

Nadia is humming a tune and the baby's eyelids are drooping. Nick turns the van right onto a small road. The sun is behind them, casting long shadows. They pass an airfield and carry on between tall conifers.

"You can drop me here," says Orca.

"It's not much further, we can take you all the way."

"I need to stretch my legs. Please."

Nick stops the van on the verge. The road is wider here, there is room for him to turn around.

Nadia gets out quickly and slides open the back door for Orca..

Nick leans over from the driver's seat. "Maybe we'll see you about. We're here for a while."

"Maybe," say Orca.

"I'd like to see husky racing."

"Take care," says Orca.

Nadia smiles, she takes Orca's hand. Orca glances up at the van, but Nick hasn't seen. Nadia squeezes, lets go and climbs back into the passenger seat.

Chapter Four

Alone between pines in the falling light Orca breaths deeply. It smells different here. The freshness of pine and also something else. Salt. She's not many miles from the sea. She leaves the road and walks between the pines. The earth is loose and granular, there is warmth in it. She remembers a word the woman in the library used – sandlings. These trees have been planted on sand.

The lines of trunks are more or less straight. Rows and rows. It might be hard to find your way as all the rows are the same, but a straight line will always lead you out of the forest in the end.

Later Orca finds herself deposited back onto the forest track as darkness is falling. There is a wooden post at the side, carved with an arrow and an alien face painted green. The extraterrestial trail.

Orca crosses the track and enters the trees on the other side. It's different here. The pines have been felled and new growth is coming, mostly birch trees. Their leaves dance on the wind. Their pale trunks hold on to the last of the daylight like ghosts. Looking back across to the pines, Orca sees them standing, a silent army in the gloom, spookily still, waiting. She finds a spot beneath a young birch, surrounded by holly shoots. She powers down as darkness spreads through the forest.

She is woken by a loud buzz, followed by another and another. Messages are coming through. Dorcas has found her.

Orca sits up and leans her back against the birch. Daylight is beginning but it's still early. The forest is loud with birdsong. The buzzes continue. She could ignore them, but now that Dorcas knows where she is, she won't leave her alone. She can't hide any more.

p.273

The first thing she does is open the identification programme. She knows the trees in the plantation are pine but not what sort. It's barely light so she'll have to get nearer for a clear image.

She stands and places her palms on the trunk of the birch. Its bark is cool and smooth. She feels its pressure against the centre of her palms.

Thank you for your shelter," she says.

She's never thanked a tree before, but she's never followed an unseen bird across the country before in order to help a stranger. She's never disobeyed orders.

She recrosses the track and she's back in the pines. She looks closely at the needles, the way they attach to the stem. She breaths them in. She remembers the baby's milk breath. These trees are children, lined up in formation, doing what they're told.

The name pops up. Corsican Pine, native of Corsica, grown in south and east of UK where the rainfall is lightest. Likes sunshine.

The floor is littered with pine cones. Orca picks one up and holds it in her hand before looking at the messages from Dorcas.

The first says *What the fuck!*

Orca smiles. She's often annoyed Dorcas, but she doesn't remember surprising her before.

The next message says *What are you doing?*

Then *I don't know what you think you're up to, but it isn't funny.*

Suffolk? Why are you in Suffolk?

There are more. Orca is about to turn the screen off but decides to answer.

Someone needed my help. I won't be checking messages for a while.

It might shut Dorcas up, though it's unlikely. Orca closes the screen and looks about her. There are squirrels racing in the trees. She remembers two mornings ago Nadia was up very

p.274

early while Nick was sleeping. It might be a good time to make contact. Staverton is near, perhaps a mile's walking.

She sets off in the right direction, but it's slow going. The ground between the trees is rough and tussocky, so when she finds herself back on another track, she follows it. She passes a brick house with roses around the door, surrounded by a garden and enclosed by a tall privet hedge. She remembers the girl with the red plastic coat, the white socks, the flash of shoes. She thinks of fairy tale wolves and grandmothers, but knows the girl in the red coat doesn't belong with them. She can't quite retrieve the tale, but the running girl is hers alone.

She recognizes the place where Nick and Nadia dropped her off, and walks faster. It's painfully straight, this road, past the rows of Corsican pine, past the airfield, past parking areas and picnic spots, past a sign warning of sled racing, until she's back on the main road, and Staverton is just a few hundred yards to the right.

Round the bend there's the van, parked on the verge.

She slows, placing her feet carefully, heel first, rounding through to the toes in a creeping walk. There is no sound from the van. There's condensation on the windows and the outside. The pattern of drops is unbroken, there's no sign that anyone has opened the door yet this morning.

Orca creeps into the edge of the wood and finds an oak tree. It's huge, its branches thicker than the trunks in the Hayes. The lowest one has dropped almost to the floor before bending up again. It is long, undulating, like an arm outstretched, calling her in or showing her the way out. The lowest part of this branch would make a great seat but is visible from the road.

She remembers the birch tree earlier and feels warmth in her palms. She places them on the oak's trunk and speaks very quietly. She asks the oak if it would mind her climbing into its branches where she will be hidden.

The tree says nothing. A squirrel has heard her voice and leaps from the branches into the next tree, creating a flurry of leaves.

"Thank you," whispers Orca.

She climbs onto the low branch and stands facing the trunk, looking for footholds. The next branch is quite a bit higher, but there are knobbly bit sticking out here and there. She reaches up with her hands and grasps hold of a protuberance on the right, some twiggy growth with her left, finds a foothold. Using the strength in her shoulders she pulls her body up, so she's folded at her stomach over the branch, then she swings her left leg up and over.

She's facing the trunk surrounded by leaves. The branch is strong, its girth more than twice her own. She swivels round and lifts her feet so they're resting on the branch, her back leaning against the trunk. As long as she stays still no one will see her from the road, and she can see the van from here. Waiting is something she's been programmed for.

The bark of the tree is warm.

"How old are you?" she asks.

With pines, she has learned to count the circles of branches, one for each year. But a deciduous tree is different. It keeps its age folded inside its rings and perhaps also its DNA. The only way you can discover the rings is to cut it down, so to age the tree that way you must kill it. Dorcas told her she must measure the tree at breast height, then do some sums. But whose breast? Orca wonders. Depending on the height of the surveyor, the tree might add or lose decades.

This one is probably hundreds of years old.

"I've come to see the holly," she says, then wonders if that's rude, if this old oak will be offended not to be the purpose of her visit. "Actually, I've come because of the people in that van. The hollies just helped me to find the way."

There is a disturbance in the high branches, a squawk and a flapping of wings, and a rook flies into the sky. Orca peers up through the leaves but she can't see anything.

"Bird? Is that you?"

A silly question, Bird never answers.

"Hello Bird," she says. "I know you helped too."

The door of the van slides open and Nadia peers out, follows with her body. She's wearing a huge black t-shirt and her legs are bare. She looks both ways along the road, then creeps barefoot behind a bush where she squats and relieves herself. She's left the van door open, but there's no sound inside.

Orca breaks a twig from the tree and throws it as hard as she can. It lands in the bush next to Nadia and makes a small noise. Nadia glances towards it but doesn't seem interested. Orca breaks of another three small pieces of oak and throws them one by one. Nadia is paying attention now. She doesn't look alarmed, but she looks up into the branches above her. The squirrel is still up there, and as Nadia looks it dashes along a branch then leaps into the next tree, further away from Orca.

Nadia smiles, then walks back to the van. She disappears inside and pulls the door closed behind her.

It's OK, Orca can wait.

She tries to remember when she last refuelled. Not since she arrived in Suffolk. Leaving in haste, she hadn't thought about the need for sustenance. Dorcas has provided regular supplies to a collection box, but now she will have to manage without her. She feels in a pocket and finds a packet of nutrition pills. There are more in other pockets, but not many, they won't last. She tears off the wrapper and swallows the pills. She's eaten hundreds of these – but this time she realises there is taste in her mouth after the pill has gone down. She looks at the packet – they are blackberry and hazelnut flavour. Blackberries and hazelnuts can both be found in the woods in autumn. She takes a deep breath. She can smell wood, leaves, earth, fungus. The pills don't smell like any of them. They smell like their wrapper.

She feels the nourishment making its way into her limbs and her brain.

The van door slides open again and Nadia comes out. She's still wearing the huge t-shirt, but she's added a pair of black jeans and some plimsolls. She is holding the baby with one arm. In the other hand she holds a carrier bag.

She walks to Orca's oak tree and sits down on the low branch. She places the baby on the grass in front of her and searches through the bag, produces a banana which she peels. She breaks a piece off, gives it to the baby and takes a bite herself. She is directly below Orca.

Orca glances towards the van. It's still and silent. Nadia is talking to the baby in a low voice. Orca imagines putting a piece of the banana in her mouth, she imagines sweetness, she imagines chewing.

"Psst"

Nadia glances sideways, then gives the last piece of banana to the baby.

"Psst."

She looks left then right, then back toward the van.

"Up here."

The baby looks up first, then Nadia follows its gaze and sees Orca.

She smiles, then looks at the trunk of the oak.

"I can't get up with the baby," she says, keeping her voice low.

Orca feels that she knows this tree now. It will look after her. She swings her body over the branch, feels out with her feet and lowers her weight. In seconds she is back on the ground. She stands on the side of the tree that can't be seen from the van.

"Shall we walk?"

"I need to feed the baby first. He needs milk."

In the carrier bag Nadia has a thermos of warm water. She uses it to hydrate the baby milk in a bottle, then lifts the baby onto her lap.

p.275

"How did you find us?" she asks. She cradles the baby in the crook of her left arm and offers the bottle with her other hand. The baby latches on and begins to suck.

"I asked the girl from the post office."

Nadia looks up. "She knew where we were going?"

Orca shrugs. "Not really. She said hollies. She said Suffolk or Sussex. I was lucky to get the right place."

"What did you tell her?"

"Nothing. Just you'd asked me for something."

Nadia thinks about this, then nods. "So you didn't tell her you were coming to find us? That you were coming here?"

"I thought you might not want to leave a trail."

Nadia smiles. It's the first time Orca has seen her smile and it changes her face. She seems suddenly very young.

"You're good with the baby," says Orca.

Nadia looks down at the child, the smile still on her face, and he stops sucking for a moment, lifts a hand to touch her face.

"He is a good baby," she says.

When the bottle is empty, Nadia takes the carrier bag back to the van. She slides the door open quietly and places the bag inside, then leans in to grab the baby sling. She closes the door again and the click of it closing seems loud between the trees. The two women wait for a moment, but there is no sound. Nadia walks back to the oak.

"He is sleeping," she says.

"When he wakes, will he think you've taken the baby again?"

"I will be back before he wakes. He will sleep for another hour. Can you hold Eli while I put on this sling?"

Nadia puts the baby into Orca's arms. He is heavy and very warm. He leans against Orca and lets her take his weight. She feels something inside, as though someone has dropped a small stone in her stomach and the ripples are circling out, rapidly filling her body. Her throat is closing. The baby has fat fingers and pushes them against her lips. He is so hot she can't hold on to him. She is going to drop him.

"Thank you." Nadia lifts the child from Orca's arms and hold him high so she can guide his limbs into the slots on the sling. "Can you just pull that up at the back?"

Orca is tingling throughout her body. She tugs the fabric of the sling so it supports the baby's back. She feels his soft hair brush her fingers like an electric shock.

"OK, we're ready," says Nadia.

Orca supposes there is a programme for mothering. There would be no reason for Dorcas to have uploaded it for her, but this is more than just an absence. She wonders if she has been accidentally given a corrupted version.

They follow a path that winds between huge trunks which bulge like swollen joints – like elephantiasis. Orca examines that thought. Where did it come from? Why does she know about elephantiasis? She shakes her head. Her brain is making connections that seem to have no purpose, she has no control over them.

The trees here are mostly oaks, their branches are heavy, their elbows dropped. The path twists to navigate around them. Sometimes Orca and Nadia have to bend their heads.

"Are there hollies too?"

"Tak. Follow me."

Nadia leaves the path and walks between the trees. The ground beneath their feet is littered with small twigs and leaves. They can't walk in a straight line, but turn right then left. They pass a birch growing inside the hollow trunk of an oak, its own trunk already thick as a post box, its canopy mingling high up with the leaves of other trees. Nadia puts a hand on it as she passes.

They reach a tall tree which has grey-brown bark, one thick trunk and lots of other smaller stems growing around it. The leaves are dark green with a shine that catches the morning light.

"Oh!" says Orca.

"It is beautiful."

Orca goes up to the holly tree and places her hands on the bark. She is still on edge from holding the baby and can feel sharp pulses rushing around her body. Now they rush to her palms, a million tiny blades pushing against her skin from the inside. She snatches her hands away.

"Are you OK?" Nadia is watching her.

"It has strong energy," Orca replies.

"Good energy."

Orca shakes her hands and the blades disperse, back into her blood stream.

"Come with me, see a place I found yesterday."

They bend beneath the lower branches of the holly. An oak has fallen and lies prone, fungus growing from its limbs, twiggy new trees shooting up in the spaces between.

There's a bank of holly shrub beyond, and Nadia slides through a gap which is invisible at first glance. Orca follows, the holly holding back its twigs to let her through.

They are in a circular space surrounded by holly, some shrubby bushes like those in the Hayes, but also some taller trees filtering the light into the glade. The ground is mossy and soft. Orca stands in the middle and turns slowly. She can feel the tiny blades circling in her body, faster and faster.

"This is amazing, yes?" says Nadia.

Orca nods. She doesn't feel able to speak, she doesn't know what would fall out of her mouth. A breeze gusts through and the holly leaves rustle. The light wavers, and the spinning blades begin to dissolve, one after the other.

"I ..."

"Yes?"

Orca sits down on the ground and hugs her knees against her chest. She lowers her head and breathes in the smell of moss and forest floor. She can see the open pages of a book, an encyclopaedia. There are photographs of diseased limbs, swollen, painful, grotesque. The heading is Elephantiasis, a disease caused by parasitic worms. Orca stares at the pictures.

The old trees are beautiful, ancient, healthy. The resemblance is astonishing. Then a hand reaches in and turns the page, a voice says 'Ughh! That's horrible!" Orca turns quickly. She catches a glimpse of brown hair, then it's gone.

"Are you OK?"

Nadia is crouching, the baby in front of her like a shield. She places a hand on the top of Orca's knee.

Orca nods. She touches the baby's hair with one finger. It is so soft she can barely feel it, but it's enough. She withdraws her hand. Her blood is flowing smoothly again now, the sun light is bathing the cells of her body.

"This place," she whispers.

Nadia nods.

They sit side by side. The baby seems to be sleeping. A small bird appears in the holly, hopping from branch to branch, its tail pointing up from its fat body, its eye shining as it trills and chatters. The database knows this one.

Orca takes Nadia's hand. "What do you want from me?" she asks.

The wren flutters up to a higher branch and trills again.

"I don't know what to do."

"Do you still want to leave him?"

"Yes!" Nadia's chin juts out and she takes off her sunglasses. The bruise has faded and the skin around her eyes has a greenish tinge. Her eyes glitter for a moment, then her shoulders drop. "But I can't leave Eli behind, he has no one else to protect him."

"And if you take him?"

"Nick has papers. The police look at it, and say he is Eli's legal guardian. If I take him, I am kidnapper, I break the law."

"His mother?"

"She is in hospital."

The wren is joined by a blackbird and together they chatter and sing. The noise is absorbed by the sunlight glancing through tops of the hollies into the glade. Orca closes her eyes and feels the warmth on her skin, the song streaming into her mind.

"It's so peaceful here." She's spoken out loud. She's with someone else and has spoken her thought out loud. Would she do that if she was on her own? She's not sure. She doesn't know if she speaks her thoughts only in her head or with her voice. Because she's with Nadia, her thought has become communication.

"Tak," says Nadia. "It is a shame we can't stay."

"What's his plan?"

"A few days here. He has his work to do, finding the beetles. He says we might also go to the sea."

"And then what?"

"We move on, to the next place. More beetles, more trees."

The baby makes a sound but doesn't wake up. He turns his head one way then the other and settles again against Nadia's chest. Orca imagines touching his cheek, his skin beneath her fingertips, smooth and soft as the inside of an eggshell. She stretches her fingers, makes fists.

"The fighting, does it happen a lot?"

"I never know when. All seems fine, then it is not."

"If I stay near?"

"It is better, knowing there is someone. Do you have a phone?"

"You can call me. I can give you a number."

No one ever had her number except Dorcas and Sylva. Since Sylva went, the only contact she has is with Dorcas.

Nadia taps the number into her phone.

"I must get back. He will be waking and I don't want him to call the police again."

They walk back through the trees.

Chapter Five

Orca walks further along the road and enters the forest on a footpath. She can't bear the idea of that long straight road again. All of the paths here are straight, but something about that tarmacked road stretching on and on, never bending, she doesn't want to face that just now. The tracks in this part of the wood are stony and potholed. In some places there are wide verges, in others the trees crowd right up to the edge of the path.

She passes an encampment with dogs and children running free. She passes the other end of the airfield. The fences look dark and foreboding, as though something mysterious is hidden behind them. Then the path opens up and there's a notice board at the side, giving information about UFO sightings, extra-terrestrial trails through the forest.

Orca wraps her arms around herself as she reads the board. The first trailmarker is over to her left, marked with the green alien head. She rocks from side to side, balancing the weight on her left foot then her right.

The feelings are too strong to ignore. She wants to hold the baby. She wants to eat the baby. She wants to crush the baby and throw it as far from herself as possible, so she never sees it again. None of this makes sense. Dorcas may have answers.

First she walks. The track leads into the heart of the forest. She marches along it, passing the numbered signposts, then takes a left turn away from the alien trail. She passes a bike park, a woman walking a dog, three cyclists. Ahead of her is a grassy bank, rubbed raw in places to show the sand beneath, at the top some tall pines. She heads for these. They are Scots pine, not Corsican. Their bark is red and crazed, their smell stinging and fresh. She sits beneath them, her back to one, her feet stretching towards the other. She breathes deeply. She opens communication with Dorcas.

Why does the baby upset me?

Dorcas doesn't answer immediately. There are ants scurrying beneath the tree, carrying objects across the sand. Orca watches them. The sun has real warmth in it now and she feels overdressed, but doesn't want to move. There must be an ants' nest nearby.

What baby?

I held a baby. I felt as though I was burned.

Ah!

What do you mean Ah! It was very upsetting and I have not regained equilibrium. My arms are still shaking.

One ant has a piece of leaf which is too large for it to carry. It pauses, and three other ants appear. Together they lift the leaf fragment and begin to move it across the ground.

You have memories.

What do you mean?

They are deep, implanted. But they can be triggered.

Why? It makes me less efficient. My system has been thrown into flux.

We wanted to see if the forest would open them, if immersion can help to heal trauma.

Orca trails her fingers across the sand towards the ants. They scurry faster. She stops, lifts her hand and traces the same line along her own thigh.

So these hidden memories are traumatic?

I don't know how they will make themselves known. They may stay hidden.

The ants have carried the leaf to the base of the tree where they vanish with it into a hole.

Am I safe?

There is silence. More ants are crossing the ground, some of them carrying small pieces of vegetation, debris. They must be building something. Orca has an urge to disrupt them, to stamp or scrape the ground, to cause an emergency in their world. She looks up at the sky. It's blue behind the pine branches. There is light up there that hurts her eyes a little. She can't focus on the individual needles at the edge of the branches, they are blurred with sunlight.

If you ever feel unsafe you can contact me. I am here for you.

Orca stands up abruptly. She doesn't want to talk to Dorcas any more. She sets off along a path. A sign points towards Scotland Fen, and she follows it. She is far from Scotland.

The path leads her past a pond and between tall pine trees. The sandy track rises slightly in front of her, and the trees form an avenue, leading to a high point where there is a crossroads. Memories. Can she access them at will? Is the girl in a red coat a memory? Can she find out more about her. Perhaps the visions she sees are like a string, and if she tugs on them, she can bring the memory towards her, into her consciousness. She's not going to ask Dorcas, she doubts she would approve.

She needs something to do while she's here in this forest. The surveying programme was designed specifically for the Hayes. She doesn't know if it will work here. Her legs move along the path, her feet fall one in front of the other, the sun warms her hair. She will try, during the day, to find out if the information she has already gleaned can be mapped onto this very different forest. In the evening she will tug that string and see what happens. She won't talk to Dorcas. She'll wait, see if there is contact from Nadia.

There are no messages from either of them that day. By evening Orca is tired. She has walked the grid of forest paths. Along one edge the forest meets heathland, one edge the road, in other places farmland, and cutting into it, the airfield. She has identified many plants which don't grow in the Hayes. The airfield is spiked with bugloss, weld, mullein, sea holly. Sandy forest rides include wild thyme and mugwort. She has rubbed their leaves and smelled a harsh sweetness. There is something about this forest that makes her feel clean, pine and artemisia, salt air from the coast not many miles away. Her airways feel scrubbed. Her legs have barely stopped moving.

There have been a lot of visitors to the forest. The sun has been warm and the breeze light. Families have cycled past, the smallest member wobbling at the back, runners in pairs and threes wearing coloured lycra, groups of adults and children with picnics. Orca has done her best to avoid them. When she has needed them, Dorcas's phrases have been useful. *Nice day for it. Morning. Afternoon. Make the most of it, while it lasts.* Nobody has said anything to her that demanded more.

Now it's evening and the sun is at the tops of the trees. The air is a little cooler. She walks through the trees near the top edge of the campsite. Children are building benders around the base of trees. A group are playing rounders in a clearing. Orca skirts out of sight. Smells and sounds waft through the air, laughter and shouts, meat on a barbeque, the strum of a guitar, woodsmoke.

She leaves it behind. The track takes her past the house with the roses. She heads between the trees. There's a place in the centre of the forest where the paths wind. Trees block the path and send it off in new directions. If she is to explore these memories, she prefers to get away from straight lines.

By the time she's found a spot the light is falling. The sun has disappeared behind the treetops, a glow through the trunks shows where it will soon disappear behind the horizon. She rubs her upper arms with her hands. It's much cooler now.

How should she do this?

She doesn't want to think about the baby. The shock of its skin still makes her shiver.

The girl in the red coat.

The glow disappears and the forest sinks into darkness. Orca looks up. Between the treetops she can see pieces of sky dotted with stars. It is very quiet. Occasionally something rustles. She has spent many nights in the dark of the forest, but this is usually the time she closes down. By the time she boots up again the light is returning. Tonight she will stay awake.

An owl calls. Orca closes her eyes and breathes.

She's running along the path which is in the Hayes but not in the Hayes. She can see the girl, the red coat, the flash of white socks. She runs after her. There's a gasp of air in her lungs, which is also laughter.

"Wait!"

The girl has vanished around a bend in the path. Orca runs faster, turns the corner, then stops suddenly. She's reached the bomb hole. It's right across the path. There are brambles growing in the base, and there is the litter again, the crisp bag, the piece of tissue snagged on spikes. The girl is standing on the other side of the hole. She has turned to face Orca and she's laughing.

"You can't catch me!"

She's a child, but there's no mistaking. Orca knows those eyes.

"Sylva!"

"Jump!" Sylva laughs out loud, then turns and runs again.

There's no way Orca can leap over this hole, it's far too wide. The bottom is a spiky mess of bramble. The only way she can get across is to creep round the edge, clinging on to the ground at the top. It can be done, but it's slow. By the time Orca reaches the other side the girl has vanished.

"Sylva!"

Orca runs along the path, but it has changed. It's straight and wide, covered with white chippings – the way it was when Orca was there two days ago.

"Where are you?"

There's no answer.

Orca feels the rush back into her body, crouched at the bottom of a pine tree. She opens her eyes. She's in Rendlesham and it's dark. Her limbs ache.

It wasn't enough. She wants to go back. She wants to pull the string and return to the memory. She has questions for Sylva, if she can catch up with her.

But it's no use. However hard she tries, she can't return to the red path in the Hayes. She imagines it, she pulls up the picture of it in her head, tries to feel movement in her limbs, but it's no good. She knows she's making it up.

She comes back to the night where she is awake. She stands and stretches her legs, listens. The bark of a fox, then a rushing sound, which might be wind in the treetops, but stops as suddenly as it starts. She remembers UFOs and smiles. If she was on one of the straight paths she could walk. She sets off anyway, feeling with her feet and hands for any obstruction. If she loses her way it doesn't matter that much, she will be able to find it again in the morning. She wants to think.

The last time she saw Sylva was the last day she came to the office. She was wearing her turquoise embroidered tunic but she looked as though she'd been crying, and that was surprising, because Sylva was always cheerful. The other strange thing was that she was late. Neither of them was ever late.

Sylva sat down at her terminal which was next to Orca's and turned on the screen. Before the start-up page appeared, Dorcas called Sylva through to her office.

Orca carried on working as normal, but she could feel the tug of the empty chair in her side vision. Sylva's screen had a screen saver, a monkey which bounced about the screen from branches that sprang up from its weight. Orca found herself staring at the monkey and having to force her attention back to her own screen.

It was nearly lunch time when Sylva reappeared. The rims of her eyes were red and her curls were subdued. She sat on her chair but she didn't start work, she turned the screen off. The monkey and its pink background were replaced with a black square.

"I have pastries," she said to Orca. "Come and eat them with me."

'It isn't time for a nutrition break. We still have half an hour to go."

"It's OK. Dorcas has given us permission."

Orca looked around, but Dorcas wasn't in the room. She had never given them permission before to eat pastries when they should be working. But Sylva seemed very certain, and Orca was uneasy about the crying, so she put her screen on sleep mode and followed Sylva through to the huge window.

The pastries had apple in them and cream. They were large and sticky. This was irregular as well. Normally Orca took her nutrition at work in the form of bars or pills, sometimes a protein drink. The breaks were short and the refuelling efficient.

She lifted the sticky triangle from the cardboard box and bit into it. Apple puree squidged out of the side and she had to catch it with her hand before it fell to the floor. Her mouth was full of pastry, fruit and cream, and she could feel there was some on her face too.

Sylva giggled, and took a bite of the other pastry. The same happened to her. She had cream on the end of her nose. Orca removed it with her finger and licked it.

Sylva put her finger into the cream on her pastry and daubed it on Orca's nose. Orca gasped, then retaliated, marking Sylva's forehead with apple. Sylva squealed.

Soon both of them had cream and apple all over their faces and crumbs of pastry in their hair. They were squealing and shouting with laughter. Then Orca realised Dorcas was standing in the doorway watching them.

She became still. This was surely a misdemeanour. There would be consequences.

But Dorcas turned round and walked away. Orca never thought about Dorcas having expressions or emotions, but for a moment the word *sad* was in her head.

There wasn't much left of the pastries, but they ate what there was standing side by side, looking out of the window.

"I'm going out there," said Sylva.

"To the distance?"

"Further than that."

"When will you be back?"

"I don't think I can come back."

"Can I come with you?"

"Not now. Maybe one day. Maybe one day you can come and find me."

She took Orca's hand. Their palms were sticky.

There's enough light from the stars to see the gap between the trees, a dirt road stretching in both directions. Her face is wet from crying and, even though it is the middle of the night, she can feel energy moving in waves through her body. She can't stay still.

A question is racing around her brain like an electrical pulse, but if she keeps walking maybe she can keep it on the move, stop it coming into focus. She strides out. Now there are no tree trunks in the way and the path is straight, she can walk fast and cover distance. Soon she is at the edge of the forest. To her right is the heath, but in front of her a road. She only pauses for an instant before continuing to walk, along the tarmac and away from the trees.

The smell of salt is stronger here. The sky is huge, a dome arching over her and the land. There are no trees to shelter her. She walks faster. In some places high, wire fences line the road, cordoning off military land. Then the fences are gone, and the world is open. The stars are bright but there is no moon.

She passes through a village. The houses are dark and heavy, except for one where a light is on in an upstairs window. Orca keeps her footsteps silent on the tarmac. She hasn't seen a single car. Past the village there's a stretch where trees line the road, and she relaxes her shoulders within their embrace. Then they are gone again, and the landscape is like none she has ever seen. Despite the darkness she can sense the broken ground, the incursions of salt-water, the fragility of land made of sand. She can hear a sound which is not wind in the trees or cars passing on a distant road. This is something else. She has never seen the sea before.

The question is racing faster, setting off bursts of emotion in her thighs, her stomach, her upper arms. It's hissing at her. Yes you have, yes you have, of course you've seen the sea before. Is this one of Dorcas's memory implants? Is there a memory of the seaside?

The road runs out and there is only shingle. Orca walks across pebbles which shift beneath her feet. She reaches a ridge and there it is before her, ink black and vast. A gust of wind catches her off guard and her hood is blown back from her face. The tie of her hood whips her cheek and she lifts her hand. She can taste salt in the air, on her face.

She can't avoid it any more.

Is Sylva dead?

She'd never questioned. She'd never wondered.

Her hair whips about her head and salt grits her skin. It could be salt from inside or out. It's difficult to tell the difference here. Her clothes balloon as the wind tries to lift her, but she's not flotsam.

She would like to see the sun rise over the water. There are still hours until sunrise, and it's too cold, too exposed, to stay here. Further along the beach are some cottages, a short, terraced row, a white smear in the dark. She can find shelter in their lee.

It's hard to walk at cross purposes to the wind with shingle underfoot. It's very different from the sea in her memory.

One of the cottages has a porch which is unlocked. Although Orca has become used to sleeping outside, respite from the salt wind is too tempting. She'll be awake and gone before anyone stirs. She curls herself into a ball beside a row of wellington boots and sandals.

Behind her eyes she can see sand so bright she must shield her eyes. A ridge of rock runs out from a cliff, pitted with rock pools. There is the salt smell, but it's warmer, less vicious. She has her back to the sea, but she knows that it's sparkling and blue. Someone throws a ball to her, and she leaps in the air, catches it with both hands. Her body is light and small. She looks down. A child's body, wearing a blue swimsuit. She can barely see the person who threw the ball as the sun is too bright. She shields her eyes and squints.

The person runs and shouts, "Here, here, Olive, throw it to me!"

It's a child's voice. It's Sylva's voice.

She didn't intend to sleep and she sits up with a start. Someone moved in the house. The night is beginning to shift.

A light comes on upstairs. Orca opens the door and creeps out of the porch. The wind slaps her hard, but she walks into it. It's still dark, only a glimmer of grey far out where sea meets sky. The stars have disappeared. Clouds are racing in front of the wind. Water hits her face and she's not sure if it's rain or seaspray. It's cold here, uncomfortable. She longs for trees, and the sunrise will likely be hidden by cloud anyway.

Although it had seemed a long way last night, she's back at the forest entrance before the daylight arrives. The weather has turned and it's properly raining now. Away from the coast the wind is not so fierce, but the world is grey and wet. Puddles have formed on the sandy forest track. The smell of wet pine welcomes her in, and Orca leaves the path to walk between the trees. She is glad of her waterproof clothes and smiles when wet pine needles brush her face. The moss shines greener in this grey light. She finds a huge tree with low spreading branches, shielding the sandy ground, and crawls underneath. There isn't room to sit up. She lies on her front and looks out at the world

She will have to contact Dorcas at some point, but what can she say to her? Is it possible to be angry with Dorcas? What would happen if she said *How dare you? What gives you the right to use me as an experiment? How am I supposed to process this information?*

Dorcas might laugh. She'd probably say *What right have you to question me? I'm the one in charge here.*

Chapter Six

A voice call comes in from Nadia. Orca answers.

"I am in the van," says Nadia. Her voice echoes in the enclosed metal space. Rain is pounding on the van roof.

"Are you alone?" Orca asks.

"He is gone to look for the beetle. He has been waiting for rain. He knows where to look for the beetle when it rains."

"You have the baby?"

"I am bored."

"What do you ...?"

"Let's go to the pub."

Orca is silent. She hears the baby hiccup in the van. The forest is heavy with rain, the pine branches are drooping with the weight and the birds are quieter than yesterday. There is an angry squawk in the top branches, but Orca imagines they are mostly fluffing out their feathers and staying near the tree trunks. She thinks she sees something move on the nearest tree and think of Bird, but when she looks only a branch is moving. Maybe the sound is just the wind between the trees.

"Are you there?"

She hasn't been indoors since she was in the office, apart from briefly in Hartshill post office, and the porch last night, but they barely count.

"OK."

"I thought you'd gone. That's great. Where shall we ..."

"Stay at the van. I'll come to you."

"Where are ..?"

"I'll be twenty minutes."

That means walking fast, but Orca needs to move. If she doesn't, she will think. If she doesn't move, she may be tempted to contact Dorcas, and say things she'd regret.

Although she can't see him, Bird is flying ahead of her, flitting from tree to tree, leading the way. She knows something with clarity – she can't tell Dorcas about Bird. Even if she tells her everything about Nadia and Nick and the pub and the dreams of Sylva, she can't tell her about Bird. If she does, she'll be brought back in from the field. She will be sent for re-examination. And although a few weeks ago she may not have minded, now she relishes movement. She wants to decide for herself.

Nadia is sitting in the driver's seat holding the baby. She leans over and opens the passenger door.

Orca's waterproofs are running with rainwater, but Nadia shrugs. "Put them on the floor."

She unzips her jacket and throws it into the footwell, climbs into the cabin. Nadia hands her the baby and puts the key in the ignition.

"You can drive?"

"At home, yes. Here can't be much different I think. The pub is one mile."

Nadia turns on the engine. The baby grabs at Orca's face.

Something has changed since yesterday.

"Hello," she says to the baby. She stretches her eyes and turns her mouth into an O. The baby's fat fingers bat her nose. Orca makes popping noises with her mouth.

Nadia laughs. She has moved the van onto the road and her driving seems fine. "I thought you do not like babies," she says.

"I had a sister once," says Orca.

"Was she a baby? Are you older?"

"I don't know."

"Where is she now?"

"I've lost her."

They are already at the pub. They could have walked, but they would have been wet. The pub is at a junction and there's a signpost to the village Orca walked through in the night.

The rain is even heavier. They get out of the van and run to the pub. Orca is still holding the baby which she covers with her raincoat.

Nadia doesn't ask Orca what she wants, she orders two pints of beer. Orca is glad that Dorcas doesn't have video or audio, that she can't watch what she's doing. There's the GPS, she can check where Orca is – but she won't know about the beer, not unless Orca tells her.

"Me and Nick made up."

"Oh."

"We agree the most important thing is Eli. We have to be good parents for him. Set him a good example."

"And you feel safe?"

Nadia laughs. It's shrill and the baby turns to stare at her. "What is safe? My life has ... I have met worse than Nick."

Orca nods. She examines what Nadia has said. Is she inviting questions? Does she want to talk about her past? She's playing with the baby now, hiding behind her hands then peeping out to make him laugh. If she does talk about her past Orca won't know what to say, whether she should give advice or if she would be expected to hug Nadia. She isn't ready. It's enough being indoors with other people and beer. Her systems are stretched to capacity.

"He's a happy baby," she says.

"I love him," says Nadia, lifting him in the air above her head so he giggles. "I don't know what I'd do without him."

Two men are sitting at the table next to them. One has just placed a pot of tea on the table with a wooden spoon marked number 7.

"Sure you don't want anything stronger?" he says to his friend.

"I found this this morning," says the other.

"What is it?"

"I don't know. It was on the floor of my porch. I've no idea how it got there."

Nadia is talking about Nick. She's telling Orca about his work which takes him around the country, and also his search for the beetles.

"He is lucky that his work and his passion match. If he had to work in an office, he would go mad. Sometimes he wants to go to find the beetle, where there is no work."

Orca asks, "What about you? Do you like to be outdoors?" But she wants to turn around and see what the men are examining at the next table.

"Does it open? There might be something inside."

"I've never seen anything like it."

"I don't mind in the summer. I think in the autumn we will need to find a house."

"Has anyone visited that might have dropped it?"

"For Eli, he can't live in the van all winter.'

Orca looks at Eli and wonders how old he is. He must have already lived through one winter.

"I need to find the toilet," she says.

"OK."

The men are drinking tea. The object is on the table between them, but Orca can't see it as their cups are in the way. In the bathroom she locks herself in a cubicle. She checks her wrist. She wears a small silver chain with three charms attached. There are only two.

She knows what the two men are looking at. It is actually a memory stick, but it doesn't look like that. It is flat and made of silver and engraved with three letters, O, D and S. The letters intertwine so it is hard to see which is which. The end which holds the connection is sealed – to open it you need one of the other charms on her bracelet. The third charm fits over the end to form a grip. The missing piece is the part that goes into the computer, and alone looks like a small silver rectangle.

She doesn't know what is on the memory stick or why Dorcas didn't just put the information on to the main drive. She knows that it's precious, that she shouldn't lose it. But how can she retrieve it from the men?

She walks back into the bar. Nadia is feeding the baby from a bottle. The two men are eating huge plates of food. One has fish and chips and the piece of fish is longer than the oval plate. The other has a meat pie.

Orca takes a deep breath and approaches their table.

"Excuse me."

The both look up. One has just inserted a mouthful of fish and batter. He looks at Orca, then quickly scans the pub.

"I was the person. It was me."

The man with the fish reaches for a glass of water which is next to him. The water sloshes. The pie man has an empty mouth and it's him that speaks.

"What was you?"

"I am sorry. Last night I was at the beach in need of shelter and I entered your porch. I have lost an object. I think you have found it."

The fish man swallows. "The beach?"

"Yes, I had walked there, then the weather became inclement. I apologise for my trespass."

"I'm sorry love, you've got the wrong people," says the pie man.

Orca feels heat rising from her chest. She pulls back her sleeve and reveals the silver chain. The attachment for the memory stick is still there, next to the other two charms.

"This," she says. "This is what I have lost in your porch. I am sorry but please may I have my property back."

She is aware of the quiet in the pub. There aren't many customers, but all conversations have stopped. Everyone is watching and listening. Nadia is watching and listening. Orca can hear the suck of the baby taking milk from the bottle.

"I don't live by the beach," says the fish man. "It wasn't my porch you broke into. This is what I found." He pushes an object across the table to Orca. It is brown, oval shaped, a seedpod or a growth. It is made of vegetable matter. "I live in the forest," he says.

The heat solidifies and rushes up Orca's throat. She turns and runs back to the bathroom where she is sick in the toilet. She's breathing fast. The memory stick is lost – it might be in the porch by the sea, or in the van, or anywhere in the forest. It's so small, how can she possible find it? What will she say to Dorcas?

By the time she returns to the bar conversations have resumed, but they are all about her. Nadia has moved and is sitting at the table with the two men.

The man who was eating fish has abandoned his food. "Are you OK?" he says to Orca.

She isn't. She doesn't know what to do with herself.

"Sit down," he says, indicating to the space on the bench next to his friend.

"I'm going to the bar," said Nadia. "Do you want beer?'

Orca perches on the edge of the bench and shakes her head. "A glass of water, please" she says.

The man has a beard and his hair needs cutting.

"Were you at Shingle Street?" asks the other man, who has finished his pie.

She knows she should check, that she has the information and can retrace her route. But the lights in the pub are very bright and she is squinting. She doesn't want to look at the men.

"I don't know," she says.

'The first place to look is in your friends van," says the man with the beard. "She says you came here in a van?'

"Yes. Yes, I will look."

Orca stands up. She follows Nadia to the bar and asks her for the key. Outside it's still raining. Orca walks across the carpark with her eyes to the ground, looking for a glint of silver. In the van, she checks the floor, the seat, down the back of the seat. The memory stick isn't there.

Back inside the pub the others are drinking beer and tea. Nadia is holding the baby again and there's a glass of water on the table for Orca. Nadia tells her that the two men are called Matt and Jack. Jack is the one that ate fish for lunch.

"Did you say it's a memory stick?" says Jack.

"A bit old school," says Matt.

"Presumably the information is stored elsewhere."

"I don't know."

"Is it very important to you?"

"I think so. It was given to me look after. I don't know what is stored on it, but I know I can't lose it."

"You'll have to retrace your steps." Jack has become the main speaker. Orca is looking at his face. She wonders if her gaze is too intense. "Would you like some help?"

"A treasure hunt!" said Nadia.

"I'm not sure ... I have to get back to work." Matt looks anxious. "Jack, don't you..."

"It's OK. I can work a bit later this evening."

"You are very kind."

"Jack, will you ...?"

"I'll be fine, Matt. We'll be outside." His eyes are grey and his lips are hidden by his beard. He had a crumb of batter under his lower lip. "Let's go," he says.

Nadia quickly drinks the rest of her beer and the three of them head out to the carpark.

"I'll drive," says Jack. "I've not had any beer."

Orca has drunk one pint of beer, but she sicked it back up. She's a bit wobbly but doesn't feel like she has poison in her system – it feels more like a malfunction. Since she discovered the loss of the memory stick she's not been running smoothly.

The drive to the camp only takes a few minutes. Nadia directs Jack, who parks the van exactly where is had been before, even lines it up on the flattened grass tyre marks.

"Which way did you come from?" asks Jack. "Did you walk about when you got here?"

"It was raining. I got straight into the van. I took my coat off."

They search the ground on the passenger side of the van. The rain has stopped now, but the grass is wet, and soon their hands and sleeves are soaked. They find nothing.

"OK, now we must retrace your steps. Can you remember the way you walked?"

"I think so."

They walk through the forest. Nadia had put the baby in a sling. She's singing to him, but the words are not in English. Orca has language recognition programmes, but she is too distracted. She doesn't verify, she doesn't ask. She knows it is not French or German or Chinese.

They reach the tree where Orca had sheltered from the rain.

"I lay under that tree," she said. "For quite a few hours."

Jack looks at her. "You're a strange one, lying under trees and breaking into porches in the middle of the night."

"It is a welcoming tree. The rain had become heavier."

Together Jack and Orca crawl under the low branches. Nadia laughs.

"You look so funny. Your bottoms next to each other."

Jack looks at Orca and smiles and she smiles back. She doesn't feel like laughing, but this smile makes her feel less scared. They pat the ground with their hands. There are a lot of pine needles covering sandy ground. It's dry under here, the branches have kept the rain out. Orca digs her fingers beneath the surface. They search up to the trunk, then to the other side. Nadia has stopped laughing.

"I didn't come to this side of the tree," says Orca.

They find nothing.

When they emerge, headfirst, on the track side of the tree, Nadia is not alone. Nick is with her.

'Are you following us?' he says to Orca.

'I'm looking for something I have lost," she replies.

He holds out his hand to Orca. On his palm is the memory stick.

"Is it this?" he says.

Orca takes it and turns it over in her fingers.

"It was lying on the path further up."

"Thank you." She pushes her sleeve up and tries to reattach the memory stick into its fastening. It's difficult with one hand.

"Here," says Nick. He pushes the stick into the holder but it slips straight out again. "It's bent, look. You need some pliers or something."

"I have pliers at my place."

"You are …?"

"Jack. I work in the forest. I have a cabin up the track."

Jack holds out his hand and the two men shake.

"Nick. Entomologist."

They are very different from each other. Nick's hair is shining golden in the rays of sunshine that are showing between clouds. He's wearing navy shorts, a bright green t-shirt and sandals. His calves are the colour of butterscotch and covered with gold hairs. Jack is wearing trousers of an indeterminate colour and a dirty overshirt. It is hard to tell what age he is.

"Visiting? Working?"

"Both. I'm doing some survey work for the Forestry Commission – click beetles in Staverton. But I'm also on a personal mission. I'm hoping to see all the types of longhorn beetle this summer, and I've just added this beauty to the list." He shows them all a photo on his phone, a close up large brown beetle crawling over moss, its back striped with grooved lines like textured leather.

"*Asemum striatum*" says Jack

"Yay, you know your stuff."

Orca has taken the charm bracelet off her arm and is trying to fit the memory stick back in place by squeezing the holder with her fingers. It's not working.

"Yeah, well I work here. It's my job to know." Jack touches Orca lightly on her upper arm. She looks up, startled. "Come with me. I can fix it."

"We'll come too," says Nadia, stepping forward.

"We'd love to," says Nick. "But we can't."

"Why ...?"

'We're leaving. We have a long drive and I want to get going while there's still plenty of daylight left."

"I didn't know we were leaving today."

"Well we are."

"Where you headed?" asks Jack.

"North."

"Can't we just stay another day? We could set off in the morning so we have the whole day for the journey."

"Nope. We're done here. Nice to see you guys."

Nick beams at Jack and Orca, then takes Nadia by the elbow.

"Goodbye," she says. Her eyes latch on to Orca's as though trying to communicate something.

"Which forest are you going to next?" Orca asks.

"Kielder," Nick gives her a big grin. "The biggest manmade forest in Europe. It will be difficult to find anything in there. Like looking for a needle in a haystack. Just in case you're thinking of it."

He and Nadia walk away. Nadia looks back over her shoulder and waves. Orca waves back and the baby gurgles.

"That was weird," says Jack.

"I don't think Nadia wants to go."

"Too right she doesn't. I wonder why she doesn't tell him to stuff off. Another day wouldn't make a difference."

"She loves the baby. She doesn't want to fight."

"He's a cute baby."

Orca turns and looks at Jack. He's smiling and he looks cleaner now that Nick has gone. "You like babies?"

"Who doesn't like babies? Come on, let's go and fix your bracelet."

Chapter Seven

Jack's cabin is made from wood. It has a porch, with two chairs and a small wooden table, overlooking a fenced patch of grass. Beyond the fence the trees are held at bay by an area of overgrown gorse. Orca sits on the porch whilst Jack goes inside to find the pliers.

The forest is quiet in the aftermath of rain. Dampness pools beneath the pines. The ground sweats evaporation. Orca can hear Jack moving inside the cabin. She sees a movement and turns her head. A hare is standing near the gate watching her. Its ears are erect, eyes glittering. She sits very still. *Have you seen Bird?* she asks the hare inside her head. *Have you seen Sylva?* The hare doesn't answer. It returns her gaze, but its body is poised for flight.

Jack comes out of the door. He's holding two pairs of pliers of different sizes.

"There was a hare."

He smiles. "He usually visits at sunrise. The rain must have brought him out. Do you want these, or would you like me to have a go?"

Orca takes the pliers. The smaller pair is for fine work, its pointed jaws narrow.

"What do you use these for?"

"I make jewellery."

She looks at him. He doesn't seem to be making fun of her, but she's not sure. She finds faces difficult to read. She uses the larger pliers to bend the fitting on the bracelet. If he really makes jewellery perhaps she should let him do this.

"What kind of jewellery?"

"I use things I find in the forest. Bits of bark, seedpods, snail shells – all sorts. I dry them, preserve them, and make them into jewellery."

She seems to have done it. She tries slotting in the memory stick. It clicks into place, and she smiles.

"Maybe if it's precious you shouldn't wear it. I mean, like all the time. When you're walking."

"You're probably right. I should keep it zipped in my pocket."

"Do you want a drink? Beer? Tea?"

She should say no. She should say *thank you for your help* and go on her way. She hasn't even checked for messages from Dorcas. It's less than two hours since the previous beer.

"Beer would be nice."

"I've got some cold in the fridge."

It tastes great – much better than the beer in the pub. The bottle is wet with condensation and the label is soggy. She pushes at the edges with her fingernail. The sun is properly shining now, drawing up all the moisture from the forest floor. The air between the trees shimmers.

"Don't you want to know what's on the memory stick?" Jack asks.

"I haven't thought about it."

"Really? I would be so curious. I am curious, and it's not even mine."

"I don't have the correct technology."

"I do."

Orca drinks from her bottle. She frowns. It's the afternoon, and if she leaves now she can walk back across the forest to the road. She can find a place to spend the night. She can think about Nadia and the baby and what she should do next.

"Was the thing you found for your jewellery? In the pub, when I thought you had my memory stick."

"Yes. Matt has a shop in Orford where he sells some of my stuff. That's why I was showing it to him. I found it here on the porch this morning."

"Is jewellery making your job?"

He laughs. "No, a hobby, a side hustle. I'm a forester." He goes back into the cabin and brings out a wooden box. Inside it's divided into compartments – some containing stones, flints, shells, pine cones; others, silvers chains and fastenings. Orca picks up a stubby white stone which marks her fingers.

"That's chalk. I probably won't use that. It's too soft."

"Can I have it?"

Jack shrugs. "You can have an actual piece. These here are finished. Choose one. You can have whichever you like."

The finished necklaces hang from a silver tree in his other hand. Orca looks at them, touching the stones and pieces of bark. One of them has a small tightly closed cone, lacquered and set in a filigree pendant.

"Is this from the Corsican Pine?"

"Yes, do you want to try it?"

He lifts it from the display and fastens it round her neck. It feels warm on her skin. She slips the chalk into her pocket.

"Do you live here on your own? Are you not lonely?"

Most humans like to have the company of other humans. This cabin is alone in the forest, nothing near except trees.

"That suits you."

"Thank you."

They sit in silence. Squirrels are racing in the branches. A blackbird is singing accompanied by the rat-a-tat of a woodpecker. Some cyclists appear on the track, dressed in brightly coloured lycra, moving fast. They whizz past the cabin at high speed. The air smells of pine and mushrooms.

"I'm not very good around people."

Orca looks at Jack, but he's rearranging the jewellery. She waits.

"Do you want some food?" he says. "I could make pasta."

"You are hungry again?"

The words come out before she checks them. She realises they could seem rude. His plate of fish and chips had been enormous.

He doesn't seem offended though. He's laughing. "Well, maybe not yet. In a bit. If you want to stick around."

"Tomorrow I might follow Nadia. I might go to Kielder Forest."

"Why would you do that?"

"She needs me. She's in danger."

"What sort of danger?"

"Nick – he is violent."

"Really? He seemed like a teddy bear to me, but I suppose you can never tell." He looks sideways at Orca. "What do you think you can do? If you even find them?"

She shrugs. "I don't know, but I feel I must be there."

"Is that what you're doing then, following them about?"

"I was surveying woodland. Not here, in Warwickshire, some woods called The Hayes. Now I am following Nadia and Nick."

"Surveying for what?"

"Holistic surveying. Recording the complete experience."

"That sounds full on."

"I should return to The Hayes, that is my intended purpose. But I think I will go to Kielder."

"Your intended purpose – you speak strangely, you know that?" He drains his beer. "Would you like to see something cool?"

They walk further up the track for about half a mile, then Jack points between the trees.

"This way."

Orca looks at the wall of trees lining both sides of the track, uniform trunks spaced three metres apart.

"How do you know it's this way?" she asks. "It all looks the same."

Jack points to the tree nearest to him.

The bark of the tree has been carved with an X, about the size of an adult hand and at elbow height.

"You go to this place often?"

"Not really, but I wanted to remember how to get there."

They walk in a straight line along the row of trees. The canopy is dense and nothing is growing on the forest floor, other than some patches of moss. The ground is loose and sandy and breaks beneath their feet. Light filters through, but it's gloomier than out on the path. Jack is counting the trees, touching each as he passes it, saying the numbers out loud. Orca says nothing, not wanting to break his concentration.

When he gets to forty-seven he turns right and continues along another line of the grid, still counting. Orca feels she might burst with curiosity. She grabs his arm and stops him.

"Twenty three. This one is twenty three. How do you know what number to count to?"

"The first time I came here, I was lost. I counted the trees until I found the path, I memorised the numbers."

"So this route – is it the most efficient?"

Jack shrugs. "Probably not. But I know it works."

"You could draw a grid of the forest and mark on the rows of trees, then plot a line which is more direct."

Jack stares at her for a moment. Then he points past tree twenty-three. "Look there."

A few meters away is a young birch tree standing in a pool of sunlight. "There's a pine missing there. It didn't thrive. Your grid wouldn't know that. I'm counting the actual trees, that are here."

"Wouldn't you like to find a faster route?"

"No. I have a route. I don't want to spend my evenings drawing grids."

"I would enjoy making the grid."

"Well we're different then." Jack is still staring at her, but suddenly he laughs. "Come on, we're not there yet."

They turn twice more, Jack counting trunks all the way. The forest has changed. The trees seem closer together, or the canopy is denser, either way it's darker here, harder to breathe.

Then they step out into the open. They're still in the heart of the forest, but this space, just a few meters across, has no trees or shrubs. The grass is short and the ground lumpy with rabbit burrows. In the middle something large and metallic catches the sunlight.

Orca steps forward for a better look. "How did that get here?"

"I don't know. Come and look."

The car has obviously been there for some time. Although parts of it still gleam enough to reflect the sun, much of it has rusted over. It's tilted at an angle on the uneven ground, two of its wheels hovering in the air.

Orca looks back at the way they've come. "There's not room ... between the trees. You couldn't drive here."

"It's a mystery. The trees here are seventy years old. This type of mini – well, it's not one of the originals, it's nowhere near as old as the trees. Come on, you have to see this."

Orca follows him to the abandoned car. She feels anxious. She didn't feel anxious before, even though she was walking with a stranger into the middle of the forest. She feels no threat from Jack – and even if she is wrong about him, she has the trees. She doesn't need to count them, she knows that if she ran they would hide her. The anxiety she feels now is not to do with Jack.

He grabs the nearest handle and opens the passenger door. The outside of the car looks like a blue mini, rusting with age. Inside it doesn't look like a car at all. The seats have been removed, and the dashboard has been replaced with a set of dials and controls that look more like the flight deck of an aeroplane. There's litter on the floor.

Jack picks up a takeaway pizza box and looks at it.

"This is new," he says. "Someone's been here since I last came."

"What does it mean?" Orca stares at the interior of the car. She steps back and looks at the outside. She walks around it. "It's ordinary on the outside, but inside ..."

"Like the Tardis."

"The Tardis?"

There must be something in the data, because an image comes into her mind. A blue box, a child laughing. She shakes her head and the image disappears.

"No, not really the Tardis. It only looks bigger in there because they've taken out the seats. And those dials and stuff – they look pretty cheap. I think it's just a toy."

"Here in the forest? Who would want a toy like this, here?"

"Like I said – it's a mystery."

"Let me lead the way back."

"You know if you get lost in here it can be hours if you don't hit one of the tracks."

"I know the way we came. 47 trees, 32 trees, 27 trees, 9 trees. Each time we turned we turned 90 degrees, right, then left, then right, then left. I can see that path in my head. I don't think we will be lost."

"It will be dark in just over an hour."

"It will make no difference. The lines of trees are straight. And if we get lost we can sleep here."

"I was going to make pasta."

"We'll be back at the cabin before dark."

Orca sets off in the direction they'd come from, but she doesn't turn after nine trees. She can see why Jack did turn here, the first time when he was lost, as there is a slightly bigger gap to the right, inviting you that way. Pushing straight ahead seems more like trespassing, but the trees do nothing to stop them.

Jack's lips are moving, and she suspects he is secretly counting the trees, but she doesn't ask. They reach a damp patch where the moss grows thick and lush, and water rises around their shoes when they step on it.

Orca turns right.

"Why are you turning here?"

"There's a landmark. This moss. I'll be able to find it again if I need to."

She knows he is mentally logging the number, but she doesn't want to know what it is. These trees are younger, their trunks are narrower and their branches don't quite meet overhead. More light can get through, but it's a different light now. The sun has fallen below the tops of the trees and the space between them is full of shadows.

Orca is in front and she nearly trips over. Jack walks into the back of her.

"What, what is it?"

They both look at the ground. A deer has been split apart, its body cut in a line down the abdomen and opened like a book, its skin pegged to the ground with tent pegs, its organs on display. It's a dissection. Orca has never had to dissect an animal, but she has information in the database, she understands what she is seeing.

"What the fuck!" Jack looks like he might throw up.

There's a knife on the floor which has blood on the blade, and near it a hammer and some scattered pegs. The smell of fresh meat is overpowering.

"I think we've disturbed them," Orca says very quietly.

"We should go." Jack pulls her arm. "Come on."

He starts back the way they've come, but Orca stops him.

"No, this way." The tools were on the righthand side of the deer and she guesses that's the way the perpetrator has gone. She heads left.

"It shouldn't be far to the track this way. Keep going straight."

They're both running now, either side of a row of trees. Jack has abandoned counting and is in full panic mode. But she's right – the trees end and they tumble out onto the track, a hundred yards or so further along than they'd gone in.

Jack bends forward with his hands on his knees panting.

"What the fuck was that? What kind of sick...?"

Orca wonders if he might cry. He is showing strong physical signs of emotion. His face is red and he's sweating – though that could be from the run. His breathing is uneven.

She touches his sleeve. "Come on, we can walk now."

Back at the cabin Jack gets more beers from the fridge. He gets vegetables out and puts them on the worktop. He picks up the chopping knife, then sighs and puts it down again.

"I can't do this yet."

They sit on the porch and drink beer as the sun sets. Jack rolls a cigarette from herbs and weed. He offers it to Orca but she shakes her head.

"Why the hell would someone do something like that?"

Orca has been pondering this question. The point of dissection is for exploration or for display – either way the intended end result is learning – either for the dissector or the observer. Presumably they had not expected to be disturbed.

"Do you think it was one person only?" she says.

Jack stares wildly at her. "I hope so. I hope there's not more than one sick fucker out there."

"It's true it would have been more difficult to hide silently if there was more than one. We might have heard something."

"This has been one weird day."

"Will you go back in the morning?"

"God, no!' Jack puts out his cigarette and sighs. His shoulders drop. "I suppose I ought to. I do kind of have some responsibility. I ought to report it."

"To the police?"

"To my bosses first. They can go to the police if they want to. But do you know what?"

Orca looks at him.

"Let's forget about it for the moment. I'm going to put some music on and make pasta and not think about sick bastards out there in the dark."

"Would you like some help?"

The pasta smells delicious and glistens with oil and tomatoes. It's a long time since Orca has eaten real food.

"Give me a small portion," she says. "My stomach isn't used to bulk."

She feels self-conscious using the muscles in her cheeks. Jack isn't looking at her though, he's eating quickly, fork in one hand and phone in the other as he changes the music.

"Marvin Gaye," she says, and he grins at her.

She swallows and puts another piece of pasta in her mouth. She thinks about the previous night and what has changed. Last night she was alone in the forest in the rain, then the long walk to the coast, the night curled in a porch – the first night spent indoors in months. And now, she has been inside a pub as well as inside this cabin. She is with someone else. Jack has finished his pasta now and he takes his bowl over to the sink. She's not afraid of him. She has stayed in his company when she could have left.

"Did you want to look at that memory stick?"

She has just put more food in her mouth.

"It's just that I've got a laptop with a USB port, so we could probably have a look if you want. When you've finished eating."

She has eaten less than half of the pasta, but it's hard work. She puts the fork down on the table and swallows the mass that is filling her mouth.

"Do you think I should?"

He shrugs. "It's up to you, I guess. I'm really curious myself. If I was you, I'd want to know what's on there."

"OK. Get the laptop."

He goes to find it, and she tries another mouthful. The pasta's cooled down and makes her think of the white fungus that sometimes grows on the sides of trees. She pushes the bowl to the side of the table, and when Jack returns he doesn't say anything. He opens the laptop. She removes the charm bracelet from her pocket and fits the memory stick into its attachment.

The anxiety is back.

Jack boots up the laptop and fits the memory stick into the port. An icon appears on the screen. The drive is named Olive.

Jack clicks on it and a box opens. It contains a folder labelled Photos.

She flattens his hand with hers. "Slowly."

He looks at her. "Are you sure you want to look?"

The food was a bad idea. Her digestive process is out of practice. She can feel acid moving in her gut, but the pasta is sitting solid.

"OK." She removes her hand.

He opens the folder before she can change her mind. There are ten photos showing as icons. They are a set – family photos of a woman, a man and two children, taken in a garden. One child is four or five, a girl, and the other a baby. There are different groupings, the two children, the father and the baby, the mother laughing with the girl on her shoulders, the parents together, and one of all four of them sitting on a bench. Jack opens this photo and it fills the screen. They both look at it. The woman in the photos is Orca.

She gets up and runs to the bathroom and is sick for the second time that day. If she's to eat human food she needs to start with something less shiny than pasta.

When she returns Jack has closed the laptop.

"You OK?"

"I've been living on nutrition pills and protein bars. And I'm not used to beer."

He gets her a glass of water.

"Do you know ...?' he nods towards the laptop.

"They must have been created. Dorcas told me I have false memories implanted."

"Dorcas?"

"My controller."

Jack frowns.

"My boss."

"Memory implants? Are they even a thing?"

"Apparently so. I will ask her about these photos and why they have been put on the memory stick."

"You don't recognise the other people in them?"

Orca drinks the glass of water and feels the cleansing wash through her gullet. She rinses the glass and stands it on the side, then turns to face Jack, her bottom leaning against the sink.

"No, I don't."

"So..."

"Let's talk about something else."

Jack puts more music on.

"Al Green," says Orca.

"You know your music."

"I have recognition software."

He fills the kettle and gets two mugs from the cupboard. "You are the strangest person I've ever met," he says. "Would you like some tea?"

"Do you have any herbal infusions?"

"Herbal ...? I have peppermint tea, or chamomile."

"Chamomile would be perfect, thank you."

The kettle boils and he makes the drinks. They sit back at the table. The laptop is closed and Orca doesn't look at it.

"So how are you going to get to Kielder?" Jack asks.

"I travelled here by train," says Orca.

"Kielder's pretty remote as far as I know."

"You think the train won't go there?"

"Let's look." He opens an app on his phone and scrolls through, then looks at another app. "You'd need to go to Hexham, but that's 35 miles away. There's a bus from there, but only a couple of times a week."

"I can walk."

"I could take you."

"I don't understand."

"I've got a van. I could drive you there."

"Don't you have to work?"

"Yeah, but I haven't taken any holiday this year. They'll be OK. I'll just have to report that ... thing ... we found. But after that, we could set off mid-morning."

"Why would you do this?"

He shrugs. "I've never been that far north. It's nearly Scotland."

She is too tired to argue. She suddenly needs sleep. He offers her his bed, saying he can sleep on the sofa.

"I would prefer the porch. I'm not used to sleeping indoors."

"Are you sure?"

"Yes."

"OK, well I'll get you a sleeping bag and a camping mat."

The air is fresh and she breathes in deeply, listening to the owls. The warmth of the cabin has dulled her senses. She lies on the camping mat. It's not as comfortable as the soft ground beneath trees, but she is soon asleep.

She wakes with first light and sits on the porch looking at the forest, silhouetted black against the pale sky. The dawn chorus is deafening. The air is chilly and she wraps the sleeping bag around her shoulders.

After a while she goes into the cabin and gets the laptop. She closes her eyes and thinks about Sylva as a girl, running in a red coat in the Hayes. Then she looks at the photos again.

The child is a girl, but it's hard to tell with the baby. The man has dark hair and skin and might be Indian. They look like a happy family. The woman who has been given Orca's face, is smiling in every picture. She tries it now, lifting the corners of her mouth. She feels like an animal grimacing.

Jack appears with a cup of peppermint tea for her. She ejects the memory stick and fits it back into the charm bracelet, closes the laptop. He sits on the step cradling his cup in his hands. Neither of them speak.

When the tea is gone, he takes the cups and the laptop back inside, returns wearing coat and boots.

"I'm going back," he says, "To see what's there, and get the coordinates. Then I'll report it before we set off. Make yourself comfortable – if you want a shower or breakfast ..."

"I'm coming with you."

"You sure?"

"You'll need me to find it. You were panicking too much to get your bearings."

Jack looks at her but says nothing. She knows that people communicate without words, but she isn't sure what he means with this look. She could ask him. Instead she rolls up the sleeping bag and camping mat and fastens her shoes.

She remembers where they came out of the forest onto the track, and that they'd followed a straight line of trees in their mad dash. She doesn't remember exactly how far they'd run, but she knows when they've gone too far.

"It's not here," she says. "It's gone."

"Maybe we're in the wrong place."

They look around for a while but find nothing.

"They must have taken it away after we'd disturbed them. Well, I'll report it, but they probably won't be able to do anything, with no evidence."

Back at the cabin Jack makes a phone call, then packs a small backpack with belongings. He eats a bowl of cereal, but Orca refuses and makes do with some nutrition pills. It's still early. The sun is above the pines and the whole forest is glowing with warmth when they set off in Jack's van.

Chapter Eight

"My grandma came from up that way," Jack says. They are driving up the A14 towards Huntingdon. Jack has chosen a disco playlist and Orca toes are twitching to Sylvester.

"Kielder?"

"Not far. Near Carlisle – a village called Croglin."

"But you've never been?"

"She moved when she married my grandad. They met at the Royal Show, both of them from farming families. She lived the rest of her life in Suffolk."

"Will we go through Croglin?"

"No. the quickest way is up the A1, the other side of the country."

There's a road atlas in the door next to Orca. She opens it and studies the route.

"We could cross over, at Birmingham, or further up on the M62. The M6 would take us nearer – we could go and have a look."

"I don't know. I don't see what the point would be really. I don't have family there anymore, and it would make the journey longer."

"We could stay overnight."

"I thought you wanted to find Nadia."

"She didn't ask me to follow. One more night would be OK."

"I don't know." They pass a water tower outside Huntingdon. "If we get onto the A1 here and go straight up, we'll be in Kielder by teatime."

"What was your grandma like?"

The song comes to an end and another starts with the flat sound of a church bell from a horror film.

"I shouldn't listen to this stuff when I'm driving, it makes me go too fast."

The bell is followed by a comedy vampire laugh and a disco beat. Orca checks the playlist. Soul Dracula by Hot Blood.

"Gran used to tell stories. She died when I was ten, so I only have vague memories. I do remember though, she said Croglin had a vampire."

"Well that's it then. We have to go. It's a sign."

Jack glances at her, then back at the road. He indicates to change lane, following the signs for the A14 on towards Kettering. "I'm surprised you believe in signs. Doesn't seem like your thing."

Orca listens to the music. She can imagine dancing to it. She can feel the shape of her body moving and when she closes her eyes she can see coloured lights, a dance floor.

"Do you dance?" she asks.

He's looking at the road, but even so Orca can see the shutters come down. "No," he says. He doesn't say anything else, and a couple of miles later he changes the music.

The drive to Croglin takes them along lanes which get ever narrower. Over to the right the Pennine hills loom darkly, but the road goes between bright fields with stone walls. It's late afternoon and the village pub has opened. Jack buys drinks – a coke and a soda water – and they sit outside.

"I'll text my mum," says Jack. "Ask her if there's anything to see. She came here as a kid."

The red brick houses glow in the sunshine. Orca sips her drink and feels the bubbles fizz at the back of her throat.

"What's with dancing then?" she says. "Why not?"

Jack looks away, but she perseveres.

"All the music you play has a beat – you seem like someone who'd like to dance."

He coughs and drinks some coke. "I used to."

"But not anymore?"

"I was at ... there was .... something happened. I don't want to talk about it."

"OK."

It's not OK, Orca wants the answer. She wants to say – *no, tell me* – even to shake the answer from him. She hasn't felt this before when talking to someone. She has never felt so curious, so ... invested is probably the word.

Jacks phone pings.

"Mum says they used to cycle to the next village where there are some old hazel trees near the moor."

Orca looks at the map. The next village is Newbiggin. She searches the data for hazels and finds a record for an ancient tree with a matching grid reference. She can feel changes in her body, a churning in her stomach, a fizzing in her veins. She's excited.

"Can we go?"

Jack nods. "Let's get some food first."

Orca doesn't care about food, but she waits while Jack eats a burger and chips. She reads about hazels in the database.

"Some people say hazels are the most magical of all trees,' she tells Jack.

He wipes the plate with the last of the chips and places the cutlery neatly in the middle of the plate. "I was in a club, with my girlfriend, and there was a stampede."

"A club?"

"A nightclub. We used to go dancing."

"I didn't know you had a girlfriend."

"I don't, not anymore."

"Did you break up? At the club?"

"There was a fire, and a stampede. Two people died. I didn't know where Becky was, she'd gone to the toilet. I was fighting to get back into the club to find her, but they wouldn't let me through. I saw the dead people. People were stamping on them, running over them, I've never seen anything like it, they were like animals."

"Was she …?"

"No not animals, not unless they're frightened. They were ugly and desperate, they wanted to save themselves and didn't care if anyone fell or if they trod on them." Jack's eyes are dark and unfocused.

She touches his hand. "I'm sorry."

He looks at her fingers and turns his hand so their palms are touching. "Becky was fine," he says. "She was already outside."

"And you?"

"I was fine too. Physically anyway. But I started having nightmares after, and panic attacks if there were many people about. I took the job in the forest because it was isolated, I wouldn't have to be around people. It wasn't what Becky wanted."

Orca squeezes his hand. "Let's go and find some hazel trees," she says.

The path to the moors is easy to find. They leave the van at the bottom and walk through a valley of ancient trees. Near the road aspens tremble, their roots sipping at a fast flowing brook. There are many hazels, and their nuts litter the ground. Most of the kernels have been eaten already, but Orca cracks one open with her teeth and chews the sweet white flesh. There are also hawthorns, rowans, birches and oaks growing in twisted shapes above lush green grass. Halfway up the path to the moor is a hazel that has grown in the shape of an arch, and beneath it is a green hollow.

"Let's sleep here tonight," says Orca.

"You and your outdoor sleeping!"

"It looks so comfortable."

"You know if you fall asleep under a hazel tree you'll wake up in fairy land…"

"I would like to see fairy land."

"You might not get back."

p.276

Orca sits down beneath the tree. The arch frames the horizon where the field meets the sky. The sun is low and the arch does look like a portal to a shining world.

"If you prefer you could sleep in the back of the van," she says.

Jack shakes his head. "No, this is an opportunity not to be missed. If you wake up in another world I want to as well."

The next morning when they set off the valley looks the same, though flushed with morning light, but since leaving the main road they haven't seen another car. No walkers or workers. No humans at all. It's been fifteen miles of emptiness. Orca says nothing. Maybe it's always like that here. She knows it would mean nothing in other parts of the world – fifteen miles with no people, fifteen hundred miles more like, in Canada, Botswana, Australia. But here it seems like something. Kielder is the most remote village in England and they haven't reached it yet.

There are signs of humans – an area of felled trees, a large corrugated building with vans parked outside, fences, the occasional house. It's not wild, this is a managed landscape. But nobody's here.

Jack doesn't say anything either. The music is still playing and the van swerves along the winding road to the sound of Curtis Mayfield's Keep On Keeping On. Sometimes the road narrows to almost single track and the verge starts to blur into the moors, then there is a stretch newly tarmacked, the white lines smart and confident. The sky fills a wide V-shape between the hills, rolling with high clouds and fuzzed along the edges by plantation trees. Orca looks at Jack's profile. He's singing along silently to the music, emphasising the notes with movements of his head. She wonders if he'd sing out loud if she wasn't here.

They cross a cattle grid and the valley narrows. The forest comes closer until trees are lining the road, peering at them as they pass. Over a stone bridge they pass a sign for Kielder

Village, Kielder Skyspace off to the right, and then a sign for a campsite. Jack turns into it.

'Worth having a look," he says.

The campsite is long and narrow, straddling the river with an iron bridge. There are wooden sleeping pods, a brick toilet block, fire pits, washing-up posts and static caravans. But no people. It's eleven in the morning.

"Maybe everyone's off for the day, at the lake or whatever," says Jack.

They park the van next to two other cars and get out. The campsite office is a wooden building with a sign outside advertising ice-creams and camping gas. The door's open but there's no one inside. The shelves are stocked with tinned food and midge repellent and there's a bell on the counter. Jack rings it and the sound fills the small space. No one appears from the back room.

"Look," says Orca. There's a notice sellotaped to the counter.

If I'm not here, I'll be out on the site and won't be long. Try again in 15 minutes.

They go back outside. Quiet air is sitting heavily above them. There's hardly a breeze in the valley. They're surrounded by trees. Nothing is moving.

"We could go for a walk, see if we can see him."

"OK," says Orca.

There are a few tents pitched on the long tongue of grass reaching down to the river. They are zipped up and silent. Orca and Jack reach the end of the field and walk on along the river bank into a gravelled carpark. There are a couple of cars parked here, as well as Nick and Nadia's van.

Orca finds she is gripping Jack's arm. She hadn't expected to find them so easily.

Jack is looking at her. She is unnerved by the quietness, and she'd like to hear a voice, see a familiar face, even if there is awkward explaining to be done. She tugs at Jack's sleeve and together they approach the van. Orca knocks on the door.

There's no answer.

"There's a pub up there, shall we have a look?"

The long car park could belong to the pub or be an extension of the campsite, sitting between the two. The building is low lying, painted white, and closed, even though the sign on the door says they open at 11.30, which has now just passed.

They cross the road and walk up the hill to Kielder Castle, a Victorian castellated manor house housing a visitors' centre. This is also closed. All the doors are locked and there is no one about.

"I don't understand," says Jack. "Where is everyone?"

"Is it a bank holiday?"

"No, it's not. And if it were, you'd expect it to be busier."

"Maybe something's happened."

Jack looks at his phone, but there's no signal.

There has been radio silence from Dorcas, but Orca is sure she's tracking her, that she knows where she is. Maybe it's time to make contact.

"Can I have a minute on my own?"

Jack looks around the empty courtyard across to the coach park. There are no cars or coaches. It is a field of empty tarmac and white lines.

"Sure, I'll wander down that way." He points in the opposite direction. A footpath is signed for the Minotaur Maze.

When he's gone Orca sits down on a low wall and calls Dorcas. Even though Jack couldn't get a signal, she's sure she will find one, as Dorcas provided her with the most advanced system. She waits. The courtyard has tables and chairs for overspill from the café, but they don't look like they've been used for a while. There is tree debris littering the wooden slats – leaves, seeds, small twigs. In a few places there are bird droppings.

Opposite her, beyond the café, is a row of windows, some of them piled up with books and files of paperwork. She crosses the courtyard and peers in. The first window looks into an office. There are three desks, each with the kind of office chair that spins round, but one of them has been overturned and is lying on the floor. One of the desks has botanical specimens laid out on pieces of blotting paper. The desk next to the overturned chair has a mug on it – Orca can't tell if there's anything in it. Everything is covered with a thin layer of dust.

Something crackles. It's Dorcas, but the signal is very weak.

"Hello, are you there? Dorcas?"

"He ...th...re...ing."

"I can't hear you. Try sending a message."

The line goes dead.

Orca walks along to the next window. This looks into a small kitchen. There is a microwave, a fridge, a kettle. There are more mugs set out on the surface next to the kettle, and this time Orca can see that they are full of mould.

She leaves the courtyard and runs down the footpath to the maze.

"Jack, where are you?" The maze is square and built of walls of caged stones. It doesn't look as though it would be very easy to get lost in there. "Are you in the maze?"

She thinks she hears his voice and goes in. She knows something about mazes. Touch the walls, with one hand only – she chooses the right – keep your hand in contact with the wall at all times. It might not take you the quickest way through, but it will eventually bring you out again. She sets off, feeling the wires with her fingertips.

"Jack, are you in here?" The wall takes her to the right then the left, into a small alcove which she traces with her right hand, then on again. At one point she has to duck under a low archway. She feels she's walked a long way for such a small maze. "Jack!"

She takes a sharp right and collides with him. She's back at the entrance and he's standing next to it. He holds her wrists and steps away, releases her.

"Are you OK?"

"I was looking for you in the maze. I heard your voice."

"I didn't go in. I was over there, sitting on a bench."

"Oh." The twists and turns must have bent the sound. "Your voice sounded like you were in there."

"I didn't say anything. I heard you calling and came to see what was the matter." They both turn and looked at the maze. "Are you sure it was a voice?"

"Yes ... no ... I thought I was sure. I expect the wind makes strange noises in there."

The day is still and warm, there's no wind. High cloud cover gives a pearl grey look to the sky, as though there's nothing up there. As though if you travelled up and up you would gradually fade away.

"Did you manage to make contact?"

Orca checks for messages. There are none. "This place is bad for signal."

They walk back down to the road, past the locked-up pub, across the carpark and alongside the river.

"Can you hear that?" asks Orca.

"What?"

"Birdsong."

"There's lots of birdsong – there's a blackbird, that one repeating itself is a thrush. Woodpigeons, a robin ..."

"No, something else ... there, listen ..."

"I don't think ..."

"I keep hearing it, a birdsong I don't know, but I can never quite catch it. I've tried looking it up, but I can never remember it."

"Is it a goldcrest? I thought I heard a goldcrest earlier"

"No. Maybe I am imagining it, like the voice in the maze. I think I have a malfunction."

Jack looks at her and shakes his head. They enter the pointed end of the campsite and walk along the path. Now that she's tuned into it, the birdsong all around is overwhelming. She can't hear Bird anymore, but she's glad he's here. Her anxiety levels have gone way up since they arrived, but Bird is familiar. He has come with her from the Hayes, to Rendlesham and now to Kielder. He's obviously attached to her in some way, and he feels like a comforting rather than a threatening presence.

"Look at the grass. Was it like that before?" Jack is pointing at a small purple dome tent near the path.

The grass needs cutting all across the site. It's five inches or more everywhere, giving the place an unkempt look, spotted with dandelions and scattered here and there with patches of daisies. The grass is growing right up to the tent Jack is looking at, forming a fringe along the base of the entrance. It hasn't been flattened.

"No one can have been in or out of that tent for days – more than a week I'd say."

"Maybe they've gone trekking."

"It's not just this one. It's all of them, look."

They walk through the campsite looking at the tents. The grass grows around every one, sealing the doors with its green blades. Orca can feel something rising in her chest like a filled balloon being forced through her oesophagus.

"Hello!" Jack shouts, but his voice doesn't carry in the still air. "Hello, is anyone here?"

Chapter Nine

Back at the camp office Orca goes inside and rings the bell. The noise reverberates then dies away. She does it again, again, again. Ding, ding ding, the noise fills the wooden building, but outside there is stillness. Nobody comes, nobody answers.

Jack picks up a Snickers bar from the counter, unwraps it and takes a bite. Orca watches.

"What? You think this is stealing? I'll pay for it when there's someone to pay. Here."

He throws her a Twix and she catches it. She looks at the shiny wrapper in her hand. Outside she sits on a fence post. She doesn't remember eating chocolate. She opens the end of the packet and pulls out one of the two biscuits.

"Nick and Nadia can only have been here for two days," she says. "That's when they left Rendlesham. So the tent people must have already gone when they arrived."

"Presuming they came straight here and didn't stop overnight – which they might have done. If they broke their journey, then they'd have got here some time yesterday."

Orca bites into the Twix finger. The sugar makes her gasp.

"We'll need to find some real food, or we'll be living on chocolate." Jack has finished the Snickers and thrown the wrapper in the bin.

It's easier to chew than pasta – the chocolate and biscuit disintegrate quickly in her saliva, though the caramel takes longer. She swallows. She feels sugar hitting her bloodstream. Can that be right? First the food needs to be processed by her stomach, passed into her digestive tract, and only then will the constituent elements pass into her circulation. How quickly does than happen? Her body isn't used to the process, it's used to nutrition pills which bypass all of that, feed the blood directly. She finishes one biscuit and starts on the other. "What are we going to do?" she says between mouthfuls.

"We have three choices – we can wait for them, look for them or leave."

"Waiting and leaving are no good. We could wait forever. They might not return. And leaving – well. We have come all this way, and it feels that something is not right."

"We could go to the police," says Jack.

"Would the police be interested?"

"Everyone's disappeared. That's interesting. And also, it's not our responsibility."

"I promised Nadia I would help her."

"But she left."

Orca has eaten the whole Twix. It's not like the pasta, it doesn't sit in her stomach. It's more like heat, she can feel activity in her gut, a burning. She stretches her arms, stands up and lifts her legs one after the other.

"Where would we even start looking?" says Jack. "You know how big this forest is? If we tell the police, they'll know what to do."

"What about the village?" She walks up and down. "This is only the campsite, there may be people in the village."

Jack nods. "Good call. We'll check the village, and we'll check Nick and Nadia's van – see if there are any clues. Then we'll see."

"Let's go."

"OK. I'm going to grab a drink first though. Do you want one?"

"Yes, but not with sugar. Water please."

There isn't much village. A few rows of houses, a playground, a school-cum-library, a fire station. There's nobody in the street or the playground. There is no noise except birdsong.

"Let's knock on some doors," says Jack.

They try the first house. Jack raps loudly on the door with his knuckles. There's no response. The move to the next, which has a bell. They can hear the ringing reverberate through the house.

Orca checks for messages from Dorcas. What they are doing is so far from her instructions. *Avoid human contact if possible, when it's unavoidable be polite and disengage quickly.* She and Jack are actively seeking humans. And what about Jack himself? She hasn't disengaged from Jack. She has been with him for over forty-eight hours now.

The next house has a sign saying Beware of the Dog, but when they knock on the door, no one barks. There's nobody in these houses. The birdsong has become louder. Amongst the trills and warbling Orca can hear Bird, but only if she doesn't focus. When she tries to tune in to his voice, she can no longer hear him.

"Let's try the van," says Jack.

A footbridge takes them anticlockwise over the river and past the maze. They cross the road to the pub.

"Look," says Orca. "I didn't notice that before." There's a tin ashtray on one of the picnic tables, the size of a tea-plate. It has some cigarette ends in it, and they're floating in water. "Nobody has emptied it since the last rain."

"When did it rain?'

"I don't know, but the ground is dry. There are no puddles."

They knock on the van door again, just in case, but there's no answer. Jack tries the side door and it slides open.

Inside it looks much the same as last time Orca saw it. It's cluttered with clothes and books and smells faintly of baby. The cot is empty.

Jack picks up the books and looks at them. They're all books about nature, ID guides, red data books, a book about forests by Jim Crumley. He flicks through the pages, but nothing falls out. "Pristine," he says. "He doesn't write in his books."

Orca picks up clothes and shakes them, checks their pocket. She looks in the sheets of the cot, under the duvet on the bed.

She doesn't know what she's looking for, but all she finds are light wafts of smell; milk, wipes, sex.

There's not much in the front of the van either. No sign of the baby sling, backpack or any waterproof clothing, which suggests they headed out well prepared. On the driver's seat there's a slip of paper with a phone number written on it. Jack gets his phone out of his pocket and stares at it. "If we had signal ..."

"Was there a landline at the campsite office?"

"I don't know. Maybe in the back office."

It's the third time they've arrived at the campsite, and this time they've completed a circle. Nothing has changed. They go behind the counter and through to the office at the back. A cubby hole really. A desk, a chair, a filing cabinet, some maps pinned on the wall. A phone.

Jack lifts the handset and listens. He nods, his face lighting up.

"There's a dialling tone. Have you got that number?"

"Try Nadia first."

She reads out Nadia's number, but it goes straight to answerphone. "She won't have signal either," Jack says. He tries the number on the piece of paper, which is a landline number. "It's ringing."

He lets it ring a long time. Orca can hear the sound even though Jack's holding the phone to his ear. The short double peals wind around the room, filling it with a long line of sound, threaded with the two beads, brring brring. How long will he let it ring for?

She goes outside. She needs to think. This place is pressing down on her and she can barely remember why she's come. To find Nadia, to help Nadia. But Nadia told her she doesn't need her help anymore. She and Nick have made up their differences. She didn't ask Orca to follow her. She didn't send any messages on the journey. Orca's brought Jack all this way, and she doesn't even know what he wants. It's probably the emptiness that attracts him. An adventure which from which all the people seem to have vanished. But he couldn't have predicted this.

She looks up quickly. Her eyes have caught movement. To the left, down the field near the small tents, there's an animal. She stills, watches. It's behind one of the tents. She thinks she can hear the grass being torn as it grazes. Soon it will appear at the other side.

Jack is speaking inside the office. She focuses on his voice. He says something then waits, then speaks again. Someone must have answered the phone. She's torn between going in to listen to his end of the conversation and waiting for the animal to appear. Jack will tell her what was said. She waits.

Horns first, nudging the ground, then a soft mouth, the head. The animal is a white goat. She can't check the data due to the lack of signal, but she dredges through to see if she has anything stored about goats. Domesticated, used for milk, meat. A bad press when compared with sheep – *separate the sheep from the goats* – this fragment is floating free, not attached to anything. She doesn't know what it means, except that sheep are meant to be better.

Very slowly she stands up. The goat takes no notice. She takes a step, then another. It keeps chewing. She keeps the pace slow and covers the ground between them. The goat looks up once and regards her with its horizontally slit eyes, then drops its head and continues to graze. She reaches the tent and is within touching distance, she reaches out her arm. The goat jumps sideways evading her hand but continues the munch the grass.

"Hello," she says, and the goat ignores her.

"Orca! Where are you?" Jack's shout rings across the campsite. The goat isn't bothered by the sound, but Orca doesn't want to shout back. She stands and waves her arm. Jack spots her and runs across the field. At his approach the goat finally decides to take to its heels. It runs across the grass and into the trees.

"Was that a goat?"

"I was making friends with it."

"Sorry. I got through, I spoke to someone."

"Who? Did they know what was happening?"

Jack frowns. "No, it was a child, a boy. He said he was with his brother, that their grandfather works in the forest."

"They were left alone?"

"He said he's twelve. He gave me directions"

"To where?"

"Their house – his grandfather's house. He said if we come up later, we can talk to his grandfather."

"You could have been anyone."

"But at least there's someone we can talk to. The man might know what's going on."

"He shouldn't have answered the phone. His grandfather should have told him to ignore it."

"Did you hear how long it rang for? He probably only answered because he was fed up."

Orca looks over to the trees. The goat is standing in the edge of the forest, still grazing. "What time is it now?"

Jack looks at his watch. "Just gone two."

"When should we go to find the boy?"

"I guess early evening. Time for the grandfather to be back from work."

"I'm going to follow the goat."

She walks towards the trees. Jack follows and puts his hand on her shoulder.

"What are you talking about? You can't."

"Why not?"

"Well for a start it's not going anywhere." The goat lifts its head and watches them. A twig with leaves is sticking out of its mouth as it chews. It doesn't seem bothered that they are so close. "And if it does go somewhere, you'll get lost."

"Only if the goat gets lost. Which it won't."

"You can't just follow a goat."

"Watch me."

p.277

The goat chooses that moment to walk deeper into the trees. Orca goes after it, and Jack follows.

"We shouldn't separate."

"OK."

The goat is walking quite purposefully, winding a path between tree trunks. The ground is mossy and soft, but quite dry. Light filters through the treetops. The goat crosses a wide path and leaps up the bank on the opposite side.

Orca scrabbles up after it, using some tree roots to pull herself up to the top. Jack gets there before her and gives her a hand. They brush the dust off their clothes and look for the goat. It is just still in sight, and they set off through the trees after it. Orca remembers the straight lines at Rendlesham. The trees here are not in straight rows, counting them wouldn't help at all.

"It seems to know where it's going," Jack whispers.

The goat doesn't stop to eat, or for anything else. The ground is sloping uphill, and it travels in more or less the straightest line. It walks fast and Orca and Jack struggle to keep up. Its white shape keeps slipping out of sight, then reappearing behind a tree further on. Then it disappears altogether.

Orca runs forward hoping to startle it. "Goat, where are you?"

The forest suddenly ends, and they are on a single-track road. The goat is nowhere to be seen. On the other side of the road the trees crowd close to the edge. They are much bigger than those they've been walking through, and there's no space between them. Their lower branches slope down to the ground, forming a barrier; it's impossible to see into the forest.

Orca and Jack are both panting from their chase up the hill.

"It could have gone anywhere," says Jack. "We've lost it."

"I'm just going to look."

Between the road and the trees is a ditch with water in the bottom. Orca takes a large step across it onto the mossy bank beneath the trees. Her foot sinks into wetness, water seeps up around her boots. She feels as though she's standing on a sponge.

She parts the branches in front of her. It's dark inside. The trees are close together and their branches low to the ground – too low for a person to be able to stand upright. There is nothing below them, no other plants growing, no squirrels or birds, no goats. It's still and dark and secret. Orca lets go of the branches and turns back to the light. Her feet are completely under water now. She steps back across the ditch onto the road.

"What sort of trees are these?" she asks Jack.

"Sitka Spruce. Most of the trees at Kielder are Sitka. The crop trees that is."

"They have a different energy than Corsican Pine."

"They are certainly denser, when they're planted close like this. These are probably seventy or eighty years old. They'll be felled in ten or twenty years."

"How long would they live if they were left to themselves?"

"Oh, much longer. Hundreds of years. In tree terms these are babies, adolescents. They're farming children here."

Orca looks at the trees lining the road, silent, dark, unknowable. They don't look like children. "We've lost the goat," she says.

"No we haven't."

She looks where he's pointing. The goat is standing in the middle of the road a few hundred yards to the right. It's looking at them.

They set off at a brisk pace. The goat waits until they have nearly reached it before leaping off the path and back into the trees on the right side of the road.

"I wish I could jump like that," said Jack.

"Let's try," said Orca. "Go on – jump into the woods like the goat."

"I'll need a run up."

He goes back a few paces, then runs down the road at an angle, past Orca to the place the goat had disappeared, then he leaps and lands in the edge of the woods. It's not as spectacular as the goat's jump, or as elegant, legs and arms akimbo. He's laughing, bent over, his hands on his knees.

"Your turn."

Orca goes back to the same spot, then a few yards further. She runs. Her arms swing and her legs power forward, the breath rushes into her lungs. She reaches the spot and pushes with all of her body, her legs against the floor, her arms against the air. Jack steps quickly out of the way and she lands beside him.

"Good jump."

"That felt amazing."

"You looked amazing."

"I'd forgotten how much I like to run and jump."

"You never run when you're in the forest?"

"I'd forgotten. And also, I'm meant to be watching and recording, not scaring everything away."

"Speaking of which, where's the goat?"

It's waiting for them further down the hill, standing still. When they start in its direction it trots off to the left.

"Where do you think it's taking us," whispers Orca.

"To its master," says Jack.

Ten minutes later they are back at the campsite. The goat is standing between the tents grazing, as though it had never left. It doesn't look up when Jack and Orca tumble out of the forest onto the grass.

"You're kidding me," says Jack.

"It was playing a trick on us."

"I made a joke, did you get it...? Oh never mind."

Chapter Ten

They get the stove out of Jack's van and make tea, which they drink with some biscuits from the campsite shop. Orca feels the hot liquid pass down her gullet, and the sweetness infuse her saliva. She doesn't drink hot drinks – when Jack made her chamomile in the cabin she'd let it go almost cold before she drank it – but the sensation is familiar. Perhaps it's to do with the implanted memories that Dorcas told her about – perhaps they include some of this everyday normality that humans share, that she didn't think she was a part of, the preparation of the brew, the infusion of the leaves, the pouring of the hot liquid, the imbibing. A ritual so commonplace that no one thinks of it as being one. A recognition of friendship, so important that people take it with them on camping trips when only essentials can be carried. The first thing to be done after a shock – the hot brew, the passing of the mug from hand to hand, the reminder that someone is there for you. She knows all of this, and not just because she's read about it. Drinking tea with Jack in the emptiness of the huge abandoned forest she understands she is no longer alone.

"Are we becoming friends?"

Jack gives her that odd look again. "Yes, I guess so." He takes another biscuit from the pack and dunks it in his tea. "Though I'm not following any more goats."

Jack had written the instructions on a piece of paper he'd found by the phone in the campsite office. He gives it to Orca.

"Can you navigate while I drive?"

"I'll do my best."

The instructions are simple to follow. Right out of the campsite, then left. Then keep driving. The road is lined on both sides by Sitka spruce, similar in size to those Orca had peered between earlier – heading towards a hundred years old, their skirts falling like evening dresses to touch the mossy floor, allowing no view into the interior. They drive for a mile, two miles. It seems much further on this narrow road, where there is no other traffic. At one point a deer crosses the path ahead, vanishing between the dark trees.

"You sure this is the right way?"

"We haven't reached a left turn yet, only that one on the right further back."

"Let's hope the kid knows his left from his right."

The trees stop abruptly and they are driving through open countryside. On the right there is a huge expanse which must have been clear-felled a year ago, maybe two. There are tiny trees sprouting, six inches high or a foot. The whole area is covered with white fluff. It looks like someone has got married, but on a huge scale. A giant's wedding with confetti covering acre upon acre. Two birds are flying across it, swooping, circling each other, flying back up into the sky.

Orca checks the data for an ID. Buzzards, cotton grass. The info had already been downloaded so it doesn't matter that she has no connection. She realises that Jack has stopped the van. Neither of them says anything, they watch the buzzards flying. A breeze ripples the cotton grass which moves in a wave, the white heads shaking and settling beneath the circles of the birds' flight in the early evening sunshine. Orca hadn't realised how much the trees held her until she was here in the open, exposed to movement, light, freedom. She'd like to scurry back, to hide, but Jack is starting the van again.

The road has been steadily climbing and they're quite high now. It's different on the left side of the road where the ground slopes down dramatically. This has also been clear-felled, but recently. The ground is red and raw, scoured with deep ruts, some filled with water like small ponds. Nothing is growing. Here and there abandoned tree trunks lie like dropped matchsticks. Orca keeps her eyes focussed to the right, on the birds and the flowers.

They reach a fork in the road. "This must be the left turn," says Orca, "Even though it's not a turn really."

There's a sign, No Vehicles beyond this point, Danger, Tree Felling in Operation. But there's no one about. The road has become mud rutted with deep tyre tracks, but it's still just about possible to drive on. Piles of felled trees rise up on the right side of the road, marked with red, yellow and blue bands. On the left, huge machines stand silently amidst the devastation. A stand of trees is still intact, like a patch missed when shaving. The road begins to go downhill.

A patch missed when shaving. Orca turns the idea round in her mind. Where did this image come from? She doesn't shave. She's not connected, so she can't be picking up on anything from the outside world, it must be something she has stored. She closes her eyes and is shocked by the clarity of the image which fills her mind.

A man, naked from the waist up, a towel slung around his shoulder, his dark hair wet. He's laughing, and there is a patch of bristles just below his jawline below his left ear. A voice says, *You've missed a bit.* It's her own voice. The man is the man from the photograph on the memory stick.

She opens her eyes.

"You OK?" asks Jack.

"Yes," she says. "I had a memory. I don't know if it was mine."

"One of those implants?"

She's not sure if he's mocking her or if he's concerned. Perhaps both. "I don't know. It's gone now anyway."

They're out of the felling area now. There are trees growing on both sides of the road. They're young, not much taller than men, and beyond them Orca can see the hills rising up around the valley. From up here they can sense of the scale of the forest.

The hills aren't near, but the forest stretches to them in every direction.

"There should be a right turning coming up."

It's barred by a gate. Orca gets out of the van to open it. The trees here are mixed in size, even mixed in type – there are young birches, holly shrubs and Scots pine mixed in with the Sitka. The road is two mud tracks for the tyres, a strip of grass between. The grass needs cutting.

The instructions say drive for five minutes. The road winds through the forest, but the trees soon start to thin out. The Sitka disappear, leaving a scrub of birch and holly, then that goes too, and they are crossing open moorland. The view has opened up and they can see the house ahead of them. A boy is sitting on the wall at the front watching their approach.

"Seems like he's pretty good at instructions," says Jack. "I was beginning to wonder."

The track ends in a parking space wide enough for three or four vehicles. It doesn't go any further. The boy doesn't move.

Orca and Jack look at each other. They haven't seen another human since they passed through Carlisle that morning. That was only hours ago, but it seems like a different lifetime. They nod at each other, then get out of the van.

"Hello," says Jack.

The boy dips his head.

"We spoke on the phone earlier."

"Did not."

"I was asking about the campsite. You said your grandad would be home later."

"That was me brother."

"Ah. OK. Is your brother here? Or your Grandad?"

"Out back." The boy indicates with his head towards the house.

"Is it OK if we ...?" Jack lifts the latch on the garden gate and gives it a small shove. The boy watches him but says nothing. Jack opens it and they walk through.

The front garden is an area of grass with a concrete path up the middle. It's in need of mowing, but otherwise tidy. The paving slabs lead up to the front door, but also branch off to the right, to the back of the house. They follow it round. The boy continues to sit on the wall, keeping his back to them.

"Do you think he's alright?" says Orca.

"Probably had a fall out with his brother, or got in trouble or something. Seems like he's in a sulk."

The back of the house is very different from the front. Here the garden is sheltered by the house from the brunt of the wind, and the garden is tended. There are shrubs planted around the edges for extra shelter from the weather. There's a vegetable patch and a border planted with tulips of various colours. They're still in bloom. Further south the tulips are over but on this northern hillside they are still jewels of red and yellow and pink. Next to the tulips is a wooden bench framed by clematis.

Nearer to the house on an open gravelled area, the boy and his grandad are brushing down a horse. The horse is huge. The boy's head doesn't reach the top of its back, and the grandad can only just see over the top to peer at Orca and Jack.

"I phoned earlier. We just arrived ..."

"Lad said."

The boy has turned, and both of them are looking at Jack with impassive faces.

"He said you were out in the forest, and if we drove up later ... well we followed his instructions, and ..."

"Where is everyone?" says Orca.

They man and boy look from Jack to Orca. The horse shifts its feet and farts.

"Clopper!" says the boy, and pats the side of its belly.

"Best make some tea," says the man. He doesn't invite them in. He disappears into the house leaving them with the boy and the horse.

"They were good instructions," says Jack.

The two boys are obviously twins. They are even wearing the same clothes – jeans and a blue t-shirt, dirty white trainers. The only difference is that this brother smiles at them.

"Hard to go wrong," he says. "Not many roads."

"What's the matter with your brother?" asks Orca.

She's surprised at herself. She hadn't expected the question. It sounds like small talk, which Dorcas had told her to engage in only if she keeps it to a minimum. But it isn't small talk. She wants to know what's the matter with the boy sitting alone at the front of the house. She's interested.

The smiling brother shrugs. "He's scared of horse, in 'e," he rubs his hand against the horse's flank. "And grandad, he called him a ninny."

"It's a big horse," says Jack, who hasn't stepped any nearer since they came round the corner of the house.

"Needs to be. Tough work, pullin' trees."

"She's a work horse.?"

"That's what me grandad does. He's a forester."

"A forester that uses a horse?"

"There's some bits they can't take them machines in. Triple SIs and so on. Need to be a bit delicate like, so you don't crush everything."

"I didn't know anyone still ..."

"There's only two. Grandad and some bloke in Wales. They have to travel."

"Do you go with him?" asks Orca. She ought to be interested in the trees, the SSSIs, the efforts at conservation. Maybe because she's not connected, the stored information is shifting, moving priorities. She's sure Dorcas didn't intend her to be interested in human stories.

"Nah. We're mostly at school."

"In the village?"

"No, that's just for the little 'uns. We have to go to boarding school."

The grandad appears with five mugs of tea on a tray, and a packet of chocolate digestives.

"Call your brother," he says to the boy. He puts the tray down on the wooden bench, then leads the horse over to the other side of the yard where he ties her halter to the fence. "Help yourself to milk and sugar."

It's the second time she's had tea that day. Orca takes the nearest mug and adds a drop of milk. She'd quite like to add sugar, but she's already had an unaccustomed amount. She doesn't know how her body will react to the onslaught.

The man opens the biscuits and the two boys appear from the front of the house. Seeing the two of them next to each other, the similarity is even more striking. Orca can't tell which is which as neither is smiling or frowning.

"These are my two lads, Keith and Kelvin. My name's Carter MacKenzie." He holds out the biscuits.

"Jack," says Jack, taking a digestive.

"Orca," says Orca, copying him.

"That's a weird name," says one of the boys.

"There's just us now," says Carter.

"Just us ...?" Jack looks at the older man. "You mean ..."

"I mean since their mother went. I've raised them two lads since they were bairns."

"It must be strange," says Orca, "living up here, so far from everything."

"We're luckier than most," says Carter.

The boys have taken three biscuits each and are sitting on the grass dipping them into their mugs of tea. Orca thinks about the chocolate melting and turns away. She sips the tea, but it's too hot to drink. She bites into the biscuit instead.

"Speaking of people," says Jack, and Orca thinks, actually we weren't. "We were down at the campsite and the village, and there's no one there. It seems like no one's been there for a while. We were wondering if you know anything. Where has everyone gone?'

Carter puts half a biscuit into his mouth and chews. He looks thoughtful.

"Is it like when mum went?" says one of the boys.

The horse shifts its feet. It's a heavy sound, hooves against concrete, the huge flanks moving slowly, the rattle of the bridle by its cheek. It sighs deeply, vibrating its lips.

"You're too young to remember," says Carter, who has biscuit crumbs in his beard. "They were just weaned when Mattie went," he says to Orca and Jack.

"But the village ...?" Jack persists.

"I don't know where all those people can be," says Carter. "I never go there. No need. If I want provisions, they ain't got none, I take the truck to Carlisle."

"What about the foresters?" says Jack. "Up the road, that's pretty near. There's no one working the machines. Surely you see some of those people."

"I ain't that sort of forester. I have Clopper here, and I have a chainsaw. I know how to take a tree down safe, and I taught these two boys. Kelvin and Keith, they know how to handle a chainsaw, I made sure of that. First time they come home from that school with their soft hands and pale skin, I got them both a chainsaw each and took them out into the forest. They can both take a tree down safe. And Kelvin, he can get the wood out of the forest. Keith will too, once he's stopped pambying around old Clopper here who wouldn't hurt a fly."

"But you must see them, see their vehicles and so on."

"What truck?" says Orca.

They all look at her.

"There's no truck out the front. You said you drive the truck to Carlisle."

"I left it in the forest, piled up with wood. I rode back up on Clopper today. It's good after a day's hard work to feel the warmth of a living seat."

"How old are the boys?" asks Orca. She feels rude talking about them when they are right there. She turns and asks them, "How old are you?"

"Twelve, miss," says one of them.

"Isn't that a bit young to be in charge of a chainsaw?"

Carter coughs and puts his mug down on the wooden arm of the bench. "You ain't one of them social workers are you? Come sneaking around. We do alright, me and the lads. They go to that school in the term time like they have to, but when they come home to me, it's my rules. I don't ask them to do anything they ain't capable of."

"I'm not a social worker," says Orca. "I was just surprised."

"Impressed," says Jack. "I couldn't do anything like that when I was twelve. I was just about allowed to walk the dog on my own then."

Carter humphs and picks up his tea again. "It's just they send people up here sometimes, nosing about. Think we're too remote for boys. Who ever heard such nonsense. It's a boy's paradise up here." He sinks into a silence. The boys' mouths are full of biscuit and the horse is still. There's a skylark high above, singing its song out loud, although its tiny body can barely be seen. The sun is on its descent and the forest below looks like a photo in National Geographic, of somewhere in Canada maybe, vast and empty. "You want to stay for supper then?"

They look at him in surprise.

"Well, you ain't gonna find anyone tonight, what with dark only an hour off. You can tell me about it over a plate of food."

It's shepherd's pie with carrots and cabbage. Orca asks for a small portion. One of the boys says, "Can I have hers?" Orca thinks it's Kelvin. The other boy is quieter, not sulking exactly, but wary, watching. Carter spoons steaming piles of meat and potato onto their plates.

"This is delicious," says Jack.

It certainly smells good. Orca puts a small forkful in her mouth. She hasn't eaten meat since ... since when? Has she ever eaten meat? She's certain that she has, but she doesn't have any evidence to back that up. The other thing that's bothering her is the National Geographic. Earlier, looking at the landscape, that was the thought she had. She could see the magazine opened, with the photo spread across two pages, the gloss of the paper. She knew if she closed it the cover would be yellow. Were there magazines in the office? If there had been, she and Sylva might have looked at them.

Jack is telling Carter about their journey up, about Nick and Nadia. He says they're friends of Orca's. He describes the empty campsite, the grass growing up around the tents.

Carter listens as he eats his food. He wipes his mouth with a piece of kitchen roll.

"People have a habit of going missing in this forest," he says.

Orca thinks of Sylva, of how she loved to look at the distance. "Do they get found again?" she asks.

"Sometimes, sometimes not." Carter looks thoughtfully at the twins, who are shovelling in the last of their food. "The boys' mother, for example, my Mattie. We never found her. She left a note when she walked into the forest. She didn't want to be found, and she wasn't. It's big enough here, so you can do that. She'd got in with a wrong 'un – I didn't know that 'til after. They let me have the boys, after it all came to light, and that evil bastard got put away."

"Did she ...?" Orca doesn't want to say the word suicide, not in front of the boys, not about their mother.

"Aye. And there's many others have done the same. Mostly they get found, but sometimes not."

"But not the whole village. Not all the people from the campsite." Jack has finished eating too. Only Orca still has food on her plate. "And Nick and Nadia, they have a baby."

"Ain't nothing we can do this evening," says Carter. "How about we drive down in the morning and see what's what."

Chapter Eleven

In the night Orca can't sleep. There are spare rooms in the house and she and Jack have been given one each. Her room has flowered wallpaper and a bed with a white padded headboard. There's a dressing table with a round mirror perched above it. It must have been Mattie's room. Orca hasn't slept inside for a long time. The bed is soft and the air feels rebreathed.

She opens the window wide and the coolness is a relief. She leans out. The world outside is a separate entity. She can hear noises – owls, the bark of a fox from across the fields. Nearer, Clopper sighs and his heavy feet thump the floor of his stall as he shifts his weight. She wants to be out there. It's hours since they all went to bed, everyone else will be asleep. She slips silently down the stairs and out of the front door.

There are stars. It's not all that dark once your eyes adjust. The forest is laid out before them, a great bowl full of non-human life. Perhaps some humans too if you knew where to look. The cool air against her skin is like a familiar hand. She touches her own cheek. It's hot from the down pillow, the green patterned duvet.

She'd like to go down to the trees, to walk amongst their presence. It's what she's used to. It seems natural to lose consciousness while they breathe the night air, filling it with the oxygen she needs, protecting her small form with their towering branches. It's quite a walk – maybe a mile – but she could easily do it. She'd wake with first light and return to the house and none of the others need know.

She can't bring herself to set off. The trees in the Hayes seemed like her friends, and at Rendlesham they stood in their rows like soldiers waiting for orders. Here she's less sure. It's as though the trees are hiding something. Maybe it's the missing people from the village, or the stories of suicides that Carter told them over dinner, but she doesn't feel that she'd be completely welcome.

She remembers the bench in the back garden. It might not be the most comfortable place to sleep, but she could sit there for a while. It's more sheltered than this windblown front of the house.

Around the bench the air is sweet scented with flowers. The sky is framed by the lilac tree and apple tree that flank her, their foliage silhouetted against the huge space above. She listens to the night and breathes deeply. As well as lilac, there's a smell of horse. Clopper's stall is attached to the house and she hears her snicker. She wonders if she's sensed her presence. She'd like to see her.

She walks across the grass and lifts the latch of the stable door, slips into the warm darkness, and immediately realises she's not alone. Someone is standing by Clopper's head, but they back into the shadows. She listens. She can hear Clopper's heavy breathing, the faint sound of her own breath. There is another, the quietest of sounds, but it's there. She reaches out and touches Clopper's nose. It's as soft as baby's hair. The horse breathes hot air on to her hand.

"Hello Keith," says Orca. There is silence and stillness. She can feel his warmth emanating from the dark corner, but she doesn't move. He has almost silenced his breathing. "Couldn't you sleep either? I was too hot in the house. The night air is better outside, don't you think?"

Slowly he moves out of the shadow, until he is standing next to her. Clopper snickers again and pushes her nose towards the boy.

"I'm not Keith?" He rubs Clopper's brow and she flicks her ears. "I'm Kelvin."

"No you're not."

"I am. Keith wouldn't come in here, he's scared of Clopper."

"He only pretends to be scared of her. Actually they are very good friends when no one else is looking."

"Why do you think that?"

"Because I can see him right now."

"I'm Kelvin."

"You have a mole beneath your left ear, Keith. Kelvin doesn't have a mole. I saw it when we arrived, when you were at the front of the house, and I can see it now in the light from the moon."

There is silence. The boy takes something from his pocket which he feeds to the horse. Clopper crunches it with her huge teeth.

"You couldn't see it before, when I was over there. How did you know it was me then?"

"Because you smell of peppermints and Kelvin doesn't."

They stand next to each other and the moon washes white light over the sides of their faces and the horse's as well. Orca scratches Clopper in between her eyes, then walks back into the garden, leaving the boy and horse on their own. She sits on the bench. The lilac blossom smells strong in the night air, which is soft and cool. She won't go back to the hot bedroom tonight, she can sleep on the bench, or even in the stable on some hay if it gets chilly.

After a while Keith comes and sits next to her on the bench. He puts a peppermint in his mouth and offers her one, which she refuses.

"Are you going to tell them?"

"No."

"Why not?"

"It's none of my business."

Keith moves the mint in his mouth and it clacks against his teeth. Something stirs in Orca's mind. Annoyance – someone else's annoyance – *don't clack your teeth* – who said that? It's a male voice. The image of the man in the photo – smiling, static, not speaking – flashes behind her eyes. Do they match, this voice and this face? Why has Dorcas given her these memories?

"Most grown-ups think everything kids do is their business."

Orca looks at the boy. He's almost, but not quite, a teenager. He seems younger now than when she'd first seen him sitting on the wall, and younger than his capable twin brother. She remembers holding Nadia's baby, the fat hand wrapped around her finger, how she felt as though she might be sick. She doesn't touch Keith on the shoulder, or put her arm around him. There is space between them on the bench.

"If you want to them to know, they will find out. I'm leaving tomorrow. I'm just passing through."

Keith sucks hard on the mint and makes a slurping sound. *For God's sake!* This time the voice and image match. The man is sitting at a dinner table, speaking to someone on his left who is out of the picture. Or rather, the picture she can see fades out at the edges, just the man is in focus, the plate of spaghetti, the blue t-shirt, the slight frown on his face. Then it's gone. She can't recall it.

"I wish you would stay."

She looks at Keith in astonishment. "Why?"

He shrugs. "Everyone else tells me what to do. There's nobody here, just Grandad and Kelvin, and Kelvin does everything right, like Grandad wants him to. It's better when we're at school."

"You enjoy school?"

"Yeah! It's OK at school. I'm kind of normal there, just a quiet kid. Kelvin's the weird one who lives in the woods and plays with chainsaws, they all laugh at him."

"Do they ever mix you up?" The two boys have identical features and hair, they are the same height and build.

"Never."

There is no sound from the stable. Clopper must have gone to sleep. Orca's body needs to rest and recharge.

"I'm sorry, I can't stay. I need to find some people I'm looking for."

"I heard a baby yesterday."

"Where?"

"On the other side of the water. Over near the Forest Head."

"Did you see anyone?

"I keep out of the way. I'm meant to stay here, when Grandad and Kelvin are working. Chop wood and stuff. Grandad gets annoyed 'cos I don't do anything, he thinks I just read books or sit about. But I go out, I walk all over the forest, up to Deadwater Fell, everywhere. I just make sure to get back before them."

"And you heard a baby?"

"Yeah. I don't want to be seen by anyone that knows Grandad."

"Thank you for telling me."

Keith tenses and turns to look at her. "You're not going to tell them that are you? That I walk around the forest.?"

Orca shakes her head. "No, I won't tell. Now you go and get some sleep."

After breakfast the five of them drive down to the campsite. It's as empty as the day before. Carter scratches his head.

"You say there's no one in the village either? Or up at Castle?"

"That's right."

"And there weren't no one up at the fell site either. It's certainly a conundrum."

"Our friend's camper is near the pub," says Jack. "And they can only have been here two days. But it looks like no one's been camping for a couple of weeks."

"I best drive over to Bellingham and speak to folks there, see if anyone knows what's going on."

"We're going to look for Nick and Nadia," says Orca.

Jack frowns. "Do you think that's the best thing? The forest is huge, we could just end up getting lost and never finding them. We've no idea which way they went."

"I don't think they'll have gone far from the lake."

"Who knows, if Nick is looking for the beetles, he'll just follow their trail."

"What beetles?"

They all turned and looked at Keith. He'd been quiet all morning, even surly. The others had paid no attention to him, but Orca had smiled at him when no one else was looking and he had almost smiled back.

"Nick is interested in longhorn beetles," she tells him now. "He's going about the country looking for them. That's why he's come here."

"So, like beetles with horns?"

Kelvin laughs. "Keith you idiot! They're not goats or stags"

His brother turns to him. "You never heard of stag beetles?"

"Well, yeah, but they ..."

"They're called that because they have horns."

"OK, OK, when did you become Mr Know-it-all?"

"That's enough boys. Kelvin, you know he reads more books than you, so just leave off." Carter turns to Jack and Orca. "You best stick to the lake, keep it in sight. Your man's right, if you get lost we'll have a deal of a time finding you."

"I know where there's some of those beetles. I can show you."

Carter sighs. "Don't be daft, Keith. Come on now, if we set off straight away we might be back to get some work in before dark."

"Down near the Forest Head."

"We ain't been down there since Christmas, and we didn't see no..."

"I'd like him to come with us. We'd look after him."

Carter and Jack both look at Orca.

Kelvin says, "If you want one of us, it'd better be me."

"No," says Orca. "Your grandfather needs you. I'd like Keith to come with us."

"What d'ya think boy. Do you want to go with these folks?"

Keith shifts his feet, uncomfortable to be in the spotlight, but he nods his head. "OK."

The walk takes them along a cycle track beside the lake. To the right the path leads across an old viaduct, built when a railway ran through the valley, before it was flooded.

"There's a station under the water," Keith tells them. "We need to go this way." He looks different than earlier. He's brighter and straighter. He looks less like his brother. It's as though they have the same raw materials, but they're animated differently. "Where the beetles were, it's near where I heard the baby."

"What baby?" says Jack.

Orca looks at Keith and he nods. "You can tell him."

When they've walked for fifteen minutes the path splits. The main route continues on the left fork, but another path leads down towards the water. There's an information board about the Forest Head, which is literally a head made of wood.

Keith bends down and looks at something on the path. "This weren't here yesterday." It's a cigarette butt. "It were down near the Head that I heard them. I went the other way."

They take the path towards the Head. When it comes into view Orca gasps. It's huge, half as high as the trees, with black holes for eyes, staring out across the water.

"You can go in through the mouth. There's stairs inside, so you can go behind its eyes and look out."

"The ears creep me out," says Jack. "They look like fungus. But made of wood."

"They have holes through, so you can shout through them."

Orca goes inside the Head. It smells of the baby. "Nadia," she calls. There's no answer, but she can smell milk and nappies. She feels in the dark for the stairs and climbs them.

Nadia is lying on the floor behind the eyes of the Head. She is asleep or unconscious, and there's blood on her face. The baby is sitting on the floor next to her chewing its fist. When it sees Orca, it starts to cry.

"Jack! Can you come up here."

She kneels beside Nadia and touches her face. It's warm, she's breathing. The blood is dry, caked on. The baby stinks.

Orca looks about the space. Nadia's rucksack is leaning against the inside of the wooden ear.

Jack appears at the top of the stairs. "Bloody hell!"

"The baby is hungry and needs changing," says Orca. "We should check Nadia for broken bones, and if possible take her outside."

"What the fuck! How did she get here?"

"I'll check Nadia, you take the baby."

"The baby knows you. Why are they the only ones in the forest? Where's Nick?"

"I don't know."

'I've done a first aid course, I know what to do.' Jack kneels beside the body on the floor. 'Look at the way her legs are. If they were broken they wouldn't lie like that, folded one on top of the other. And this arm ..." He lifts Nadia's left arm and bends it at the elbow. "That's fine. It's hard to tell with the other one because it's underneath her."

"What about her ribs?"

"I don't think we can tell. You need an *x*-ray. You only know they're broken because of the pain."

The baby's crying is getting louder. There are footsteps on the stairs and Keith arrives. He looks at them, taking in the situation, the two of them bent over Nadia's body. "I'll take that baby outside," he says. He picks him up and goes back down the stairs. The crying quietens.

"Shall we try?" asks Jack. "One of us can hold under her shoulders and the other take her legs."

"I'll take the shoulders."

When they lift Nadia, a sigh escapes from her mouth but she doesn't wake up. Jack goes backwards down the stairs holding her legs. There aren't many stairs, but they spiral round, and it's dark, so it's tricky. Orca, going forwards, has to bend her knees to step down them, whilst keeping Nadia lifted out of the way. They get down though, and soon are back outside, where the sunlight is blinding after the dark interior of the Head.

Keith is holding the baby which is no longer crying. Orca and Jack lay Nadia down on the ground beneath a tall pine.

"I don't think anything can be broken," says Jack. "It would have woken her, the pain of moving like that."

"This baby needs changing," says Keith.

"I'll get the stuff," says Jack, and goes back inside the Head to collect Nadia's rucksack.

Keith lays the baby on the ground on a patch of grass. When Jack returns, Orca looks in the rucksack and finds nappies, wipes and cream.

"Have either of you changed a baby's nappy before?" asks Jack.

Keith and Orca shake their heads. Orca wonders if she is lying, or misremembering – but why would she have ever changed a nappy? – why would Dorcas have imprinted such an unnecessary memory? Still, she is the one who kneels in front of the baby and undoes his trousers, which open with handy poppers for this very purpose.

The smell is revolting and gets worse when she undoes the nappy. Keith and Jack are both watching. Jack hands her the wipes.

"That's disgusting!" says Keith.

Orca wipes the baby clean and rolls up the nappy, fastening it with the tapes so it stays closed.

"You have done this before haven't you?" Jack has found some plastic bags in the rucksack and hands her one.

She puts the nappy inside and ties it up. Her hands are shaking. "I don't know." Her voice trembles and she feels pressure in her chest. She fits the clean nappy and does up the tapes.

"Hey, hey, it's OK." Jack puts his arms round her and presses her face against his shoulder.

Her eyes are leaking water. Jack saw she was crying before she even realised what was happening. She's making a noise, and Jack is rubbing her back, telling her it's OK. She doesn't know why she's crying. She didn't even know she could cry like this.

After a few minutes it stops. Jack holds her arms and pushes her away from him. She tries to identify his emotions in his face. Concern, worry, sympathy. She remembers the tree tests at the lab when she had to recognise the tree from the bark or the shape of the leaf. Here she's looking at the contraction of his eyes, the size of the pupils, the line of the mouth. But it wouldn't work on a chart, there something else going on here that couldn't be listed on an emotion identification chart. It's all the things together, and also something you can't see, but only know, about the person's intentions. What about trees? Is it the same for them? Is identification just as pointless? Do you need to get to know them? She laughs.

"That's better."

"I don't know what happened."

"It's been really stressful. Everyone has gone missing, then finding Nadia like that. You did really well with the baby, it all caught up with you."

"I think I have a malfunction."

"You're just tired. You didn't even sleep properly, out in the garden all night."

"Where's the baby?"

The place on the grass is empty. Jack points across the clearing. Keith is showing the baby to the trees. Orca can hear the rumble of his voice as he talks.

"It will get hungry."

"There's some food in the rucksack. We'll manage. First we need to decide what to do about her."

Nadia is still lying in the position they left her. Jack takes one of the babywipes and dabs at the blood on Nadia's face. It doesn't come off easily, but in a moment the wipe is red. He takes another and keeps going. After a few minutes there is a small pile of babywipes and Nadia's face is clean.

"It's not as bad as it looks. Jack is examining Nadia's face. "I think she's bitten her lip. That's where the blood has come from. Her mouth is swollen. If she fell against something ..."

“Or if someone hit her ...”

“Yes, or if someone hit her... then her own teeth might have gone into her lip.”

“But why is she unconscious.?”

Jack looks at Orca. Worry, fear, concern. “If she fell ... she might have knocked her head ...”

“We should check for bumps or swellings.”

Orca raises Nadia gently by the shoulders and Jack slides his hands under her head, probing gently with his fingers. He shakes his head. “I can’t feel anything.”

“What should we do with her?”

“She’s too heavy to carry far. We’d need something – a stretcher or something. We could wait to see if she wakes up.”

“What if she doesn’t? What if she needs to get to a hospital?”

They are both quiet again. They look at each other, then at the unconscious woman. Keith has come over with the baby, which is grabbing his nose and making cooing noises.

“I hope she doesn’t die,” he says. The soft space beneath his eye twitches and he blinks.

“We’ll make a stretcher,” Jack decides. “We’ll need to find a couple of long branches, then we’ll use our clothing – we’ll carry her back to the van and take her to hospital.”

They find a branch that’s long enough, but they can’t find another.

“Take the baby,” says Keith, and puts the child into Orca’s arms.

He takes a knife from his pocket, and selects a young tree that’s just the right height, its trunk slim as a wrist. He makes a sharp nick in the bottom of the trunk then pushes hard from the weak spot. Jack helps and they bend the tree until it cracks. There’s a sudden strong smell of resin. Keith uses the knife to cut through the last attaching fibres, then starts to strip away the branches. Jack also has a knife in his pocket and he helps.

The baby says “Muma,” and grabs hold of Orca’s hair. She’s meant to be recording data in Hartshill Hayes, making a dispassionate record, noting and noticing. She's hundreds of miles away, with a man and a boy who carry pocket knives. She's holding a baby and its fat fingers have pulled some of her hair free from the band that ties it back. There's an uneasy feeling in her stomach again.

Jack and Keith lay the stripped trunk parallel to the other branch they found, and they begin to tie on pieces of clothing, using the arms; Nadia's hoodie which was in the rucksack, Orca's coat, Jack's top and Keith's jumper.

"They'll stretch differently," says Jack. "Use the jumper for her head, it will be more comfortable."

It looks strange and precarious.

"What if they come undone and we drop her?" says Keith. "We might hurt her even more. We might kill her."

"We won't kill her," Jack touches the boy's shoulder. "Let's test it. You lie on it."

Keith looks over at Nadia then at himself. "I'm not the same size. She's heavier than me."

He's right, Nadia is slim, but she's a grown woman, and Keith is a child. Orca is nearer in size to Nadia. She suspects she's heavier as her muscles are more developed. She gives the baby to Keith then lies down on the stretcher.

"I can't pick it up on my own." Jack laughs. "You'll have to put the baby down for a minute."

Keith has a strange look on his face. His skin seems to be pulled too tight and his eyes are moving quickly. The tips of his ears look white. Orca watches him sit the baby down gently on the ground. He's anxious she thinks. She remembers what Carter told them about Mattie, how she'd walked into the forest and never returned. She was Keith's mother. Orca feels herself being lifted into the air. The clothes support her, but the coat is firmer than the fabric of the hoodie. The jumper is soft and her head lolls backwards. She's tipped, her feet lower and her head higher because Jack is taller and stronger than Keith.

They lay her back down and she gets up. They adjust the knots and lift Nadia onto the stretcher. She's still unconscious, her body is limp and unresisting, but as they lie her down some sound comes out of her mouth.

"Did she say something," asks Keith.

"I couldn't tell."

"It sounded like, Eli," says Jack.

"No, it didn't." Orca frowns. "It was just air escaping from her mouth."

Jack shrugs. "Can you manage her rucksack as well as the baby?"

Keith nods.

"OK then. We're set. Lead on McDuff."

Keith stares at him then hoists the rucksack onto his back. The baby has fists full of dirt and pine needles. Keith unfolds the fingers out, one hand then the other, and brushes them clean, then he picks the baby up.

Jack takes the foot end and Orca the head. They lift Nadia off the ground. Jack has his back to the stretcher and walks at the front. Orca has a view of his back in his blue t-shirt, his muscles moving beneath the fabric. She has a view of Nadia lying on the makeshift stretcher with her swollen mouth. She can't see her own feet as she walks.

It's a bit awkward to begin with but they get into a rhythm. Orca watches Jack's body. She can see the length of his spine, his arms and shoulders, the back of his head. Below that he is obscured by the stretcher. She fits her stride to match. Right leg, left leg, they are walking in time. Keith is behind with the baby. He said he wanted to be able to see, to be sure they don't drop Nadia. Orca is aware of him. She wonders if he is matching his stride to hers. She also feels as though she's being watched from the sides of the path. As she settles into Jack's rhythm, she throws glances left and right, but sees nothing. The trees are younger here, they don't have the long skirts of the older trees, and she can see between their trunks. Beneath them is mossy ground, whole mounds of moss tumbling in wet masses, a tiny stream cutting a line through. She can hear birds, she can hear their footsteps, Jack, herself, Keith, a steady march, one two one two, she can hear the soft sounds of their clothes rubbing together as they walk. Nadia is silent. None of them speak, even the baby.

Chapter Twelve

At the carpark they lay Nadia down next to Nick's van. Inside they find more baby food, bananas, nappies. They find chocolate, and whisky. They find tobacco and rolling papers, a lighter and a bag of weed. In Nadia's coat pocket they find two mobile phones.

They shove everything into the ruck sack and cover Nadia with a blanket.

At the campsite they unlock their own van. There's not a lot of space in the back, but Jack shoves things aside to make a long gap for Nadia.

"Keith, you'll need to sit in the back with her. Make sure nothing falls on her."

"OK."

"It won't be very comfortable."

They lie another blanket down first, then manoeuvre Nadia into the back of the van. Keith gives the baby to Orca and climbs in, sits in the small space hugging his knees. Jack and Orca get into the front of the van and Jack turns the key. The engine doesn't start. It doesn't turn over, it does nothing.

"What's wrong?"

"I don't know." He turns the key again. It makes a small click as it moves, but nothing happens. "Bugger." He presses a button that opens the bonnet and gets out to have a look.

Orca gets out as well. "Do you know about cars?"

"Not really. I don't know why I'm looking."

"We filled up with petrol in Carlisle."

They both stare into the engine. Nothing is obviously wrong, no leaks or burned areas, nothing cracked or broken. Orca checks through her stored data, but there is nothing on car maintenance.

"Could there be a leak?" she asks.

"I don't think that's it. It's not even turning over. It's not the fuel."

Orca places the baby on the ground and looks underneath the van. There is no oily patch beneath the fuel tank, no smell of petrol. 'We could take their van," she says, "Nick's van."

"Not a bad idea," says Jack. "I'll drive it over here." He sets off across the campsite.

Keith gets out of the van and sits on the grass next to the baby.

"Do you want some chocolate?" Orca asks him.

In the campsite shop nothing has changed. She grabs a Twix, a Mars bar and a Twirl. She grabs three cans of coke. She grabs a bag of buttermints. Her hands are crammed full of sugar.

Keith chooses the Mars bar. She opens the Twirl and lays the other things in the shade beneath the edge of the van.

When she's eaten the chocolate and the inside of her mouth is coated with the sticky sweetness, she takes the mobile phones they'd found, and turns them on. They both have some charge and light up. One of them needs a fingerprint to open it. She crawls into the back of the van and lift's Nadia's right hand, presses the forefinger to the screen. Nadia sighs and moves her head, but she doesn't open her eyes.

The fingerprint works, but there doesn't seem to be anything very interesting. There are messages between her and Nick, but they are a few days old, and purely of a practical nature – *how long will you be? Nearly done – at the checkout. Did you remember wipes?* There are some between Nadia and a person named Katsia which are in a different language. There is the conversation with Orca herself, the messages they sent at Rendlesham – nothing more recent than that. There are no apps such as facebook or whatsapp or instagram. She looks at notes, but there are none, and then at the photos. There are a couple taken since they got here – one of the baby laughing in the back of the van, one of the goat, and a selfie of the three of them sitting at a table outside the pub. They have beer and empty plates of food, leftover chips smeared with tomato sauce. Orca frowns.

She opens every app on the phone. Weather, banking (unused), health (unused), voice memos. There are two voice memos, and they have dates and times – they were made two days ago.

Orca opens the first and listens to it.

"What's that?" says Keith.

"I don't know."

It's a sound, perhaps singing or humming. It starts off quietly and gets gradually louder, lasting for just over a minute in total.

The baby begins to cry. Keith lifts him up and bounces him and he quietens.

Orca opens the other voice memo. This is a voice, Nick's voice, and he's shouting, *you stupid, fucking bitch*. That's it. The sound recording is only four seconds long.

Jack is walking back across the campsite shaking his head. "Their van won't start either," he says when he reaches them.

Orca plays him the two sound recordings. "Do you know what that sound is?"

"It sounds like equipment when it's switched on – speakers or something."

"Why does it get louder?"

"I think it's a person," says Keith. "That's someone making that noise, not a machine."

They listen to it again. The baby doesn't like it and Keith walks away along the path.

"Which was first, the sound or Nick?" asks Jack.

Orca checks the times of the recordings. "Nick was first, by a few hours. What happened with the van?"

"Exactly the same thing. The key was there – they'd even left it in the ignition. But when I turned it there was nothing."

Orca shows him the photo of Nick and Nadia and the baby taken outside the pub.

"Does that have a time on it?"

"18.30, two days ago. After the recording of Nick shouting, but before the other one."

"What the fuck is going on here?" Jack puts his head in his hands

"I don't know. What are we going to do with Nadia?"

"I guess we have to wait until Carter gets back. We can make sure she's comfortable, that she won't choke or anything."

"The recovery position." Keith is back with the baby. "I learned it at school in first aid."

Jack nods. "She can stay in the van. There's no point in moving her anywhere else. Do you want to do it, Keith?"

Orca is holding both of the mobile phones, so Keith puts the baby into Jack's arms. Jack is astonished. He looks at the baby's face as if it's the first time he's realised it has one.

Orca laughs. "You're as bad as me," she says.

The baby bats Jack in the face, and he crosses his eyes at it and sticks out his tongue. The baby looks at him intently, then sticks out its own tongue. The baby says, "dada"

"O my god!" says Jack.

"He likes you," says Orca.

In the back of the van, Keith is rolling Nadia onto her side and moving her limbs into position. He appears at the back of the van. "This fell out of her mouth."

He is holding his hand out, palm up, with a small gold coloured object. Orca and Jack both peer at it.

"It's a sim card," says Jack.

"Is there no sim in her phone? Has she taken it out?"

They check both of the phones from the van, and both already have sims inserted. Nadia's phone takes a different size card, but the other phone has an identical card.

"Have you checked this phone"

Orca shakes her head.

They fetch a paper cup from the campsite shop and put the new sim in that while they check the phone.

"I assumed it was Nick's." Orca looks at the screen cover photo of mushrooms growing in a bed of moss. "But it might not be."

This phone doesn't need a fingerprint, or even a passcode. They get in straight away. There's barely anything on the phone, no apps, no photos, no files, no contacts. There are two messages.

Use the golden sim to make contact.

Don't look back.

"What does that even mean – don't look back?" Jack frowns. "And why the fuck was the sim in her mouth?"

Orca checks the sim in the phone and it's silver in colour. "Shall we try the gold one?"

"What can happen? Go for it."

She removes the silver sim card and replaces it with the gold one, then restarts the phone. It all looks pretty much the same – except for one thing – there is a phone number stored on this sim. There's only one, and it doesn't have a name attached – it's labelled – *Call this number*.

They look at each other.

"Put it on speaker," says Keith. "Then we can all hear."

"Is there signal?" asks Jack. "There's not on any of the other phones, and there wasn't with the other sim in this phone."

Orca checks and there are five bars. "Full signal."

"This is fucking weird." Jack walks away a few paces and walks back.

"I got you a Twix, from the shop. And some drinks." Orca points to the stash by the van.

Jack grabs a can of coke and opens it, takes a long swig. "Go on, dial the number."

Orca put the phone on speaker and dials. Keith and Jack come closer. They can hear a phone ringing, a small tinny sound in the outside air.

"We should have done it inside," says Jack.

"Shh!"

The ringing has stopped. There is silence.

"Hello." Orca speaks loudly into the phone. "Is somebody there?"

No answer.

The three of them lean in closer.

"Is this a prank?" says Jack. "If there's someone there, tell us who you are?"

"Do you have my mum?"

Jack and Orca look at Keith in surprise. He has tears in his eyes.

Then someone speaks. "Listen well."

"We're listening," says Jack.

"Listen well. You must choose of the three paths. You have only one chance to choose."

"What paths? Where? What are we choosing?"

"You have only one chance to choose."

"You said that."

"Don't look back."

"Don't look back, what the fuck does that mean? Look, can you just tell us who you are?"

"It's gone dead," says Orca. "They've gone."

"I don't think you should have been so annoyed with them," says Keith.

"Annoyed? I'm not annoyed! I just want some answers." Jack glares at Keith then at Orca, then he walks away across the campsite.

"What do you think it means?" Keith sits down next to Orca on the wall, quite close to her. She's not quite comfortable with how close. He's still holding the baby and she can smell it. It needs a bath.

"Why did you say that, about your mum?"

Keith shrugs. "People go missing in this forest all the time. Some of them are never found. I just thought, maybe there's a place where they all are."

"You think this place ..." she holds up the phone. "you think it's another ... a different ...?"

"No one can get signal here. No one."

They are both quiet. The baby says 'muma' and lurches towards Orca.

"He wants to go to you," says Keith, and he puts the baby into Orca's lap. She's still holding a phone in each hand, and she grabs hold of the baby with her elbows, hands the phones to Keith.

"Call them again," she says. "Ask them what they mean."

Keith calls the number, but this time it just keeps ringing, no one answers. Jack has disappeared into the woods at the end of the campsite. There is nothing to do except wait. The baby lays its head on Orca's chest. She looks down at him. His eyes are closing, and the lashes lay across his cheek.

"He's going to sleep," says Keith.

There's something familiar about this. She can't remember holding a sleeping baby, she can't bring an image to mind, but her muscles hold memory, her arm tightens very slightly behind the baby's back, and her thighs gather the pool of body heat. She wonders about the memory implants, that they should be this subtle, this advanced. There is something else going on as well, a tender yearning wiping away her disgust at the unwashed smell. Her arms want to circle this baby with bands of iron, and also to press him hard against her chest until they meld and become one. The baby lets out a long breath like a sigh and Orca relaxes a little.

Keith brings her a can and opens it for her. She holds it with the arm that isn't supporting the baby, and drinks. The fizz fills her nose and makes her want to sneeze. The edge of the drinking hole scrapes her lip. She's consumed so much sugar she feels she must smell of it, she can imagine a cloud of bees following her.

"Shall I go and find him?" asks Keith.

"I don't think so."

The baby's sleep has affected them. The sun is warm and they are both drowsy. Keith is still sitting close to her, and she feels his weight leaning against her shoulder. She imagines putting her can on the floor then putting her arm around Keith, letting him sleep against her in the same way as the baby. Would he be pleased?

He sits up straight and alert. "He's coming back."

Jack is running. His face is animated and he's out of breath. He reaches them and bends over with hands on his knees, gasping. "I found them." He manages to get out.

"What, Nick?"

"Did you find my mum?"

Jack shakes his head. "The paths ... three ... the goat, that's where it was taking us."

"What goat?" asks Keith.

Orca hands Jack the can in her hand and he takes a drink, calms his breath.

"I went back the way we went yesterday when we were following the goat, but the other way round. Up by the road, on the other side, there's a sign with three paths going in different directions, it's right by where the goat stopped, but yesterday I didn't see it."

"How do you know it's the right place? There must be lots of places where there's more than one path, lots of signposts."

"That's the weird thing. There's a sign –carved in wood – and it says, *Three paths, Choose wisely, You may choose only one.*"

'We didn't see that yesterday."

"I don't think it was there."

Orca looks at his face. Excitement, energy, determination. It makes him look different, she feels like she's meeting him for the first time. "What are we going to do?" she says.

"Well we'll have to choose. If we go up, we can look at the three paths and see which seems the most likely, and either we could all take the same path, or we could take one each, as there's three of us and three paths ..."

"There are five of us."

Jack stops and looks at her.

"And we can't leave Nadia."

He deflates visibly, but the shine is still there on his skin. "Of course," he says, "you're right."

"Someone will have to stay here with her, and the baby too. The baby should stay where Nadia is."

"I can stay."

They look at the boy. He's showing signs of lack of sleep, with dark shadows under his eyes. His shoulders are thin and bony, and Orca can feel an ache in her bicep where it would lay across those sharp bones if she gave in to the impulse to hug him.

"You're the one that knows the forest," she says to him.

He shakes his head. "I've never seen that sign or those paths. I don't think anything I know would help you."

He's twelve years old. Not old enough to be left in charge of an unconscious woman and a baby.

"Eli's gone to sleep. We can get in the back of the van. My grandad will be back in a bit, it would be better if I was here when he gets back."

"He's right," says Jack. "Nadia is OK, she's breathing and she's in the recovery position."

"One of us should stay too. He's only a child."

"Which one of us?"

There's no way she could persuade Jack to stay, he's rocking on his feet, clenching and unclenching his hands. But this is her journey – even though Jack has found the entrance to the paths, it was her that followed the goat yesterday, it was her that brought them to this forest in the first place. She can't let Jack go on his own, she has to go too.

But that means leaving Keith on his own.

"I'll be fine," he says. "I'll have a nap as well."

It feels like an impossible decision.

"We'll be back as soon as we've found out what it's about," says Jack.

"You go," she says to Jack. 'I'll wait until Carter gets back, then I'll follow you."

"How will you know which path I've chosen?"

"Leave me a sign," she says.

Keith is drooping visibly. They make a space for him in the back of the van. Jack unrolls his sleeping bag and Keith lies on top of it. Orca lays down the sleeping baby and Keith snuggles next to it. He's practically asleep already. She closes the van doors, makes sure the windows at the front are open so there's a free flow of air.

"You sure you're OK with this?"

"I can't leave them."

"I'll make an arrow on the ground," says Jack, "to show which way I've gone."

"Don't use breadcrumbs," says Orca.

He looks puzzled.

"Like Hansel and Gretel."

"Oh, OK. I'd forgotten that story. What do they use instead?"

"White pebbles."

"I'll find something."

He touches her arm when he leaves, and she can feel the spot warm and glowing as she watches him walk away. It's become his adventure. Something stronger is holding her here. She's surprised. Her purpose is to investigate woodland, but the deeper programming obviously takes precedence. She cannot make choices that will put human beings in danger. Keith and Nadia and Eli might not be in danger, but the possibility that they could be has activated something in her original coding. The forest will have to wait.

She feels the sleepiness creeping over her again. It couldn't hurt to rest for a short while. She lies down in some grass under a tree a few yards from the van and closes her eyes.

Chapter Thirteen

She wakes to the sound of voices. She sits up. The back of the van is open and Keith is with his brother and his grandad. They're lifting Nadia out of the back of the van. Orca gets up and goes over to them, but as she approaches her legs begin to feel strange, as though there is less gravity than normal and at each step her knee lifts higher than it should.

"Hello!"

None of them turn around. They lie Nadia on the makeshift stretcher from earlier, making sure she's still in the recovery position, and lift it, Carter at the front and the two boys at the foot. Orca looks for the baby, and sees he's sitting in the grass beside Carter's truck.

"I'm glad you came back." Her voice sounds strange, as though something is snatching the words as soon as they leaves her mouth, wisping them away. She's quite close to them now, but it's clear they can't hear her.

They load Nadia on to the back of the truck.

Their voices sound thin as though they're coming through a radio. Carter is grumbling about wanting to get back to work, and Keith is insisting they take Nadia to hospital. Carter lifts the baby and holds it in front of his face. It makes a grab for his beard and she hears him say *now you're a fine little fellow.* Keith says, *his name is Eli.*

Orca can't get any closer. She lifts her feet but they land in the same place. No amount of pushing makes any difference. She can see Kelvin making faces at the baby, who laughs at him. Then they all get into the truck. As Carter hands the baby in to Keith, it looks over in her direction and says *Muma,* but then the boys are giving it all their attention and she hears it laugh. Carter starts the engine and they drive away, leaving Orca completely alone in the empty campsite.

She doesn't hesitate. She goes into the shop and grabs handfuls of chocolate bars which she stuffs into her backpack, along with some bottles of water, then she heads off to follow Jack.

There's been a malfunction and she isn't able to check the time. She doesn't know how longs she's slept. She follows the path uphill through the strip of woodland to the forest road. She can feel the presence of the trees all around her, whispering high above in their young branches. In tree terms, these pines are just infants, but they've been alive for more years than her.

She reaches the road and is relieved to find Jack's gateway is still there. She's certain she didn't see it yesterday, but here it is, hard to miss. The sign is on a sturdy wooden stake, embedded in the ground. The words are carved into wood, and darkened, perhaps by burning. *Three paths, Choose wisely, You may choose only one.*

And there they are, three paths leading off in three directions.

The path on the right appears to run alongside the road, carving a line through tall bracken, its hard mud surface dips and rises, and Orca can imagine it would be fun to run along. Further ahead it disappears between another stand of tall trees.

The path on the left heads into trees almost straight away, and these trees are older. The path is less well defined, less used. The gap where it enters the trees is narrow and it looks dark beyond. The third path, the middle one, leads along the edge of this stand of old trees, going steadily uphill.

Orca looks for a sign from Jack to show which path he has taken, but there's nothing. She looks in the grass on the verge at the side of the road, in the gateway, on the sign itself, and on the ground around the start of each path. She's not surprised. She's sure this is a decision each person must make for themselves. She is drawn to the path on the left, she feels a strong pull from the dark forest interior, but she can't imagine Jack would have taken that path. She remembers him at Rendlesham counting the trees, the panic rising from his skin. He wouldn't choose the route that felt crowded. And he probably wouldn't have taken the path by the road, as it doesn't seem to go anywhere new. He'd have chosen the middle path. She doesn't need a sign, she is sure.

She sets off. The pull from the dark forest is like a magnetic force, and her legs shake, her head and torso turn towards it, but her feet keep moving forward. She sees movement between the silent trees, small scurrying bodies, she sees faces peering out, imagined from shadows, there and then gone. She keeps along the path, the forest on her left, open ground on her right, her left side in shadow, her right bathed in sun. There's movement on this path too. Up ahead of her the goat is trotting along, moving at about the same pace as her, not looking back. Could the goat be Jack's sign? Surely not.

The path veers out away from the trees and cuts across moorland to another part of the forest. Cotton grass is growing here, trembling in the air, and high above a skylark is riding its song. She knows it's a skylark, there must be some connection to data. It's shaky though, she has limited access to stored information, no way at all of uploading anything new. She feels light, insubstantial. Ahead of her the goat disappears into the trees.

These trees are similar in size to the forest she just avoided, but the path is wider. Soon she's leaving sunshine and heading into shade. It takes her eyes a moment to adjust, but the path winds uphill between the trees. There's moss everywhere – huge mounds of it filling ditches, making its own terrain beneath the trees, climbing up the trunks, devouring fallen logs. The damp it exudes fills the air, and she feels it in her lungs. It's silent here. Even the goat's feet on the path ahead are muffled. She walks on, still looking for any sign which Jack might have left.

But why would he have left a sign here? She's already made her choice. If she's wrong and he took one of the other paths, there's nothing she can do. If she turned now and went back, changed her mind, what would happen? Maybe the paths would just not be there anymore.

It's then that she sees the sign – or at least proof that Jack went this way. His phone is lying in the middle of the path. She picks it up and presses the screen. It's on, and it has some battery. She opens it – not wanting to pry but wondering if there might be a message. There's no signal here, but he could have recorded something. And there it is, in voice memos. He's even labelled it – *Orca, please listen to this.*

She presses play, and Jack's voice is whispering to her, the sound not dissimilar to the breeze moving the pine branches. "Orca, you won't believe what I've found. This place is amazing, just keep walking until they call you. I'll wait for you." She scrolls down and up, but there are no more messages for her. There's nothing in notes and there are no photos. That's all she has. She listens to it again. The first time she was concentrating on Jack's voice, this time she listens for background sound. There is the hush of branches, which she can hear around her in the forest as well as on the phone. There is a bird. She replays it. It's not a bird she knows, but it's very clear. A long note rising at the end, repeated three times.

The message ends and she listens to the forest. The goat is standing further on, at a bend in the path, waiting for her. She hears someone laugh. It sounds like a child, a high note, rising at the end, then repeated. It's not on the path, it's off to the left, between the trees.

The child laughs again, and Orca steps off the path. She hears the goat bleating. It sounds distressed, and she knows it wants her to follow it along the path. She pauses at the edge. She could get lost. It would make sense to find out where the path leads, and if she sticks to the path she can always turn around and retrace her steps. She can hear the goat's hooves on the path, it's coming back for her.

Orca closes her eyes. She can see a child's face. It's a girl and she has long, lumpy plaits from the side of her head, with bits of hair escaping. She's smiling, she looks cheeky, mischievous, there are sparks in her eyes. She hears the laugh again, immediately followed by a loud bleat from the goat.

She feels in her pocket, thinking of Hansel and Gretel and the white pebbles. Is there something she can leave, a trail so she can find her way back? Her fingers close around something hard and powdery. It's the piece of chalk from Jack's cabin.

"It's OK goat," she says out loud. "I'll mark the trees. I'll be back in a few minutes. I just need to see this child, make sure she's alright."

The goat looks at her. Its horizontal pupils have narrowed to a line and she wants to laugh. She never knew goats could look disapproving. She's reminded of Dorcas.

She draws a big white X on the tree nearest the path, then heads in the direction of the child's laugh. It sounded as though it were OK. She can almost hear the goat saying this. But what's a child doing alone in the woods?

It might not be alone.

The child was laughing – if there were something to be afraid of it wouldn't be laughing.

She hasn't heard it again, but she knows where the sound came from and heads that way, marking each tree she passes with an X. Her feet are saturated – each time she puts her foot down on the moss, a pool rises up around it. She concentrates on the direction, the chalk Xs, the wet moss. She pays no attention to the shadow flitting from tree to tree above her which she knows is Bird, there's his familiar call which she can never catch. A call, which if she let herself listen, she'd realise was not dissimilar in tone to the goat's.

The moss gets higher, rolls of it reaching above her knees, climbing up the base of trees as though it's trying to devour them, suck them down into green depths. She can feel intention in the profusion, the desire to return the trees to the earth, sink them deep beneath the surface, digesting them, turning them into peat, returning the land to open moorland. Is the land hungry enough to take more? To take people, memories, stories? What has already been covered by moss, swallowed by the ground?

She shakes herself and looks back the way she's come. She can't see the goat anymore, or tell where the path is, but she can see a line of white Xs showing the way she's come. In front it's more of the same. She continues, ignoring the calls from the treetops.

The trees end abruptly at a clearing. The child is sitting in the middle on a large rock, cross-legged, looking at her hands which lie in her lap. She's wearing the red coat with the fake fur trim, knee-high white socks with a pattern of holes, brown leather buckled shoes which don't look wet.

"Hello."

The child looks up when Orca speaks, but she doesn't say anything. Her eyes are dancing.

"I heard you ... laughing. I wondered if you were OK."

The child shifts across the rock making a space beside her. She looks at Orca and pats the rock for her to sit down.

The space between them is a green expanse with no tree roots to give solidity to the moss. Orca wonders if she might sink, if this is some kind of trick. It's too far to jump, but perhaps she could do it in two large leaps.

She tries, and finds it's easy, her foot barely touches the moss, and she's in the middle sitting next to the girl. She crosses her legs.

"What's your name?" she asks, knowing what the answer will be.

"Olive."

The girl's voice is light, and Orca wonders if she'd heard it properly, or if it was just the creaking of the trees.

p.279

"I thought you were called Sylva."

The girl shakes her head. She takes something out of her coat pocket and hands it to Orca. It's a photograph of a baby lying in a Moses basket. The baby has fluffy black hair and dark brown eyes. There's a yellow rabbit in the basket too. Orca touches the photo with her fingertips.

"Is this you?" she whispers.

She turns to look at the girl, but she's gone.

Orca looks back at the photo. Somewhere she's seen it before. The baby is looking at the camera. The yellow rabbit is at the side of the basket, where the back of the baby's hand is touching it. Orca's gaze moves beyond the square of the photograph to her own legs, crossed beneath her, and her throat tightens. She is wearing the white patterned socks, and the brown shoes. She touches her arms and feels the plastic of the fake red leather. She moves her head and feels plaits next to her ears.

She puts the photo back into the pocket of the red coat and stands up. The moss is solid beneath her feet. Ahead of her she can see the trees with the white Xs marking the line back to the path. She listens.

There is a faint distant sound, which might be the. goat bleating. But there is something much nearer, a bird call which she knows.

"Bird," she whispers.

He seems to be saying, *What did I tell you? Why didn't you listen?.*

But he's also saying, *Pay attention to me if you want to get out of this.*

She looks up and sees a dark shape at the top of the last tree she marked with the chalk. It flies across the clearing and lands in the middle branches of a tree on the other side. He's a large bird, but difficult to see clearly. More like a shadow than a bird. She hears him call from between the branches of spruce. *This way.*

She follows and reaches into her pocket for the chalk to mark the tree. It's not the same coat, and the chalk isn't there. In one pocket there's a packet of sweets and in the other, the photograph. Bird has moved on to another tree, further into the wood.

Her body feels strange. She's much shorter now, and lighter, and her steps don't seem to have any weight. She moves forward but there seems to be no effort needed. Her feet move, one then the other, but it feels more like gliding. She follows the shadow that is Bird as he flits from tree to tree leading the way.

They travel like this for some time. She's come a long way from the path. They're travelling gradually uphill, through dense forest, where the skirts of the trees overlap and light only gets in through small chinks. The ground is deep in moss. However, Orca – if she is still Orca – has no difficulty making her way. The trees seem to pull their branches, allowing her passage. She senses there are others in the forest, that between the straight trunks and the dark branches, eyes are watching her progress. She isn't afraid though. She has lost all connection with data, there is no way she can contact Dorcas, that's all been left with her other body. There's no panic, just steady movement, following Bird as he leads her. The trees whisper her name, but they think she is Sylva.

The forest comes to an abrupt end. Orca steps between two trees and out onto a track which leads uphill away from the trees. On the other side of the track are some young spruces dotted about, shorter than an adult human. Bird is in the highest branches of the tree behind, to her right, and he calls. She thinks he says, *keep going, and you will see everything.*

She looks down at her feet. They've changed again. She's not wearing the brown leather shoes any more, she's wearing black doctor marten boots and patterned leggings. She touches her head, and the plaits have been replaced by a ponytail. She takes a step, and there's the same effortless glide. She moves uphill away from the trees. She can feel the memory of this body awakening within. The implants must be very sophisticated. She wonders if they are prone to malfunction.

She reaches a drystone wall. Beyond is open moorland with a narrow path leading up to the summit. At the top there are the buildings of a weather station. She can see Jack. He's standing beyond the buildings, looking in the other direction.

Chapter Fourteen

Jack doesn't move, even when she's near enough for him to hear the sound of her boots on the path. She reaches the place where he is standing and stands next to him, looking out across the hills.

They seem to continue for ever, hill after hill, some wearing wisps of cloud wrapped around their tops or draped along their slopes, green and grey. No buildings, no roads, no people. This place has names; it is Scotland, it is the Pentland Hills, it is the Borders, it is Deadwater Fell. These words drift about the summits like scraps of cloud, then disperse into the air.

"It's an otherworld," Orca says, and her voice is fine – clear and strong, and definitely her own.

She turns to look at Jack. He isn't moving and his eyes are closed. He doesn't turn to her, he doesn't move any part of his body or his face. A breeze lifts a strand of his hair and drops it at a different angle, then balloons through his clothes.

"Jack?"

She touches his arm. It isn't stiff, she can move it. It's as though he's playing statues. She slides her hand down his arm to his hand. It's warm. She interwines her fingers with his, and he lets her, but there is no reciprocation, no response. She removes her hand.

"Jack, are you messing about?" She looks at his chest. It moves slightly as the breath goes in and out of his body. "It's not funny Jack, I'm not a child."

But she had been, only a few minutes ago, in the woods. If she hadn't changed again, her head would only reach up to Jack's chest. She hasn't got any of the phones anymore as they were in the pocket of the old coat – the two from Nick and Nadia, and

Jack's which she'd found on the path. She wishes she had one so she could take a selfie, see what this new version of herself looked like. Her hands seem the same. She realises she's hungry.

Jack isn't moving. She searches through his pockets to see what she can find. He has his pocket knife, some chewing gum, a lighter and a half empty packet of cigarettes.

Her own coat is ex-military, green canvas, way too big for her. It has many pockets. She searches through and finds she still has the photo and the packet of sweets from the red coat. The sweets are in a brown packet with white writing on the side – Spangles. She takes one out. The waxy paper has stuck to the sweet, and when she tries to remove it, the sweet is soft and sticky. She doesn't want to put it in her mouth. She rewraps the paper and puts the sweets back in her pocket. She takes one of Jack's cigarettes and lights it. There's not much wind up here, which she guesses is unusual.

Smoking, she walks slowly along the path, inspecting the view. To the south she can see the reservoir, huge and blue, reflecting the sky, enclosed on all sides by the forest. She and Jack had read some of the facts, how it was the largest manmade lake in Europe, how the forest stretched for twenty, thirty miles in each direction. She can see it all from up here. The huge squares of trees of different ages, the shorn patches of clear-fell, the raggedy edge where the forest meets the water, where visitors are encouraged into areas of continuous cover.

She has smoked before. Or at least it's included in the memory implants. Drawing in smoke, holding the cigarette between two fingers, it's familiar. She holds the smoke in her throat, then lets it out through her nostrils.

Whatever Dorcas had done was going seriously wrong. She can't have really turned into a little girl and then a much younger woman. In reality she must have the same body and the same clothes. But it didn't alter the fact that what she has access to now is this body, these clothes. The data, the phone, the nutrition pills – things that could help her in this situation

– are not available. She has a photograph, some inedible sweets and stolen cigarettes. Jack's knife – but she can't see how that would help.

She wants to talk with Jack, to hear another human voice. She wants to go back through the forest to the campsite, but she can't leave him here on his own. At the moment it's warm enough, but it won't be later. If he stays here, he'll get chilled, or worse.

She walks back to him and blows smoke in his face. He doesn't respond.

"Jack! Wake up!" She shouts it, and she pushes his shoulder. His body takes the impact, but rights itself. She tries to shake him, but he's difficult to move – his head wobbles a bit, but nothing more. "Jack, wake up, I need you. I'm scared."

This surprises her. Fear is only useful when you are in danger, because it makes you remove yourself from danger. She hasn't felt fear in the forest before, and wasn't sure if Dorcas had programmed the capacity. Now she has spoken it out loud, it fills her. Her hands start to tremble and she's crying again.

"Jack, please." She grabs at his hands and lifts them with her own. Tears fall from her face splashing on to her skin and his. "Jack, why won't you wake up."

There's a noise. At first she turns around, thinking someone has come up behind her, but they are alone. There aren't even any birds calling. The noise is coming from Jack, and it gradually gets louder. He's humming, and as it increases in volume she recognises it – he's humming the first few lines of *Sitting on the Dock of the Bay.*

She drops her cigarette on the ground and grinds it with the ball of her foot. She joins in, humming at first while she searches through her memory. Do the implants include the words to *Sitting on the Dock of the Bay.* She finds the first line, and then the second, and when Jack starts again, she sings the words. The third line comes naturally, but she sticks at the fourth, and hums along. This is where Jack's loops finishes and goes back to the beginning. She sings more clearly this time, three lines, then a line of humming.

"Jack, I've forgotten the words, do you know the words. What comes next, after the ships roll in?" She sings again, and Jacks' humming gets louder. "Come on Jack, help me out." She sings *da-da-da-da-da-da-da-da-da* for the last line. "You know the words Jack."

He goes back to the beginning. The breeze has dropped and there is no sound in the landscape other than their voices, his a deep humming and hers ringing out. She didn't know she could sing. It feels good

The loop goes on. She sings the first three lines then goes silent. Three times round, and on the fourth it works. Jack sings. *Then I watch 'em roll away again.*

"Yay! Jack, you did it." She grabs hold of his hands, but they are as unresponsive as before.

He's started again, but this time he's singing the words. She sings along. Three times through the first verse, then the fourth time he continues into the next. Orca falls silent, listening to his voice in the still air. He gets to *Wastin' time* and opens his eyes.

"Jack?" she whispers.

The song has stopped, but he's not moved other than his eyelids. She takes his hand, and this time it doesn't seem so limp, there is some responsive energy. She gently tugs at his arm.

"Come on Jack, let's go." She pulls a bit harder, and he takes a step. "Great, keep going." He takes another and soon they are walking, quite slowly, back down the path. He still doesn't look at her. He doesn't seem to be looking at anything, his eyes are unfocused, but he lets her lead him, and after a while they move a little faster.

They reach the place where she came out of the forest. She looks up. "Bird, are you still there." There is an answering cry, which she thinks means, *this way this way.*

She tugs at Jack's arm to lead him between the trees, but he is resistant.

"Come on Jack, this is the way." He won't move. When she tries a step or two along the path, he steps forward. "You want to walk along the track?"

The track leads downhill, which is the right direction. It might take longer, but if she can't get him to step into the trees then she doesn't have a choice. She can hear Bird calling *this way, you came this way* but she ignores him. When Jack doesn't want to move, he's as solid as a tree trunk.

The track winds down the hill, through increasingly mature forest, until they are walking between two walls of tall spruces whose branches block the view of the interior. Orca feels that there are eyes watching from within, but here on the road everything is quiet. They reach a gate across the path. Jack stands immobile while she opens it, then he allows her to walk him through and stands still again while she closes it. She takes his hand and they continue. Bird is flying behind them, moving from tree to tree, calling out occasionally in disconsolate tones.

Something in the air feels different. There's a lot of birdsong, but she doesn't think it's that. Her skin feels different – as though previously there had been a lot of static and now it has gone, the hairs on her arms are lying flat. She looks down at her boots and they are her own. She's wearing her own trousers too, her own coat. She feels in her pocket with her free hand, and finds the chalk as well as Jack's mobile phone.

"We're holding hands." Jack lifts both of their hands up into his vision. "Where did you appear from?"

She pulls her hand away from his.

"Hey, I liked it."

"Where have you been?" she asks him.

A frown passes over his face like a shadow. "I don't know. I must have been dreaming."

"Dreaming what?"

"I can't remember. But I was there a long time." He shakes his head as though to loosen the memory. "Do you have those dreams where you feel like you've lived through a whole film or book, a life even – all the details, all the emotions? Then when you wake up you can barely remember one thing. You just know it was immense."

Orca isn't supposed to dream. There would be no point in programming that, but there must be some processing going on during downtime, and sometimes she feels as though something has shifted when she boots up. Updates maybe.

"What's the last thing you remember?" she says.

"We fell asleep under that hazel tree – then we came here and everything was strange, the people were gone. We stayed at Carter's house and we found Nadia. There were three paths, and I chose the middle one." He stops and his gaze floats off across the wall of trees.

"And then?"

He looks back at her face. "I don't know."

"I found your phone, you'd left me a message." She shows him the words – *Orca please listen to this* – but when she plays the message it's just the sound of the wind in the trees.

"Where did we meet up?"

"At the top of the hill, on Deadwater Fell."

Jack frowns. "Was I there?"

"You were ... "

"I think I can remember the view. Hill after hill. Mist. Like something from Lord of the Rings."

"Yes. But you were somewhere else, in your head."

"You were different ... younger ..."

"So you could see me? I couldn't tell."

Jack shakes his head again. "Ridiculous. This is nonsense. How could you be a different version of yourself?"

"How could you be a walking zombie who couldn't speak, only sing?"

He stares at her for a moment longer, then turns away. "Come on, let's get back to the campsite, see if there's any news."

They walk in silence. The road does a big loop and then another, winding down the hillside. The forest seems different now. The trees are just trees. A squirrel scampers out across the road, but Orca has no sense of being observed.

"Did you see that? A red squirrel!" Jack is excited.

It vanishes into the trees on the other side of the road, an area of Scots pine. There is a wooden sign on the right with a picture of a footprint, and a footpath winding down through the trees to a cute wooden bridge over a stream. They hear a shout of laughter, then another – children playing.

Jack and Orca look at each other, then they both head down the footpath, hurrying. There are people in the forest.

The path takes them though a patch of woodland which is populated by sculptures of children's storybook figures. The Gruffalo and the Mouse watch them pass. The path is made of woodchip and rough steps have been made to help them down the slopes. They're almost running. They come out of the other side of the wood and are at the Castle. There are coaches in the carpark and people walking about. The bike hire shop is open and has customers. A family have just been kitted out and are strapping on helmets; mother and father, boy and girl, four different sizes of bike. The café is busy.

Jack hesitates for a moment, but he says nothing, and they take the path down to the pub. There are shouts of laughter coming up the hill from the maze, and when they reach it, people sitting outside the pub eating plates of pies and peas and drinking beer. They hurry past.

Nick and Nadia's van is still in the carpark, and Nick is there, pacing up and down. When he sees Jack and Orca he rushes over to them.

"Thank god you're here, I don't know what to do. I've lost Eli and Nadia."

"They're ..."

Orca puts her hand on Jack's arm. "Where did you lose them?" she asks.

"In the forest. We were down at the Forest Head – I was looking at beetles. She went to change Eli, and then they were gone. I looked everywhere. I've been calling them and calling them. I thought they might have come back to the van."

"How long ago was this?" Orca still has her hand on Jack's arm, she can tell he wants to speak.

"A couple of hours maybe. We went down there first thing after breakfast. I lose track when I'm on the trail."

"Was she alright when you last saw her?"

"She was just going to change Eli, over near that Head thing."

"We found her," said Jack.

Orca lets go of his arm and shoots him a glance.

"Where?" asks Nick.

"She'd hurt herself. She's been taken to hospital."

"What about Eli? Where's Eli?"

"Eli is fine," said Orca. "Are you sure Nadia was OK when you last saw her?"

"She was just normal. What hospital? Have they taken Eli too?"

"The nearest," says Jack. "Wherever that is."

Nick looks at his phone, but he has no signal.

"There's probably information in the campsite office," says Jack, "and our van is there too. Let's walk over."

They walk along the river towards the campsite. Nick walks as though he's on hot coals. Energy is creating a haze around his body. Orca can see it. She shakes her head and it disappears.

The campsite is busy with life – people walking to and from the toilet block, setting up cooking stoves, washing down bikes. Someone is mowing the grass on a sit-on mower, and the sound is the background for voices and laughter. The smell of cut grass is sharp and sweet in the air. Orca and Jack look at each other, but they don't say anything.

The campsite office is open and there's a man behind the counter who greets them cheerfully. They ask where the nearest hospital is and he's concerned. They explain that a friend was taken there, and they need to visit her.

"Hexham's the nearest. They have an urgent care centre."

"Thank you."

Nick is leaving the shop. Jack and Orca hesitate.

"Have you been open all day?" asks Jack. "And yesterday."

"All day every day, I'm here or somewhere on the site. Was your friend staying on the campsite."

"No, she wasn't," says Orca.

"It's just that we popped in yesterday and couldn't find you." Jack is fishing in his pocket and pulls out his wallet. "We owe you some money for chocolate and drinks."

The man looks puzzled. "I didn't notice anything missing."

Jack hands him a ten-pound note. "You must have been busy somewhere."

The man looks at the note in his hand. "This must be too much, do you know how much ...?"

"It's OK, see it as a donation."

Jack turns to follow Nick out of the shop.

"Do you know a man named Carter?" asks Orca, "and two boys, his grandsons, Keith and Kelvin?"

The man smiles. "Oh yes, everyone knows Carter. I've not sure I'd call them boys though. Big lads these days, the both of them."

"Have you seen them?"

He frowns. "Not recently. No reason for them to come here, and our paths don't cross often. Are they OK?"

"As far as I know. We met them yesterday, that's all."

"I thought Keith was off away somewhere. Is he back?"

"I don't know."

The man gives Orca a puzzled look. She thanks him and follows the others outside.

Jack is sitting in the driving seat of his van with the door open. He turns the key and it starts perfectly.

"Are you coming to the hospital?" asks Nick.

"Do you need us?"

"Yes, we are," says Orca.

"We should probably head back, I need to get back to work."

"I want to check Nadia's OK. You can drop me at the hospital. You don't have to stay."

Nick nods. "OK, I'll see you there then." He heads off across the campsite.

Orca gets into the passenger seat. "I want to get there before him," she says. "Let's go."

Jack doesn't say anything, but he closes his door and fastens his seat belt. As they pull out, he has to pause to let a group of children run past. There's a smell of burning charcoal as someone gets a barbeque going.

"I wonder if people are back in the village too," says Orca.

"I just want to leave."

"The whole feel is different. The trees are different. They just seem like trees."

"They are just trees."

"But earlier ..."

"I think we were both dreaming. Lucid dreaming maybe, as we were both in it."

Orca looks at his face. He's concentrating on the road, but his face is tight. His jaw is rigid and tension is holding his skin taut. She is surprised to realise that she wants to touch him, to place her hand on one of his limbs or her fingertips on his cheekbones. He must realise she's looking at him but he doesn't glance her way.

"Shall we have music?" asks Orca.

He shrugs, but fiddles with the dials and after a moment the van fills with sound. Orca finds that her recognition data is working again, and they are listening to Isaac Hayes. The van moves through the empty landscape alongside the lake. Jack is driving fast, turning the van around the bends. Once they meet someone going the other way, and once they have to slow for some cyclists. When Orca looks behind there's no sign of Nick.

Chapter Fifteen

They reach a village and slow to thirty miles an hour. Soon after there is another village. The countryside around them now is farmland.

"What are you doing after this?" asks Jack. "Are you going back to Suffolk?"

"I don't know. It depends on Nadia."

"I'll wait, if you want a lift."

"Thank you."

There are road signs for Hexham now. Isaac Hayes has been followed by Betty Davis and Curtis Mayfield. Orca closes her eyes. She could forget about Nadia. She could stay in the van, ask Jack to keep driving, listen to this music as the road winds. She'd like to see Jack smile again. See him laugh. She remembers the moment in the forest when they'd jumped the ditch.

His phone pings into life. Numerous messages all arrive at once, and the screen lights up as it buzzes in quick succession.

"We must have found signal," says Orca.

Jack glances to where his phone is resting between front seats. Orca looks too. The name on the screen is Becky. Jack frowns. "I better pull over," he says.

They are on a country road between villages. He stops the van by a field gate, and looks at his phone. There seem to be a number of texts, but also some voice messages. He starts to listen to them and Orca hears a female voice *Jack, where are you? I've been calling and calling* – the voice sounds distressed, tearful. Jack gets out of the van and continues to listen to the messages whilst pacing up and down. Then he's making a call and talking. He's gesticulating with his free arm, he's walking back and forth along the verge. Orca looks at the cows that have come to peer over the gate. Their big brown eyes look wet, and their round noses soft as velvet.

Jack gets back into the van. "I'll drop you in Hexham," he says, "but I've got to go."

"Is it Becky?"

"Her dad's died, she needs me." He hits the steering wheel and inhales sharply.

Orca nods. Jackie Wilson is singing about the sweetest feeling. She watches the fields pass and thinks about time. Six months ago she was working in the office with Sylva. Every day was the same and she always knew what to expect. If you'd asked her then what she'd be doing in six months she'd have said, the same, why change it, it works. If someone asked her now, she couldn't answer. In six months, it will be winter, that's about as much certainty she can summon.

They're on a dual carriageway, moving fast. They'll be in Hexham in minutes. Jack has lines around his eyes. There are grey hairs in his beard that she hadn't noticed. She feels the movement of the van as it reaches a roundabout and changes direction. She listens to The Dramatics, their voices filling the space in the van, leaking through the open windows. She can feel warmth from the sun on her belly as it shines through the windscreen.

"Does she have nightmares too?"

"No. I don't think so. She never said."

"Did she see ...?"

"I don't want to talk about it."

Jack's voice is sharp and his face is pinched, white around the nostrils. Orca looks out of the window. She wonders if Becky's father's death will change things. There are more roundabouts. They're moving slower through town traffic, and The Delfonics take over. They haven't finished singing when the van pulls to a stop. They are in front of a huge building made of glass and brick.

"I'm sorry," says Jack.

Orca grabs her backpack and opens the van door. "Thank you for driving me. And everything."

"I hope Nadia's OK."

Orca nods, then she's out of the van and walking across the forecourt towards the glass doors. She hears him shout behind her.

"Orca, wait!"

She stops and turns. The engine is still running, but Jack has got out of the van and is waving at her.

"Don't forget this."

He's coming over. He has the necklace of Corsican Pine. He lays it on her palm and it feels cold. She closes her fingers around it.

"Thank you," she says. She allows the fingertips of her other hand to do what they've been wanting to do. They rest lightly for a moment on Jack's cheek, and she can feel his warmth in the five circles of her fingerprints. Then she turns and walks into the hospital.

Inside smells familiar. She waits at the desk. The receptionist is on the phone, but she lifts her hand to Orca to acknowledge she's seen her. Beyond there is a waiting area where people are sitting in twos and threes, children and parents, couples, friends.

The receptionist replaces her phone, and Orca explains she'd looking for a friend who'd been brought in earlier, who had a baby with her. Immediately the woman's eyes light up.

"And you are ...?"

"I'm her friend. She was brought in by some people we met in the forest."

"She was left on the forecourt."

"Oh ..."

"The baby too. She has no id on her, no phone."

"Is she OK? ... Are they OK?"

The woman's face softens a little. "I think so. She's been taken to the wards. I'll just check which one, the doctor might speak to you."

Orca is directed to the sixth floor. She takes the lift, which lets her out at the end of a long corridor. On one side there's a plate glass window overlooking the crowded carpark. Nick's van has just arrived and is moving slowly as he looks for a parking spot. Orca hurries on.

The doctor is waiting for her. She's wearing a hijab and round glasses. She looks Orca up and down, and Orca realises she's covered in dust and particles from the forest.

"How do you know the patient?"

"I'm her friend."

"What is her full name, please?"

Orca doesn't know. "Her name is Nadia. We have never exchanged surnames. We've only known each other for a few days."

The doctor glances at her then writes something on her clipboard.

"And the baby?"

"His name is Eli."

"She is his mother?"

"I don't think so. She is seeing his father, who will be here in a moment. Can I see her?"

"Visiting is for family and close friends only. Until we know more..."

"Have you examined her? Does she have injuries?"

"Really I can't say, until we have more information."

"Nick will be here in a minute, her boyfriend. He will know her name and might have her id, and also the baby's. Will you let him see her?"

"If we are satisfied that he is her ..."

"Please, ask her how she got her injuries. I don't think she is safe with him."

The doctor looks at her again and this time she makes eye contact. "You think the boyfriend is violent?" she asks.

Orca nods. "Nadia is scared of him. I have text messages from her, a note ..." But she didn't keep the note. That is in a bin somewhere in Woodbridge, Suffolk. The messages from Nadia never said anything specific, nothing that couldn't be explained to Nick if he looked at her phone. "She told me she is scared of him. I have no proof."

The doctor is still looking at her. Orca can't decide if her eyes are understanding or disapproving. The light from the corridor is glinting from her glasses. "Thank you for that information," she says, after a moment. "We will bear it in mind."

Back down the corridor there's a ping as the lift arrives.

"Can I ...?"

"Do you have a number I can take?" The doctor looks at Orca over her glasses, and Orca feels her muscles relax a little. She recites her number and the doctor scribbles it down. "Thank you," she says.

The doctor inclines her head in acknowledgement as Nick appears beside them.

"Where's Eli?"

"You are Nadia's boyfriend?"

"Yes."

"I'd like to ask you some questions. She has not regained consciousness yet, and there some things we ..."

"What about Eli?"

"You are his father?"

Nick pulls out his wallet and produces a photo of himself and Eli. "Yes, I'm his father. Is he OK? Can I have him?"

The doctor taps a message onto a device which is hanging from her belt. "I would like to ask you some questions. Perhaps we could go somewhere more private." She looks at Orca.

"I'll wait downstairs. Please let me know if there's news." She says this to both of them, but Nick doesn't have her contact details.

A nurse appears holding Eli, and he lurches towards Nick. He says *dada*. Nick takes him in his arms and buries his face in the baby's neck. He has tears in his eyes. The doctor makes eye contact with Orca, who shrugs.

In the cafeteria many of the tables are full of doctors and nurses grabbing a bite mid-shift. Others are occupied by families and visitors. Some people are laughing, some look stricken.

Orca buys tea and chocolate cake from the counter. The surface of the tea quakes as she carries it to a table in the corner. She's been focussed on Nadia, but now she's found her other feelings are surfacing. She tries to think about Jack and how she feels about him leaving. She wonders if she's sad. But there is something else. It started the moment she stepped through the hospital doors, and she ignored it. It's a rising panic that's connected to the smell of the hospital, the disinfectant and cleaning fluids covering the stink of illness and grief, the soft hush of long corridors and feet on linoleum, the swish of double doors. She can feel these things taking hold of her. When she thinks about Jack, she sees him sitting in the front of the van, but he is very far away, at the other end of a long tunnel, through the wrong end of the telescope.

She shakes her head and takes a bite of cake.

Another image comes into her mind. A woman is screaming. Nurses are holding on to her by the arms, and she's fighting to get away. Her hair is a mess and her face is covered with black smudges. She looks frantic, furious, incandescent. She smells of burning, of thick black smoke, of terror. She's repeating two names, a boy's and a girl's, in hoarse screams.

The woman is her. She can feel the screaming within herself. She can smell the smoke in her clothes and hair. This must be another of Dorcas's implants, but she can't dissociate from the feeling. She tries to examine the memory calmly, but the panic is spreading through her body, as though the image has released a poison into her blood stream and the burning smell is reaching every part of her. The feeling is unbearable, it is pain. She takes a large bite of cake, and then another. She stuffs her mouth with cake and chocolate icing. Someone at the next table is looking at her but she doesn't care. If the sugar can stop this pain, then she wants more. She goes to the counter and buys two chocolate bars and a piece of flapjack. Her arms and legs feel awkward moving at a normal pace. She wants to run. She wants to punch something; the woman's face at the till, the person at the next table, the formica table-top. She wants to sweep everything onto the floor so it smashes. She wants to scream.

She sits down and looks at her sugar haul. She's even picked up sachets of sugar to add to the tea. She eats the flapjack.

Another image surfaces, this time of the clearing in the forest and the girl sitting on the rock handing her a photograph. Orca feels into her pocket and the photograph is there. She pulls it out and looks at it. The baby with its dark hair curling on its forehead, the yellow rabbit. The pain becomes focussed, no longer through her whole body, it's now in her hands and her throat.

"I never got to know you," she whispers.

She watches her hands tear the photograph in two, then again into four, then again until there are tiny pieces of it all over the table. The person at the next table gets up and goes to the counter. They talk to one of the staff and they both look over at Orca.

Her hands are balled into fists and energy is making them shake. She's struggling to keep herself from punching the table. Any moment they are going to come over and talk to her. She shoves the chocolate bars into her pockets and leaves the cafeteria. She manages to keep her footsteps to a hospital pace, but it's hard, following the arrows painted on the floor towards the exit. The adrenaline makes her arms twitch, her head jerk on her shoulders.

Outside she crosses the carpark at a fast walk, and when she reaches the road, she runs. She knows it's not the place for it, but she needs to move fast. She needs to expend the force which has built up in her so completely that she feels her skin will split. She runs as fast as she can in her walking clothes, avoiding other pedestrians, keeping her gaze on the ground in front of her. She runs until her breath hurts her lungs and her body comes to a stop. She rests her hands on her knees and gasps air, revelling in the burn in her throat, the shooting energy through her calves and thighs.

She's by a junction. There's a grassy verge next to a bus stop and an empty bench. She sits down and send a message to Dorcas.

Why the fuck? There's no point in swearing at Dorcas but she does it anyway. *Why the fuck did you give me these memories? I can't deal with them. They are too much. It's unethical.*

Dorcas doesn't respond for a few minutes. Traffic slows as it approaches the junction. People sit in their cars, their eyes forward. Orca's breath gradually calms. She realises she's left her pack in the hospital cafeteria and she has to go back. She gets up and walks, retracing her steps. She can control her body now, but it feels light, insubstantial. She's glad she doesn't have to cross the road, she doesn't fancy her chances against traffic.

Come back. Dorcas's reply arrives as Orca steps off the kerb to let two women pass with push chairs that fill the pavement. *Come back to the Hayes and continue with the job you're meant to be doing.*

Her pack has been put behind the food counter. The woman who hands it to her is stern. "It's a security thing, we're meant to hand them in. It could have been destroyed."

"I'm sorry. I was just … it was too …"

The woman's face softens. She works in a hospital after all, she must see people teetering on their emotional edge all the time. "Well you're lucky, we hadn't had time to call security yet."

She offers Orca a cup of tea, says it's on the house. Orca looks at the table where she had been sitting. The pieces of photograph have been tidied up and someone else is sitting there. She takes the tea to a table by the window. She holds it in both hands and feels the heat against her skin. When she drinks, the hot liquid relights the burn from the run. She puts the mug on the table and checks for trains. There are various routes from Hexham to Nuneaton, all involving two or three changes. She purchases an open ticket. She's not trying to hide anymore, so it doesn't matter if she's traced.

Her phone pings. It's a message from the doctor. Nadia has woken up and wants to see her.

She finishes her tea in two scalding gulps and goes back to the lifts. This time she's allowed to go through into the ward to where Nadia is lying in bed looking pale but smiling. Nick is sitting on a chair at the bedside with Eli on his knee. He's talking and the baby is waving its arms. They look like a perfect family.

Nadia calls her over. "Orca, you'll never guess what happened. I am the princess in the fairy tale."

"And I am the handsome prince." Nick lifts his chin in mock regal pose and Nadia giggles.

"I was unconscious, and they couldn't wake me up, then Nick came along and kissed me and I opened my eyes straight away. Can you believe it?"

Orca doesn't stay long. They don't need her, and she wants to get going now she's made the decision. On her way out she sees the doctor.

"She says she fell," she tells Orca, "and her injuries are consistent with that."

"So you're sure?"

The woman shrugs. "There are many reasons for someone to fall, but she insists that it was accidental."

"Will you talk to her? When Nick isn't there?"

The doctor looks at her over her glasses. "Yes, we will talk to her."

"Sorry. I'm telling you how to do your job. I'm just worried about her."

The doctor smiles. "Thank you for informing us of your concern."

There's something in her expression, sadness and understanding, Orca realises she's seen it all before. That women who arrive in hospital with injuries often tell only part of a story. Maybe some men too. That trying to fit the story together is part of this woman's job, particularly difficult when some of the pieces have been hidden. So many layers of fear to unwrap, masquerading as other things such as love, loyalty and shame.

I was lucky with Eric.

The thought drags with it a weight of loss that Orca isn't able to carry.

Chapter Sixteen

The station is only a few minutes' walk away, and a train is due soon. Orca finds the chocolate from the cafeteria in her pocket and eats it. Maybe all the sugar in her system is causing the malfunction. She's been surviving on nutrition pills and energy bars for a long time. The onslaught of sugar in the past couple of days might have changed her internal chemistry. Dorcas will bring new supplies though. Once she's back, things can return to normal.

At Newcastle Station she buys a packet of jellybeans, which she consumes on the train south. Gazing out of the window, she pops the beans into her mouth one at a time. Some she chews and some she sucks. She times how long it takes her to suck one away to nothing, feeling the piece of jelly getting softer and smaller between her tongue and the roof of her mouth. She'll have to scrub her mouth. She'll have to scour her teeth. The train rushes through the landscape, through Yorkshire, Derbyshire, Nottinghamshire, Staffordshire. By Tamworth the bag is empty. That's it. The last change. She's nearly there.

She sees a man waiting on the platform. He has a beard and his hair is tied back and she thinks of Jack. The sugar has made her jittery. Her eyes itch and she flexes and clenches her hands. Jack will be with Becky now. He'll be consoling her. Orca paces up and down the narrow platform. She hasn't told Dorcas she's coming, but she hasn't hidden her movements. Should she go straight to the Hayes? She's breathing faster than normal and she can feel her heart beating. She's too warm.

The train arrives. She sits across the aisle from the man with the ponytail. She closes her eyes. She is the prodigal daughter returning, overstimulated, exhausted, uncertain how she will be received.

Why does that bible story surface in her mind? Why is it even there? What possible use could Dorcas have foreseen for such a thing. Orca is too tired to follow the thought. She looks out of the window. This part of the journey is only twenty minutes. They pass through Atherstone, then back out into fields. Past quarries, and the triangular spoil heap, which she knows is called Mount Judd. Information is jangling in her mind, but she doesn't try to make sense of it. She lets it rush past her. The canal, the River Anker, the outskirts, then the centre of the town. Then the train is pulling into the station and Dorcas is waiting for her.

They drive to the city, and she's taken to the office for a debrief and overhaul, but she's so tired her eyes keep closing. In the end Dorcas decides to leave it for another day. She tells Orcas to go home and sleep. *Home.* Orca presumes she means the house she used to return to after the office each day. She'd forgotten about it, is surprised to know it's still there waiting for her, that it hasn't been assigned to someone else. She knows the walk from the office well enough to do it with her eyes closed, but this time it feels as though the streets have just been unrolled, as though the buildings are made of polystyrene blocks painted to look like bricks and stone. The ground feels hollow beneath her feet. Rooks are chattering in the trees and she looks up. Their black shapes are scattered through the branches. She wonders if they remember her, then sends the thought away. She listens for Bird, but she can only hear the rooks.

Inside the house there is a thin layer of dust over everything. She should clean it, but she's too heavy. Her limbs are drenched with lethargy, it pools in her hands and beneath her tongue, it makes her feet feel as though they're stuffed with wet sand. She trails a finger through the dust as she passes. She climbs the stairs, one at a time, with her hand on the wall. She goes into the room with the bed and lies down. She misses the smell of sap and fungus. She misses the damp softness of moss. She misses Jack. She sleeps.

She has no idea for how long. She didn't check the time when she arrived. It was probably early evening. When she wakes it is early afternoon, but she doesn't know if one night or two have passed. She could find out, but for the moment she doesn't care.

Downstairs she looks under the sink in the kitchen and finds cloths, dusters and cleaning products. In a cupboard she finds a mop. Next to the kettle there's stash of nutrition. She takes some pills. Her stomach growls at her and she eats a cereal bar as well. She looks in the rest of the cupboards, but they are empty other than a couple of glasses and a pair of scissors. She can't make tea. She drinks some water, then spreads out all of the cleaning products on the worktop. She will use them all. She'll start with the dusters, and get rid of that dry layer of neglect, then she will clean and polish and shine.

The house isn't dirty, only a bit dusty. There isn't much to clean up, but she works hard for the rest of the afternoon. Under the stairs she finds a vacuum cleaner and she hoovers every bit of floor. She scrubs the toilet and the bath, she even cleans the windows. When every bit of the house is shining and every speck of dust has been banished outside or sucked up by the hoover, she drinks more water and takes more pills, then goes back to sleep.

When she wakes up next it's early evening.

Dorcas is there. "That's enough," she says.

Orca goes back to the office. She answers all of Dorcas's questions. She tells her about Nadia and Nick, she tells her about Jack and the music he likes, about Becky who needs him, she tells her about Sylva and about the memories that keep flashing into her mind. She tells her about her anger in the hospital. She tells her about the trees and the mosses and the goat. The only thing she doesn't mention is Bird.

Dorcas inputs all of the data, then she says, "What are you going to do now?"

Orca frowns.

"Do you want to return to the forest? Would you prefer desk work?"

She shakes her head immediately. There is no way she wants to return to the office. Day after day of coming in to the same four walls, the same screen, the same callers asking the same questions. Never waking up with dew in her hair and a beetle scurrying across her knee. The empty house with its layer of dust which reforms each day.

"I'll go back to the Hayes. I'll do the work properly."

"You're sure you're ready?"

"What else would I do?"

Dorcas offers to take her the following morning but Orca doesn't want to spend another night in the house. They collect the things she needs, replenish her backpack, and order a car to take her to Hartshill.

"Do you want me to come with you?" asks Dorcas.

"I'll be fine."

"Keep in touch then. Let me know if you have problems."

The car drives along roads which decrease in size. The motorway, then a dual carriageway, then the car is driving though the town centre of Nuneaton, they pass Mount Judd and drive up the long road where Orca remembers walking in the hot sun. The car drops her off at the visitor's centre. She walks out onto Oldbury Hills and watches the light fade from the sky as the sun sets, then she goes down to the dark edge of the wood and slips quietly in between the trees. She hears an owl hoot and it feels like a welcome. The trees close around her and enfold her. It's not completely dark yet. She finds a stand of young holly, pushes her way through, and in the centre she closes her body down.

Chapter Seventeen

She's woken by Bird. She lies still and listens to him. There are other birds singing but she can tell his voice is among them. She can't catch what he's saying, but she's comforted to know he's there.

She refuels then sets off for a circuit of the wood to remind herself. She retrieves the data, reassesses where she'd got to. The early morning sun has some warmth. The woods will be busy later, it makes sense to get some work done now before visitors start arriving.

By the time she sees the first dogwalker she's already done a couple of hours. She's down at the bottom end of the woods where they meet the Hollows. She checks the data. There's nothing on the map to say that this area is called the Hollows, nor anything in the list of quadrants in her scheme of work. So why has she just called it the Hollows?

She looks through the fringe of trees into the open area with its gorse and brambles, its marshy bottom. There are more dog walkers on the paths. There are flowers growing amongst the grasses, valerian and mallow, fox-and-cubs, tormentil and scarlet pimpernel. She turns back into the woods. The trees here are wild service trees. She takes readings and measurements, photographs the jagged leaves, places her hand behind one leaf to show the size. It fits neatly over her palm. The fruits are forming in hard clusters, and she reads that they are called chequers and taste like dates, but only after they have been bletted – which means to have been left out in the frost. She holds one between her thumb and forefinger. It's hard and doesn't look tempting.

p.280

The sun is building heat. She feels energy and needs to move. She walks into the Hollows. This is not strictly the woods, and she is aware of Dorcas's instructions – no more going rogue, stick to the task. But a few minutes exercise can't hurt. She walks quickly. Above to her left she can see the back of a housing estate, but down here butterflies are darting in the morning sun. She identifies viper's bugloss, ragged robin, harebell. She thinks about their names, and that each probably has a story connecting the flower to the viper, the robin, the hare. The Hollows opens into an abandoned quarry on the left. The base has been fenced off and a white pony is grazing on the grasses. A path on the right leads steeply back to the woods. She's only been gone for ten minutes, but she feels the morning has moved on. The sun has warmed her. Back amongst the trees the liminal sense of early morning has dissipated, day has established itself and the air is still.

Her body still wants to move. She can't really gather data when she walks fast, but her body wants to run. If she expends this excess of energy maybe she'll be able to settle. She walks up the red clay path, which dips down to a stream then on up to the main ride, where she turns right and marches back up to where the woods spill her out onto Oldbury Hills. She still can't stop moving. She crosses the field, with the view opening up on her left like the ocean.

She briefly closes her eyes then opens them again. When has she walked by the ocean? She was by the sea at night in Suffolk. One of the memory implants was of a ball game on a beach. But here is another, of walking along a clifftop with the sea stretching out on her left. She isn't alone. There is someone walking on the path behind her, and ahead there is a child running. It's not Sylva. This child is dressed in shorts and a stripy t-shirt and has dark curls. It's the girl from the photos on the memory stick. Orca turns, and for a moment has a glimpse of a man walking behind her, wearing shorts and sandals, a baby carrier on his back. The image

p.281

is gone before she can grasp hold of it. She didn't get a proper look at the baby, but even though it was brief she recognised the man.

She looks at the view that is not the sea. She can see cars moving along a main road, they are like small creatures with no sound moving between the fields. She can see church spires standing tall. She remembers Sylva in the office, looking through the gap between high rises. Here, Orca can see distance in every direction.

There's another bit of woodland further on and separate, St Lawrence's Wood. Outside the entrance is a tree memorial garden where trees have been planted in memory of loved ones. There's a board with plaques showing the names of the deceased. Orca looks at them for a moment, reads some of the names out loud. Most of the trees are still very young. Some won't thrive. She wonders what people do, if the memorial tree dies. Do they plant another one? Some of the trees are decorated with flowers and ribbons.

St Lawrence's Wood is so tiny that she's reached the other side before she realises she's decided to go in. The path continues beyond across fields, and she can feel its pull. She'd like to spend the day walking, marching, burning off the restlessness that's fizzing beneath her skin. It's her first day. Would it be OK, just for one day? She'd be more settled for the task.

It's just then that Dorcas makes contact. *Why are you in St Lawrence's?*

Just walking the boundaries, Orca replies. She turns away from the field and walks the path along the bottom of the woods, along the stream. Where the path bends to the right is a huge ash tree. Orca places her palm on it and looks up. The tree has retrenched; only the branches near to the trunk have leaves, beyond that the bony branches poke their bare twigs in silhouette against the sky. She puts both hands on the trunk and steps nearer, until her forehead rests against the bark. She turns her head and listens to the sap rising. This tree isn't dead, it is fighting against die-back, it's putting all its resources into survival, into beating the disease. She's seen smaller ash trees that have lost the fight, but this one might make it. She looks at her own fingers resting against the bark. She whispers to the tree.

She walks fast after that, following the path steeply uphill, completing the circuit of St Lawrence's and back out past the memorial trees and across the fields. Her legs feel strong and her arms swing by her side. She nods to the early risers as she passes *Morning.* No lingering. She leaves the open field and the view like the sea, goes back between the trees where it is lighter and airier than it looks from the outside. There are foxgloves standing straight in the sunshine. She nods to the hollies which sheltered her in the night. She'll start at the lime tree.

She shoves the backpack up into the place where the lowest branch meets the trunk of the lime tree. Now she can run.

She checks the time and sets off for the first circuit. She runs down the narrow path to where it meets the main ride and turns left. This path is wide and well used. Early butterflies are dancing in sunlight, two together, flittering around each other. Speckled Wood, Orca notes as she runs past. She passes a man with a Labrador and a woman with two Lakeland Terriers. A wood pigeon is calling. At the top of the wood she turns and takes the path that follows the inside of the fence. She's just inside the woods here, on her left are fields and that view. She nudges through hollies, past hazels and larch. She passes the seedheads of bluebells and remembers the wash of electric blue which blurred the forest in May. The path is narrower here, crossed by tree roots. She keeps an eye on the ground, takes a small jump now and then, keeps her footing.

In no time she is at the bottom corner and the gate to the Hollows. This time she stays in the woods and runs along the bottom path. She doesn't stop for the wild service trees. There's a makeshift bridge over a stream – barely a stream, a trickle, a sweat of water against the mud, the bridge a plank laid across it. Further on some steps and the path twists. The compacted earth is redder here. Willows mark the boundary between the

p.282

woods and the Hollows. On the other side a swathe of nettles. The path runs along the boundary until it reaches a junction between the boardwalk she crossed earlier, and the red path uphill. She runs up, feeling strength in her legs, the muscles in her calves and thighs bunching and releasing. She holds on to her abdominals, lets everything else go.

She turns along the path with the clay pipe, parallel to the main ride but narrower. It's been covered with loose white gravel, but she knows it's red underneath. It brings her to another edge, where the woods meet the cemetery and the housing estate. She stays inside the boundary, takes the path back to the main ride.

She passes dogs, an Alaskan Malamut, a Gordon Setter, a whippet. She passes small-leaved lime coppices, hazel coppices. A butterfly flies across the path and she follows it with her eyes. She should note that one, they are uncommon. White Admiral. Further on more Speckled Woods, ragged robin, bladder campion.

Back at the lime tree she checks the time. It's taken ten minutes. She's warm but not exhausted. She could do it again.

Main ride, down the side path past the fields to the bottom corner. Along the bottom, over the slimy mud, the makeshift bridge, back to the junction, uphill, left along to the housing estate, through the hollies to the main ride. A golden retriever, two springers racing back and forth, up the small path back to the lime. Nine minutes.

She's panting a bit now, but she's sure she can do it faster. There seems to be a message from Dorcas, but she'll check it when she's done another circuit. Main ride, side path, bottom path, bridge, red mud, claypipe, cemetery, hollies, speckled wood, she's back on the main ride but carries on, goes around again. Past the fields, past the Hollows, uphill, left, past the housing estate, past the springers who are still playing, back to the lime. 17 minutes for a double circuit.

She's properly out of breath now. She can feel the burn in her chest. She sits down at the bottom of the tree.

What are you doing? Dorcas asks. *Are you running? Why did you leave the woods earlier?*

Speed data collection, she replies. Reconnaissance. It's getting busier and soon the families will be arriving. I'm going to close down for a while. She doesn't wait for Dorcas to reply. She swings her body up into the lime tree. She finds water in her pack and takes a long drink.

She eats a cereal bar. She leans her body against her pack, her head against the tree trunk. She could refuse to come down. She could stay in the trees. She could leap from tree to tree like a squirrel. She could move around the woods through the canopy, higher than people's heads. They wouldn't know she was there. They would sense movement, hear a rustling, but when they looked up she would freeze, and the tree would hide her with its leaves. She could eat berries, nuts, chequers, insects, food the trees provided. She could drink the rain drops that rolled across leaves. She need never set foot on earth again.

The fantasy plays through her head and she smiles. Winter would come, but she doesn't follow the dream that far. She rests.

A message comes through from Dorcas. *Enough!*

Save closedown for night time. Orca can hear children's voices, dogs barking in excitement, adults calling after them. It's Sunday and the weather is fine. Not many come up this path.

A few times she's heard the murmur of conversation, looked down and seen the tops of heads. She stays in her tree. *You have work to do*, says Dorcas. Don't I get a weekend? asks Orca. She turns off notifications.

In the evening she climbs down. There are still some people walking in the last of the light, but not so many – no families with laughing children and babies in carriers. She walks slowly, noting the species, the path types – artery, tributary, feeder, deer, rabbit. She logs every sign, notes the new plants that have appeared since she was last here – wood avens, marsh marigold, hedge garlic, bugle. The wood pigeon's call caresses the evening.

p.283

A cuckoo is singing its two note song. Orca works, logging everything she sees, takes photographs, records the birds. By the time night falls she's done a day's work.

p.284

Chapter Eighteen

She works solidly for three days, crossing and recrossing the Hayes, checking everything against the map, adding and annotating. She'd done the trees and higher plants already, but new things have appeared since she was away, so she's updating, while also getting a sense of the lower plants, where they grow and the variety. She marks all the deer paths on the map with thin red lines. It starts to look like a map of the circulatory system of the body. She follows the paths, treading where the deer have trod, but she rarely sees them. There are many of them in the wood, and she hears them barking in the hour before dawn, sometimes sees a movement off to the side amongst the trees. But for the most part they stay hidden. She watches squirrels and notes which trees they run through. She sits by the pond and watches the boatmen skimming, the dragonflies and damselflies flashing blue and green in the air above the water, frogs hopping at the edges. She walks up to the hills and looks out across the sea that is actually Warwickshire, Leicestershire, Staffordshire, Northamptonshire, Nottinghamshire. She doesn't stay too long, she answers Dorcas's messages and sends regular data reports. She stays on the surface. At night she sleeps in the lime tree.

On day four she's up at the top of the wood, not far from the visitors centre. She's examining some moss at the base of a stump when she feels someone watching her.

She looks up. A young woman is standing a few feet away. Between them is a huge hole in the ground. The bomb crater, Orca remembers. The hole has brambles growing in its base. The woman is wearing embroidered jeans and a cheesecloth blouse. She is wearing huge glasses.

"Sylva!"

"Hello Olive."

Orca looks more closely. The Sylva she knew was much older and wore her curly hair pulled back into a tight ponytail. This woman has it loose about her head. The sun is glinting on her glasses and it's difficult to see her eyes.

"You were a child when I saw you last."

Sylva shrugs. "What are you looking at?"

Orca looks back to the stump. "Orthodontium Lineare. It's got these cute capsules. Come and look."

Sylva edges her way around the edge of the hole until she is next to Orca. Together they look at the moss.

"Like a tiny forest for the fairy folk," says Sylva.

"Yes. And look up close." Orca has a lens for close inspection which she hands to Sylva. "Look at the ends of the leaves, the way the light shines through."

"Like glass."

"There's a whole world there, that you can only see if you have the right lens."

"It's amazing." Sylva is crouching close to the moss, bent forward with her eye to the lens. Orca is close enough to sense Sylva's body heat almost as though it were a smell. "Thank you." Sylva rocks back on to her heels and hands the lens back to Orca. Their hands brush in the exchange. Sylva is not a hologram or a ghost, she is solid.

"Why are you here?" says Orca.

"You were looking for me."

"And why did you call me Olive?"

"That's your name."

Orca sits with the answers. Neither of them make sense to her, but the way Sylva spoke them was deliberate and certain. Perhaps there is meaning hidden beneath them which she might discover if she turns them over and waits.

"Are you my sister?"

"If you want me to be."

Orca nods. She wishes Sylva was less substantial. If she shimmered like a hologram, if she vanished to the touch, if she were only partially saturated, then Orca could find explanations which showed she came from her own mind. She can hear Sylva's breathing, gently in and out. Can her other senses be fooled as easily as sight?

Sylva stands up. "We have work to do. Show me the forest. Show me where you've got to."

She walks off down the forest path, and Orca follows. Could they be sisters? Sylva has the same colour hair and eyes as Orca, but is certainly not identical in her features. She is talking, and Orca isn't listening. She catches a word here and there – *herbs medicine signature witch burning*

Orca hasn't any data uploaded on the folklore of plants, and Dorcas never mentioned it. But if she is to map the mark of people within the forest, then this information is relevant, as well as the stories people tell. It's all part of the shared human perception – she can't study the forest and be separate from it. She tunes in to the sound of Sylva's voice.

"... have you noticed how dock always grows near nettle? It's all there if we look for it."

"Do you have data uploads on folk knowledge?"

Sylva grins at her. "I know some things." Her eyes are glinting – she seems – mischievous? – yes, Orca grasps at the word. The look is familiar. Orca blinks and sees a child in an orange swimsuit holding an ice-cream. She's sticking her tongue out with that same glint in the eye, the sense that at any moment she will collapse into giggles.

"What about lower plants?" Orca says to the adult Sylva. "Do you have folk lore on them?"

Sylva thinks with her head on one side. "Not much," she says. "Something about Romans stuffing sphagnum into their sandals, something about Catherine the Great. Very little."

"I suppose people don't recognise the different types so easily, they don't have the same relationship with mosses as with types of flowers."

"We must make it up,' says Sylva.

"You can't make up folklore. The whole point is it gathers over time, accumulates, gets passed on from one generation to the next."

"Like moss."

"What?"

"It gathers, covers things over, softens the edges and makes everything more beautiful."

"Whatever, we can't just make it up."

"A rolling surveyor gathers no folklore."

"I just think we should stick to the facts."

"But do facts give the whole picture? If you are doing a holistic survey, facts aren't enough."

Orca couldn't remember if she'd told Sylva this was what she was doing. Sylva seems to know things about her. Again she is tempted to touch her, to check that she is made of solid flesh. She looks as solid as Orca herself, as the trees and the earth beneath their feet.

"Do you remember working in the office?" Orca asks.

"You've landed on your feet here," says Sylva.

Orca looks around. They're in a stand of larch and the trunks are tall and straight. The branches begin way up, so you have to lean your head back to look at them, and at the mosaic of sky pieces amongst them. If you look straight ahead you can see between the trunks, but they're not in straight lines. She looks down at her feet. The earth is hard and compacted after a period of dry weather.

"Yes," she agrees. "I like it in the woods."

"I knew you would." Sylva grabs her hand and her grip is firm. "I have an idea," she says.

Orca isn't sure whether to grip Sylva's hand in response, or to let her fingers lie limp.

p.285

"What?"

"Let's do a different sort of survey of the wood. Let's forget facts and just see what we like, what takes our fancy. Let's make a note of all the things that call to us."

"But that's ..."

"Not instead – you still have the facts you've collected, you can collect more another day. But if you want the whole picture this is part of it."

Orca extracts her hand from Sylva's and smooths her palms across each other. The hand that's been in Sylva's is warmer than the other.

"How would we do that?"

"We walk along slowly, looking, listening, smelling, being aware. When we have to choose which way, let our bodies choose. When something sparks us, we go to it, stop, examine."

"What if your body and mine choose different ways?"

Sylva shrugs. A slight breeze ruffles the thin cheesecloth of her top and lifts a curl of her hair across her glasses. She brushes the hair away. Her eyes are shining and she's lifting up onto tip toes. She's wearing white converse trainers on her feet, embroidered with flowers which match the flowers on her jeans.

"OK, we can try it."

Sylva does a little jump into the air. "This is going to be so much fun."

"I don't want to bring my backpack though. I'm going to hide it."

Back on the path Sylva is crouching, watching a beetle crawl across the path. Orca crouches next to her

"That's a..."

"Shh!" Sylva puts a finger on Orca's lips. "No facts. Just experience."

The beetle shines green and purple. Orca knows it's a violet ground beetle – she can't not know that. Part of her experience of this beetle is that knowledge. She watches it navigate a stone in its path.

"Let's go." Sylva stands up. "Let's survey these woods."

They walk very slowly, side by side. Every now and then Sylva grabs Orca's arm and stops her. "Listen," she whispers.

It's usually a bird. Orca wishes she could identify more birdsong without the data, but today she realises that doesn't matter. Sylva has her eyes closed, she's reaching out each foot to feel her way, her face a mask of concentration.

Then she opens her eyes and turns to the trees on her right. "This way," she says softly. "I'm being called this way."

It's not a path. They walk between larch trees, through bracken. Orca wonders if deer come this way, if there's a possibility of getting ticks. She doesn't say anything, but makes a note to check herself later – even to suggest Sylva do the same.

The space opens up and they are in an expanse of bluebells, all gone to seed or dying back. Orca wants to say something about them to Sylva, to tell her about the blue shimmer beneath the trees at dusk, but she doesn't know how to without including the *fact* that these are bluebells.

Sylva is walking slowly with her hands stretched in front of her, as though feeling her way. It's not easy to walk here, the ground is uneven, and the undergrowth covers it so you can't see where you're putting your feet. If Sylva wants to leave the path and explore, Orca knows much better places. They could follow the stream. Sylva stops. She stretches her arms above her head with her palms together. She lifts one leg and places her foot at the top of the other thigh. She has her eyes closed.

This is a yoga pose called the tree. Orca's done the pose herself, she's felt her own leg become a trunk, her arms the branches, fingers twigs. She could do it now, mirror Sylva, but she doesn't want to. This is Sylva's moment, not hers. She is uncomfortable and worrying about deer ticks. She feels as though she has angles compared to Sylva's curves. Sylva has opened her arms wide and her head is thrown back. Orca leans her back against a larch and closes her own eyes.

This trick can be done in your mind as well as in a wood. Turn off all intentions and let what wants to come, come. She can watch the screen of the back of her eyelids, see what images her mind projects. If she doesn't like what comes, she can open her eyes again, come back into the moment.

The first thing is Jack, getting into his car at the hospital in Hexham, the anxious crease between his eyes. She touches the necklace at her throat. Jack will be with Becky now. Maybe he'll tell her about Kielder, about the emptiness, the three paths, the goat, about Orca. His hair has come loose of its band on one side of his head, and is bunching out above his ear. A strand is caught in the silver hoop of his earring. She probably won't ever see him again.

Another image, of the child Sylva sitting in the middle of a clearing in the red coat, then running along the path in the brown shoes. Then it's a different child and a different path. The child with black curly hair on the clifftop. She is running towards the man who has his arms open wide to receive her. When she reaches him he scoops her up, lifts her and spins her around, and both of them are laughing.

Orca wants to open her eyes, but she also wants to stay with the image. The man and the child stop spinning and turn to her. They call out, but she can't catch the words. Are they calling her name? She feels as though she is walking. She feels as though she has a weight on her back which is warm and alive. Something moves, and she feels a small hand touching her ear.

She opens her eyes and she's back in the Hayes, in the dead bluebells beneath the larches. Sylva has stopped doing yoga and is looking at Orca. "Let's go back to the path," she says.

Later Orca leads Sylva up the stream bed, away from the path, between mossy banks and hazels and ash saplings which lean down to the stream. There isn't much water. There's a lot of mud and Sylva's white shoes get covered with brown slime which

Orca doubts will ever come off completely, but Sylva doesn't seem to mind. They climb a steep bank, pulling themselves up by tree roots, and they find a bender far from the main ride, in a small clearing surrounded by young limes. Inside there is a book and a coat. The book is The Idiot by Fyodor Dostoevsky. There is no sign of the owner of these items.

"I want to meet him," says Sylva. "Or her."

Sylva picks up the coat and examines it. It's a denim jacket, but it's lined with sheepswool and has a black jersey hood. It has red plaid cuffs.

"What a weird coat. It doesn't know what it wants to be."

Orca has seen the coat before a number of times. A man wears it. She's passed him in the woods, and sometimes they nod a greeting to each other. Once she had been examining a beetle in the cracks of a lime trunk, and he'd stopped and asked her what she was looking at. She'd told him politely, but she'd not engaged in further conversation. She had noticed signs – the slight widening of the eyes, the smile, the increased smell of pheromone – that he was interested in talking to her for longer. She wasn't interested in him.

"I'd like to meet this guy," says Sylva. "Do you think he lives here? It's definitely a guy – smell this collar."

"Let's go," says Orca. "This is his space – we're intruding."

"It's a public wood. He doesn't own it. If we wait, he might come back and we can meet him."

Orca doesn't want to meet him. She has enough with the men already in her head, Jack and the dark-haired man with the child and the baby. She doesn't need more.

"Let's try something else," she says. "Let's follow our noses. Be led by our sense of smell. Try to take no notice of the other senses, but follow smells that interest us."

It works, Sylva is hooked. They spend an hour or more following the scent of pine, rotting earth, freshly cut trees, wet mud, dead bluebells. By the time they tire of it they're far from the bender. Orca hopes Sylva can't remember the way back to it. They're at a spot in the middle of the wood where Orca once found a tent pitched. Three paths meet and there's an open area leading down to the stream. It's lighter than most of the Hayes, there is more sky.

"This place is like a gift," says Sylva, "after being hemmed in by all those trees."

Orca has never stopped here. She always passes through to the safety of tree cover. She and Sylva sit on a bench and look at the sky. It's approaching evening and there's a softness to the blue, an awareness of coming dark.

"Sylva."

"Yes, Olive."

She's been calling Orca by that name all day, and Orca has almost stopped noticing.

"Do you know anything about a man with dark hair and dark skin. Good looking, about my age. And two children, a girl of about four or five and a baby?"

"You mean Eric."

"Eric?"

"You were married to him. Those were your kids."

Orca stares at Sylva, looking for signs that she's teasing. Her gaze is steady. she's looking at Orca with clear eyes, her mouth is in a neutral position, her hands are still, resting on her knees, not twitching or touching other parts of her body. Orca had thought Sylva was her friend, someone she could trust. She must have known about the memory implants all along. Maybe she helped Dorcas choose them, maybe they came up with the ideas together.

Sylva reaches out her hand and takes hold of Orca's. "The little girl is called ..."

Orca snatches her hand away and covers her ears. She presses hard blocking out all sound. She closes her eyes and bends forward over her knees. She can hear the little girl's voice now. She's calling out *Mummy, Mummy, look what I can do.* They're in that grassy field next to the sea and she's hopping on one leg. The man Sylva says is called Eric is laughing. The sun is shining. Orca shakes her head, trying to dislodge the image, but the two of them won't go. Eric starts hopping too. He and the girl are holding hands, and she says *Mummy, you hop too.* Her voice is like clear water. Her hair is dark like Eric's, and curly. She's wearing orange shorts and a white t-shirt.

Orca gets to her feet and runs. Sylva calls after her. Orca knows the paths in these woods and she runs faster. She turns and turns again. She doesn't look back, she doesn't know if Sylva is following her. She heads for the holly where she'd hidden her backpack, but she doesn't take the straightest route. Her muscles burn and her chest hurts. She keeps her eyes wide open so she can see trees, larch, hazel, lime, ash, she can see the path, she can see when there are people ahead and turn before she reaches them. She can't see any people in her head, no men called Eric, no girls with dark curly hair.

When she reaches the holly she pushes through to the middle. She sits next to her backpack with her arms around it. She rocks back and forth, and wonders if she wants to cry, but her eyes are dry, her ragged breath is from running. She doubts Sylva will be able to find her here, she doesn't know the woods well enough to know one holly from another. Orca will wait here until it's dark.

When her breathing has returned to normal she phones the hospital in Hexham and asks about Nadia. As she doesn't know Nadia's surname, they don't want to tell her anything, but Orca remembers the name of the doctor and asks to speak to her, and eventually they put her through. The doctor tells her that Nadia discharged herself, that she left with Nick and the baby, and they said they were going south to London, though she knows nothing more specific.

Chapter Nineteen

When it's nearly dark, Orca leaves the holly and walks through the woods to the lime tree. She climbs into the tree and folds herself into the crease of its branches and closes herself down. The leaves of the tree whisper as she rests, its lizard bark is warm to the touch, the branches enfold her.

In the early light she calls Dorcas and tells her that Sylva is in the Hayes, that she finds her presence disruptive, that she would like to leave.

"Come in to the office," says Dorcas. "We'll talk about it. I'll send a car. Be at the visitor's centre in an hour."

Orca stays in the lime tree until the last possible minute. She throws her pack down, then jumps after it. She wraps her arms around the trunk and presses her cheek against the bark. She can hear the sap rising to meet the new day. When she looks up the leaves are translucent with sunlight, and the air she's breathing is green with chlorophyll. The tree will be here if she returns.

At the visitor's centre Sylva is waiting for her, sitting at one of the picnic tables. She's still wearing the cheesecloth top and embroidered jeans, but they're grubby now, streaked green with algae from tree bark, brown with mud. Her hair is tangled with twigs and there is a smear of something – berry juice? – on one cheek. Before Orca can hide, Sylva sees her. Orca walks up the path and sits at the next table. The car will be here in a moment, she doesn't have to sit with Sylva for long.

"You can't keep running for ever."

Orca doesn't respond. She looks at her hands, clasped on the table in front of her.

"You have to acknowledge the past at some point, Olive. You were married, you had two beautiful children, you can't just pretend none of that ever existed."

Orca grabs hold of the pinecone on her necklace and holds it. She tries to think about Jack, to block out this deranged woman sitting at the next table. Jack and Becky. She wants to wish them well, but she wishes Jack was here with her, in this present moment.

"You're not going to get over it if you keep blocking them out. The memories won't go away, they'll keep ambushing you, and you won't be able to recover."

Orca turns to Sylva. She's gripping the pinecone in her fist. "How dare you! How dare you speak as though this were my fault. You know as well as I do that these aren't real memories. They're implants. Dorcas is experimenting, it's part of the project. I think you have a serious malfunction. If you've been taken in, if you think these memories relate to something real, then you need to go back in for reprogramming."

Sylva stares at her. Her jaw has dropped and her mouth is slightly open. Orca can see the neat white row of her bottom teeth. "Jesus!" says Sylva.

"And what the fuck are you doing here anyway, following me about, trying to trip me up. I thought we were friends. Back in the office, we used to laugh together. I thought you'd gone away to do something important. But now you're trying to sabotage my research. Did Dorcas send you? Is it a test?"

If she pulls any harder the chain will break. She relaxes her grip. Jack and Becky will probably get married and have children who will grow up playing in the forest. She should hand the necklace over to Dorcas. It's a distraction. She should never have gone away in the first place. She should never have let herself get involved with Nick and Nadia.

Sylva has come to sit at the same table, opposite Orca. She touches Orca's hand, but her skin is cold and clammy like a fish.

"Olive," she says. "I'm sorry."

The fish is flapping about, worming its way into Orca's sleeve. A cold wave washes across Orca's body. She looks at their two hands and they've both become fish, flailing, gasping for air on the wooden table. There's a rushing feeling though her gut, she leaps up and vomits on the floor between the tables. Sylva's face has changed. She's covered with iridescent scales which flash pink and blue in the light from the newly risen sun. She opens and closes her mouth but no sound comes out.

Just then the car arrives. Orca sees gill flaps opening in Sylva's neck as she runs to the car, opens the door and throws herself on to the back seat.

When the car stops Orca is lying on her side hugging her knees to her chest, her head bent. Dorcas puts her hand on Orca's hip and rocks her.

"Come on, you can't stay there."

"Sylva turned into a fish." Orca is speaking into the dark hole between her chest and her knees. Dorcas leans forward to catch her words.

"Don't worry about Sylva. I'll deal with her. We need to get you warmed up."

She tugs Orca's sleeve, and slowly Orca allows herself to be eased out of the car into standing position. Dorcas wraps a blanket around her and walks her inside. They are at Orca's house.

"Why not the office."

"I thought you'd be more comfortable here," says Dorcas.

She settles Orca on the sofa wrapped in the blanket and goes to the kitchen. She returns with two mugs of tea. Orca holds her mug with both hands and feels the heat passing into her body. She remembers the boy Keith and wonders briefly where he is.

"I'm sending you to London," says Dorcas.

Orca sips the tea but it's too hot. She doesn't say anything.

"I want you to visit Dr Morgan. She's a specialist and she will be able to take all the information you have so far and make some sense of it. I'll arrange somewhere for you to stay."

"How long will I be there?"

"I think Dr Morgan will want a number of sessions with you. I don't know – maybe a couple of weeks, maybe longer."

"It's summer."

Dorcas frowns.

"Everything is changing all the time. It's warm. New plants are appearing every day. It's the worst time to be in a city. I'll miss what's happening in the woods"

"It won't be for long. It will do you good to have a change of scene." Dorcas has that blank face, no expression, no flexibility. Her mind is made up.

Orca drinks more tea. "Is Sylva OK?" she asks.

"Sylva will be fine. She's more robust than she looks."

Orca knows this is true. Sylva was always the stronger one. If she's become a fish, she'll find water and swim strongly, she'll find joy in her fish nature.

Dorcas has brought new clothes suitable for the city, jeans and shirts and canvas shoes. Together they pack a small suitcase. There are new stocks of bars and nutrition pills. "If you need more, you'll be able to buy them in London."

"I don't sleep well indoors."

"You can't sleep outside in London, it's not safe, the police would move you on, they would think you were homeless."

Orca thinks she wouldn't mind. She doesn't care what the police think of her, but she doesn't argue with Dorcas. At least she will be in an anonymous room – not a dead woman's bedroom like in the house in Kielder, where the air was thick with desperation and fear.

Later, after she's showered, changed her clothes and replenished her nutrients, Dorcas drives her to the station. The train will take her to Euston, and from there it's a short walk to her lodgings, which are near the university. Her first appointment with Dr Morgan is in the morning.

At the station she turns to Dorcas. Some of the panic lodged in her body rises, clutching her throat and oesophagus. She's still wearing the necklace from Jack, hidden under the neck of her shirt. She wants to touch it, but she doesn't want Dorcas to ask her about it. She doesn't want to hand it over. She remembers deep breathing, slow breathing. She remembers *Sitting on the Dock of the Bay* and hums to herself, silently, *feeling fine ...*

"Are you OK?" asks Dorcas.

"I'm OK."

"Dr Morgan is the best in the field. She'll look after you."

"Couldn't we just have downloaded the information and sent it to her? I have it all stored."

"She wants to be able to ask questions."

Orca nods. The train leaves in five minutes. She wonders what Dorcas would do if she hugged her goodbye, if her skin would be warm or cool. She doesn't try.

The room is airy and light. There is a bed and a desk, a small bedside cabinet and a wardrobe. The bed has a white candlewick cover, and the floor is brown carpet. It has a monastic feel. There is no cross on the wall, but a painting of St Francis of Assisi. Orca unpacks her suitcase and hangs her clothes in the wardrobe. She's meeting Dr Morgan tomorrow at 9am. She doesn't need to eat as she's already taken her nutrition pills. She opens the window and the noise is overwhelming – cars and buses, people talking as they walk, heels on tarmac, the city hum. She leaves the window open and sits on her bed. She calls Nadia's number, but there is no answer.

She writes a text message. *Hi Nadia, I'm in London for a few days. What are you up to?* If Nick looks at Nadia's messages, there's nothing he can object to, it's just a question. She writes another text. *How is Becky? Are you OK?* She sends both messages before she can change her mind, then she lies down on the white cover and listens to the sound of London through the open window. She breathes cool air.

Chapter Twenty

Dr Morgan has long blue jeans and short brown hair. She's wearing red trainers and a t-shirt with the word *bold*, in a bold typeface. She's younger than Orca expected. She could be thirty, but not much more than that. She smiles and offers tea. Orca asks for water.

When they've settled, Dr Morgan says, "OK, tell me everything."

"Do you want me to talk through the data?"

"No, I want your version. How it's felt to you. I can look at the data later."

"You want me to tell you about living in the woods.?"

Dr Morgan smiles and sits back in her chair as though she's about to listen to a story. Orca looks at her hands lying in her lap.

"Shall I begin when I arrived, the first time. When Dorcas dropped me off at the top of the woods?"

Dr Morgan makes a small note on the pad in her lap. "Start at the beginning," she says.

Orca tells her about that first morning, the surveying, getting to know the trees, the dog walkers, the first time she closed down for the night in the forest, the deer. Dr Morgan listens. When Orca gets to the part where she met Nadia she stops.

Dr Morgan smiles at her encouragingly.

"Do you want to hear this? About the people I've met?"

"I want to hear everything."

"I went away for a while. Should I just stick to the Hayes?"

"Tell me everything you remember."

So Orca tells her about following Nick and Nadia to Suffolk, the night on the beach, then meeting Jack in the pub and going home with him, opening the memory stick files on his computer.

"Do you have the memory stick with you now?"

Orca lifts her arm and shows Dr Morgan the bracelet on her arm.

"Can I have a look?"

Orca hesitates. She'd thought they would focus on the survey work, the information she'd gathered. "Is it relevant?"

"You say you have memory implants?"

"Dorcas told me she'd buried memories which might be triggered by things I experienced. It's happened a lot. I wish she'd told me, or asked me if I minded."

"Have you noticed any particular triggers?"

"Sometimes an image or a thought sparks it off, or a word. It can be a smell."

"And what are the memories like?"

"Flashes, pictures, short video clips."

"Do you feel emotion attached to them?"

"I can tell there is very strong emotion attached to them, but I try not to let myself feel it."

Dr Morgan makes more notes on the pad. Then she looks up and smiles at Orca. Her smile is wide and friendly. "Shall we have a quick look?"

Orca unfastens the bracelet from her wrist, detaches the stick and clips it into its holder. Dr Morgan watches her. When Orca holds out the stick, she takes it and examines it.

"What a beautiful object," she says.

She moves to a chair by her desk and invites Orca to sit next to her. She turns on the monitor and fits the stick into the drive. A moment later a photo fills the screen. It's the family photo, the man and the dark-haired girl, the baby, and Orca.

"Sylva told me he's called Eric." Orca points to the screen.

"Have you seen him before?"

Orca shakes her head. "Only after. Since I first saw this photo, I've had memory flashes. But that night in the forest with Jack, when we looked at the photos, that was the first time I saw him."

"Do you like him?"

Orca looks at the man. He's very good looking, and he's smiling. He looks very happy to be crouching next to Orca with a baby on his knee, a child between them. His smile holds love.

"He looks nice."

"Do you wish you could meet him?"

"I wish I was still with Jack."

Dr Morgan nods and clicks on to another photo. This one is of the girl riding a purple bike.

"I didn't know I was going to say that," says Orca. "I didn't know I thought that."

"What about the children," she asks. "Do you feel any emotion when you look at them?"

Orca looks at the girl on the screen. She has the same smile as her father. She is wearing a cycling helmet decorated with flowers. She looks very pleased with herself.

"She's just ridden without stabilisers for the first time."

Dr Morgan scribbles something on the pad. "Do you remember that?" she says.

"No. Of course not. It's not real. I just know it."

"Are you happy for her?"

"No. I can't be. These pictures, these memories, they have deep wells next to them, deep dark holes of emotion. I can sense it, I know they're there, but I can't step close to them. I know if I fall into the well, I'll be stuck there, I'll never be able to get out. It was unfair of Dorcas. It's a dangerous thing to have inside you. I don't know when one of the implants will be triggered, I don't know how to protect myself. I felt safe when I was with Jack."

Orca realises she's crying.

Dr Morgan closes the screen. "I'm sorry," she says. "Maybe that's enough for today."

p.286

Back on the street and it's only 10.30am, the whole day ahead of her. She's meeting Dr Morgan again tomorrow. She gravitates towards trees. In Gordon Square the plane trees have mosaic patterns on their bark. She knows this is a reaction to polluted air. She knows that London planes are planted in cities because they cope well with pollution, that they create defences where other trees might die. She traces the edges of light and dark, feels the smooth bark against her palm, then realises people are looking at her. She walks the paths of the square, criss-crossing the small space. It's an oasis of green, but behind those hedges the traffic still roars. She can feel the blood moving in her veins. She needs to cover more distance.

She walks out of the gate at the bottom corner of the square and briskly along the street. Other people are walking, but no one pays attention to her here. Not like the dog walkers in the Hayes, she doesn't have to pass the time of day with these city people. She reaches Tottenham Court Road and beyond is Goodge Street tube station. She goes in, buys a pass, and descends to the platform. She doesn't remember visiting London before, but she knows what to do. Dorcas must have programmed her with the necessary information, the basics of how to get about in the city. She looks at the map on the curved wall opposite. She's on the northbound platform. She reads the names of the stations, Warren Street, Euston, King's Cross, Camden Town, Kentish Town, Tufnell Park, Archway, Highgate. Highgate. A train roars into the platform and she gets on.

At Highgate she leaves the station and turns left. Her feet seem to know where she's going. Within moments she's standing in front of a sign which says Welcome to Highgate Woods. The words are wrought from iron and painted a bright and cheerful blue. She steps through the portal into the trees.

For the next hour she walks the paths of the wood. They are broad and well used. She sees people running, walking dogs, lots of families. In one place the wood opens out into a playing area, sports field and café. It's busy, and Orca quickly moves away. It would be hard to lose herself in this wood, she is never far from other people. She can see the city buildings through gaps in the branches. The trees stand in open spaces, with little growing beneath them. They feel aloof, she doesn't get a sense of their personalities. They must see so many people passing through.

She feels out of place with no fitbit, children or dog, and she returns to the tube station. Tomorrow she will come back. She will find a tree, one that will speak to her. She will get to know it.

Back in her room she checks her messages. There is one from Jack. *Funeral next Weds. Becky in bits. You still at Kielder?* There's nothing from Nadia. She replies to Jack – *Hope it goes well on Weds. In London atm.*

Dr Morgan is wearing a check shirt today. It's done up to the level of her breasts and sometimes when she shifts in her chair, Orca can see the edge of her white bra. She's wearing the same blue jeans and red trainers. She wants Orca to tell her about Kielder.

"I don't know what was real."

"As opposed to ...?"

"I don't know. Jack was in it too. It can't have been a dream."

"Why don't you just tell me your experience. Don't try to explain it."

Orca closes her eyes and brings up the memory. She tells Dr Morgan about the smell of the piney air. She describes the empty forest, the deserted campsite, the night at Carter's house and meeting Keith.

"We can find out if they're real," says Dr Morgan. She types Carter's name into Google and there he is. Itinerant chainsaw tutor, based in Kielder. He has a basic website with contact details, but no photos. The company name is Carter MacKenzie and Son.

"Try Keith," says Orca.

Dr Morgan types in Keith's name, and this time there is a photo. It's of a young man in his twenties. He works in Scotland for something called Cairngorms Connect. He's recognisably the same person Orca met at Kielder, but he has a beard. He's not a child. Orca rubs her upper arms. She feels cold.

"Interesting," says Dr Morgan.

"I don't understand."

"Don't worry. Carry on with the story."

Orca tells her about finding Nadia, unconscious at the Forest Head, the makeshift stretcher, and then the strange phone messages, the choice of three paths, and how she didn't choose for herself, but followed.

"But that was your choice."

"What do you mean?"

"The choice you made was to follow Jack, to check he was OK, to be with him."

Orca remembers the other path, off to the left, that went directly into the dark wood. How it had pulled her and scared her. She had been relieved to have a reason not to go that way.

"I wasn't ready," she whispers.

Dr Morgan is holding a pencil and she twirls it in her fingers near to her ear. "What do you think you might have found if you'd taken the left path?"

"I don't know." She meets Dr Morgan's eyes. "I'm still not ready," she says.

She continues with the story, of how she found Jack immobile on Deadwater Fell, and how singing brought him back. The return to the forest which was suddenly full of life and people. Nick. Then the drive to the hospital and the call from Becky.

"I'm worried about Nadia. The doctor said she and Nick were coming to London."

"London is a good place to hide."

"Could you google her and Nick?"

"I thought you didn't know her last name."

"But him. He's an etymologist, and he's working for English Nature. You might find him."

She could have done this herself of course. She doesn't know why she never has. Now that Dr Morgan has begun it, Orca wants to google everyone. She wants to google Jack and see if he's listed as forest warden in Rendlesham. If there's a photo. If there's a website for his jewellery.

"Is this him?" Dr Morgan has found Nick's website. Consultant ecologist, freelance, specialism entomology. There's a photo of him smiling. He looks like a big boy with his friendly smile. Dr Morgan is looking at him with her head slightly to one side. "He looks nice."

"He always looks nice. No one believes he's dangerous.'

Except the doctor. That doctor in the hospital, she hadn't been taken in by his charm. She'd seen it all before and knew the signs. She couldn't keep Nadia, but she'd spoken to Orca on the phone. She probably spoke to Nadia and gave her advice, even if Nadia was pretending not to listen.

"A good disguise," says Doctor Morgan.

"I've only ever seen him being friendly. He's great with the baby. I only know about the other stuff because Nadia told me."

"And the mother? You say Nadia isn't the baby's mother?"

"Nadia said she was in hospital."

Dr Morgan nods. "Let me do a bit of digging. I'll see what I can find."

Orca returns to Highgate Wood. In some ways it reminds her of a corner of the Hayes, with its coppices and broad rides. But the coppices here are hornbeam, their trunks are sinewed like runners legs. She leaves the path and walks between the trees. She can hear Sylva's voice in her head – *follow what pulls you, let instinct take over.* She's hoping that a tree will pull her, guide her to it, so she can put her hands on its trunk and learn to know it.

She comes out on another path. A couple are walking along, leaning their weight against each other, each with a hand in the back pocket of the other's jeans. They don't see Orca. They only exist for each other. They're not looking at the trees, they don't see the drinking fountain by the bend in the path. It's all just a backdrop for them. Orca feels an emotion which she can't quite place but doesn't like. Does she disapprove of the couple, lost in their romantic bubble? Does she think they should be more aware of the trees, pay attention? Or is it something else, connected to the memory implants. The memories are muddying her thoughts. She's finding it hard to be objective.

"The memory implants are causing dysfunction."

Dr Morgan nods and pokes her ear lobe with her pencil. "Why Highgate?"

Orca frowns. She's getting to know the wood. It's just a scrap, a tiny patch compared to the forests at Rendlesham and Kielder.

"There are so many woods in London. Epping Forest is huge. What made you decide to go to Highgate?"

She didn't really decide. Her feet just took her there. She was at the tube station and the train came, and that was the stop she got off at.

"Let's meet there tomorrow," says Dr Morgan. "It will be good to get out of the office. We can talk and walk."

There have been no more messages. Nothing from Jack, nothing from Nadia. In the evening Orca lies on the bed in her room and listens to the traffic. Through her window she can see the branches of a plane tree against the sky. A breeze passes through and the tree shifts, like an animal moving in its sleep, picking up and putting down its thousands of leaves. Pedestrians on the street below don't hear it, don't look up, are unaware of the ecosystem held above their heads within the trees' branches.

Orca turns onto her front and opens the laptop she's borrowed from Dr Morgan. She types Jack's name into the search bar and finds him mentioned on the forest website. She does an image search, but there are no photos of him. He might have social media pages, but Orca has no profiles, and she doesn't want to set anything up. Dorcas wouldn't approve, and it would be impossible to hide them from her, unless she did it under a false name. She searches again, this time adding the word jewellery, but nothing comes up. She tries Rendlesham and jewellery, and this time she finds the site. It’s called Forest Gems. There are no photos of Jack, and his full name doesn’t appear, but she recognises the necklaces and earrings, and the contact email is jack@forestgems. She closes the laptop and lies down again. She doesn’t know why she looked. She has Jack’s phone number, she can contact him if she wants to.

She meets Dr Morgan at Highgate tube station and they walk to the woods together.

“Call me Sarah,” says Dr Morgan.

Trees arch over their heads, watching them pass.

“I’ve never been to this wood,” says Sarah Morgan. “I’ve lived in London for fifteen years, but I’ve never been here.”

If she came to London for university when she was eighteen, that would make her thirty-three. She looks younger.

Orca walks up to a hornbeam. It was coppiced a long time ago and its four stems lean against each other. She puts her hand on the trunk where it bulges like calf muscle. It is cool to the touch. “The trees here are like exhibits in a gallery or something,’ she says. “It’s like the dirt on the ground isn’t real. It’s like somebody made the woods.”

“I suppose they were planted. Most woods are planted at some point.”

“It says, in the leaflet, that it’s a remnant of ancient woodland. It just feels like it’s been following somebody’s rules.”

“Let’s go this way,” says Dr Morgan. They take a smaller path to the left. On one side is a fenced off area which has been coppiced more recently. There’s a lot of holly growing between the young coppice and Orca smiles at it. It’s like an old friend in an unexpected place. The hornbeams are holding back from her, but not the holly.

p.287

"I think I found Nick's wife."

Orca stops walking. "He's married?"

"It seems so. She's called Melinda,
and she had Eli eighteen months ago. She
went into hospital over a year ago."

"What sort of hospital?"

"A secure unit. She was sectioned, supposedly dangerous."

"How did you find out. Aren't records like that private?"

"There was an incident. It was in the local paper."

"What happened?"

"She went out with the baby, at night. She was only in a nightie. She walked onto Dartmoor, and they were reported missing. There was a police search."

"Was the baby OK?"

"I think so."

"Is she still in hospital?"

Dr Morgan shrugs. "I could only find the one story."

They walk in silence for a while. She'd told Dr Morgan that the trees were remote, but actually she can feel their presence today. It's as though on this third visit in three days, they have begun to recognise her.

"Do you know that trees communicate with each other?" she says.

"In what way?"

Orca shrugs. "No one knows. Through their roots, through the air, via fungus in the ground. If a tree on one side of the forest is attacked by a parasite, soon the trees on the other side start producing defensive enzymes, even though the parasite hasn't reached them. The first tree has sent out a warning."

She puts her hand on the bark of the nearest tree. A runner passes them. Orca pictures calf muscles bunching and releasing. She feels the movement of sap beneath her palm.

"That's incredible," says Dr Morgan, call-me-Sarah. She puts her hand on the bark as well. Her fingers are long and narrow, the knuckles slightly too large, the nails cut short and straight.

She's wearing a plain silver ring on her forefinger. "What about you?" she says, "have you seen any evidence of tree communication while you've been in the forest?"

"Feel it," Orca says.

After a few minutes they both remove their hands at the same time. Dr Morgan doesn't say anything. Orca doesn't know if she felt what she felt. They start walking again. They've reached another wide path and further ahead is the bright green space of the playing field.

"There's a café," Orca says, "if you want tea."

"Would you like tea?"

Orca considers this. Her palm is still tingling from the contact with the tree. She could press it against the side of a hot mug, feel the burn again her living skin. She nods.

They sit outside, the woods behind them, the open grass in front. "Who'd think we were in the middle of London?" says Sarah Morgan. They drink tea and watch dogs chasing balls across the grass. "Have you had any more memory flashes while you've been here?"

"No, not really."

"What do you mean?"

"Well, no images, no pictures or video clips. Just a feeling."

"What sort of feeling?"

"This place." Orca waves her arm in a circle. "Coming here. It seems normal, like I've done it before. I knew where to go."

"You said the trees were holding back from you."

"Yes, and that's frustrating, because I know that the memories here are good. I know that once I was happy here."

Chapter Twenty One

That night she dreams. She supposes it's a dream anyway. It's like one of the memory flashes triggered by the implants, but it can't have been put there by Dorcas, because Jack is in it. He's with her in Hartshill Hayes. They're walking down the main ride, and Jack is carrying a baby on his back in the carrier. It keeps pulling strands of his hair out of the pony tail and the sun is catching the stray wisps and making them golden. The girl with dark hair is with them. She's running in front on the path, throwing her arms in the air in some imaginary game. Jack and Orca are holding hands. A goat appears on the path, and the girl stops. She calls *Daddy, Daddy, look!* Orca turns to Jack, but he isn't Jack, he's the man with dark hair, he's Eric. She pulls her hand out of his and stares at her palm. It's shining hot.

She sits in Sarah Morgan's office and twists her hands in her lap. Sarah is typing and peering at her screen. Orca thinks maybe the doctor needs glasses. She holds one hand with the other to keep it still.

Dr Morgan finishes typing and swivels her chair so she's facing Orca. "Sorry about that, I just want to finish typing up the report about yesterday's meeting before we got started today."

"I've had a memory,' Orca blurts out. She's squeezing her hands so tight that her knuckles have gone white, the blood is all in her fingertips.

"Tell me."

"It was this morning, while I was getting dressed. I was trying to decide whether to go back to Highgate Wood or not, and then suddenly I was there."

Dr Morgan nods.

"I was younger. I was wearing boots, Doctor Martens. I was carrying loppers. There were others gathering near the entrance, all with tools, and we were going to work in an area of the wood, between the playing field and Archway Road. I knew all the other people and we were laughing and joking. Then, just as we were about to set off a new person arrived."

Orca unclasps her hands and sits on them. Dr Morgan is holding her pencil in her long fingers. Today she is wearing a dark blue t-shirt with a picture of a chicken etched in white on one side. She's wearing a piece of stone on a thong around her neck.

"He came straight up to me. He said, "Is this the volunteer party? Are you Olive?" and I said yes. I said I was in charge, and I started telling him what to do. He said his name was Eric."

Dr Morgan has stopped twirling the pen and it is threaded through her fingers. "And was it...?

"Yes, it was the same Eric. He didn't have a beard, just some stubble. He was younger. But I felt something, physically. I was attracted to him. There in the woods I could feel it, deep in my belly. I wanted him."

"What happened.?"

"That was it. I was back in my room sitting on the edge of my bed. But I could still feel the feeling in my body, and it made me angry. I am really angry. I'm angry with Dorcas for giving me these memories. They're really difficult to cope with and they're messing up my research. They're affecting my choices. You asked me why I went to Highgate Woods, and that's obviously why. Because I have a memory implant about meeting Eric for the first time, about being a volunteer leader in the woods. It would have been better to go to Epping, that's actually a forest."

"The reasons we make choices is often obscure. Buried memories affect what we do, and that's interesting within itself."

"I'd like you to speak to Dorcas and ask her if she can remove the memory implants."

"I don't..."

"They are impairing me. I can't function properly."

"I'm afraid I have no influence over Dorcas. There's no reason she would listen to me. It might not be possible to remove the memories. Now that they have entered your consciousness, they've become a part of who you are."

"But there will be more. I never know when one will spring up, and they ambush me. Even though I know they aren't real. This one ..."

"Was it more powerful?

"It took me by surprise. The other memories – they have been like watching videos, but this time I was there. I could see the way Eric's smile showed the edges of his teeth on one side, and that the muscles in his arms are like hornbeam whips. When we talked about helmets and safety, we were saying something else with our eyes, and I knew that before the end of the day I'd be touching his skin with my hands and my mouth, that he wanted it too. It was instant and shocking."

"It's interesting that the memory surfaced when you weren't actually in the wood. Orca?"

Orca has slid off her chair onto the floor. She pulls up her knees and pushes her head between them. She hugs herself and rocks. She has begun to wail. She can hear it, but there's nothing she can do to stop it. There are tears too, lots of them, and snot in her nose. Dr Morgan comes across the room and puts her hand on Orca's shoulder. The wailing gets louder, and there are words stuck in it, like grit. The words repeat themselves in bursts and variations. The words are "I miss him ... I miss him so much ..."

She doesn't go to Highgate that day. It's Friday and she feels her time in London is nearly over. She will soon be back in the Hayes. The forecast is good, and Dr Morgan suggested she go to Epping Forest. "You could do some proper walking. It's big and spacious, it would be good to move." But Orca heads into the middle of the city. She walks from Bloomsbury to Oxford Street, then into Soho. She crosses green squares and walks along back streets. She reaches Piccadilly Circus and picks a line through the crowds of tourists. She walks down Haymarket and onto The Mall, through St James's Park, Green Park, Hyde Park and back up to Marble Arch. She looks at the trees. There are a lot of trees in London, it feels like a very green place. She's returned the laptop to Dr Morgan, but back in her room she looks at the data. There are over eight million trees in London, and the canopy covers twenty one percent of the city.

She refuels, but she's still restless. She goes out again and walks in the other direction. Red Lion Square, Holborn, St Pauls. She crosses the river to the Tate Modern and walks along the South Bank back to Hungerford Bridge where she crosses back, then winds up the lanes from the Embankment through Charing Cross, Covent Garden, St Martins and the past the British Museum, and then she's lying on her bed again. She's managed not to think. Her feet have known where they were going. The map of London is uploaded in her data, but she hasn't been using it. She hasn't checked the data once. It must be related to the memory implants, this knowledge of which streets connect to which. She hasn't once been in danger of getting lost. She sleeps.

In the morning she goes to Highgate. The sun is shining, pooling into the wide spaces of the woods. There are so many people, it reminds her of the parks and squares in the centre of the city. The people here are not tourists though. They are runners and dogwalkers and fathers with their weekend children, families here for sports day and ice-cream on the playing field. The air is ringing with voices, children high with excitement, the encouraging shouts of parents, dogs barking. The sun glares off the white buildings that tower beyond the trees. Orca has no dog or child and she isn't running. She feels the glances of people as they pass. This is their weekend wood. She touches a hornbeam, thinking of Eric, of the shape of his arms revealed below the line of his t-shirt. A man asks her what she's doing.

"Just looking at the trees," she says. "They're so beautiful."

"You should come in winter," he says, "after snowfall. It's magical then."

She walks away from the busiest area near the playing field and café. She leaves the path and walks along the fence. There's a small pond, and growth in profusion – holly and birch saplings, hornbeam whips. It's dark here, and smells of damp earth, rotting wood and car fumes from Archway Road. It's just a thin strip, she can hear the traffic on the other side, roaring past. She wonders if she cut some of those coppices herself. If she and Eric had worked together. If the others in the working party had noticed the charge between them, if they'd laughed at them and said, get a room. She can't remember any of this happening, but she can imagine it. She can't remember if they did get a room, or if they went back to her place, or his. But in those other memories, the ones that appear like video clips, they had two children, and the oldest, the girl was perhaps five years old. She looks at the coppice stands. They were probably cut ten years ago.

It's too much to take in. She checks to see if anyone is nearby. Most people stick to the paths, but you can't get far from the path in this scrap of wood. Two men ran by a few minutes ago in brightly coloured running clothes, one of them holding a phone and calling encouragement to the other. She'd seen them ten minutes earlier, so presumably they were running laps of the wood. Nobody else is nearby. She climbs over the fence and picks her way past the pond, behind some holly growth, and into a dip where she can crouch, hidden from the road as well as from the path. She wants to go back into the memory. She wants to see Eric again, and feel the buzz of excitement which began the moment he said her name. She wants to remember the first time their skin touched.

A memory comes. They are sitting opposite each other at a table in a restaurant. He is wearing the same t-shirt as he was in the woods. There's a bottle of wine on the table next to a basket of bread, and the air smells of garlic, tomatoes, olive oil. She knows they still haven't touched, but the air between them is so thick with desire that it slows every movement. He puts a piece of bread in his mouth. She watches his hand touch his lips, the bite of his teeth. She takes a sip of wine, still looking at him. His eyes are glittering. If she stretched her knees beneath the table, they might touch his. But without saying anything, they've invented this waiting game. Their talk has been about the woods, the trees, her work with volunteers, his day job as an engineer. Neither has given voice to the magnetic pull which feels as sweet and thick as chocolate. Later. They both know there's going to be a later, and she can feel the build-up of heat between her legs. Swallowing her wine feels like an erotic provocation.

It ends. She's back in the woods with holly leaves prickling the back of her neck. She can feel sensations in her body reflecting those in the memory. She touches her throat and squeezes her legs together. Her lips feel fuller than normal, her ears warm. She'd like to go back to the memory, follow it through to the later they'd been anticipating.

A dog is barking. Its owner is on the path calling its name, but it's smelled her and knows she's there. It comes nearer.

"Ruby, come here. Ruby!" The dog gives a final bark, then gives up. The voice of the owner fades as they move on. "Good girl, come along."

It's time for Orca to leave. Hidden by hollies she feels safe, but these aren't her hollies, they are cousins of those in the Hayes, and although she feels comforted by their familiarity she needs to get back to her home ground. She won't see Dr Morgan again.

She's woken at midnight by a call from Nadia. Nadia is obviously drunk, but also crying.

"You need to help me. I've lost my stuff."

"Nadia, where are you?"

"The bastard left me here. You must come?" There are background sounds, voices, music, traffic. Nadia lowers her voice to a loud whisper. "I'm thrown into the street."

"Tell me where you are."

She's at a club in Soho. Orca could walk there in twenty minutes, but she gets a taxi and is there in five. Nadia is leaning against a lamppost outside the club. She has a bottle of beer in her hand. When she sees Orca she throws her hands up in the air, and some beer sploshes out of the bottle onto her hair.

"Whoops!" she says, and laughs. Then her face falls and she looks like a clown pretending to be sad. Her mascara has smudged beneath her eyes. "I lost everything," she says.

"Your money?"

"Everything was in my bag, and I left it in there," she gestures at the club. "Thieves!" she yells at the top of her voice.

Orca tells Nadia to wait, then she talks to the doormen. They tell her Nadia was smashing glasses and shouting, and they'd had to eject her, but they allow Orca to go in and look for the bag, tell her where Nadia had been sitting. Amazingly it's still there, and everything is in it. Phone, wallet, keys. It had slipped down the side of the banquette, and no one had spotted it.

Nadia smiles when she sees it. "Than queue," she says. "I knew you'd save me." Then her legs give way, and she's sitting on the pavement, legs akimbo.

Orca can't get her up again. Each time she manages to get her into a half standing position, Nadia starts giggling and sits down again.

"We need to get you home," she says.

"No home," says Nadia.

"What do you mean?"

"I have no home. I come with you."

Orca imagines Nadia back in her room, the spartan white room in the quiet hotel. She might be sick. She might start shouting again. There is only one narrow bed, and the chair is not comfortable enough for sleeping. The floor is hard.

"I've lost everything," Nadia wails, and she starts to cry loudly. Passers-by look in their direction.

"I found your bag," Orca tells her, holding it up.

"Not that, Eli, Nick, my clothes, the van. This is all." She gestures at her body. "He took everything." Then she is sick on the floor next to her. Her hair falls forward as she retches and gets stuck to her face with vomit. She laughs.

Orca takes a couple of deep breaths, then she phones Dr Morgan. She has her number in case of emergencies, and this feels like an emergency

It takes half an hour for Dr Morgan to arrive. By that time, Orca has persuaded the doormen to give her some tissues and she's cleaned Nadia's face, done her best with her hair. She's got her to lift her knees up and lean forward. Nadia had become quiet, although her shoulders are shaking and Orca suspects she is crying.

Dr Morgan is in her car. She's brought towels and a blanket. Together they manoeuvre Nadia into the back seat. Orca gets in the front. Dr Morgan drives through Holborn and continues east.

"Where are we going?" asks Orca. She had imagined Dr Morgan would take the two of them to Orca's room, and that then Orca would just have to deal with Nadia on her own. But they have passed all the possible turnings.

"Back to mine," says Dr Morgan.

She has a flat on the sixth floor. They wake Nadia, gently rocking her shoulder. Dr Morgan wets the corner of a towel with water from a bottle and wipes Nadia's face. They get her out of the car and manage to walk her to the lift, where she slumps next to the buttons and gurns at her own reflection. In the flat she falls back onto the sofa and is asleep in seconds. Together,

Orca and Dr Morgan turn her onto her side, and adjust her arms and legs so she is as comfortable as possible. She looks like a puppet someone has dropped.

"Thank you, Dr Morgan," says Orca.

"Call me Sarah."

Orca nods. This is different. She's in Dr Morgan's home at two in the morning, and both of them are streaked with Nadia's vomit. "Thank you, Sarah," she says.

Sarah makes tea. Orca thinks about telling Sarah she's leaving on Monday, but she finds she's too tired to speak.

"We should get some sleep," says Sarah, echoing Orca's thoughts. She brings through a t-shirt for Orca to sleep in. It's huge and has the number 63 on it in massive red and gold letters. There is only one bed, and Nadia is on the sofa. "Do you mind sharing?"

The bed is huge, with plenty of room for both of them, but Orca lies as near to the edge as she can, her body in a straight line. She thinks she won't sleep, but she closes down immediately.

Chapter Twenty Two

When she opens her eyes, the sun is well above the horizon, and the room is sliced with light from the blinds. Sarah is still sleeping. Orca slides out of the bed and pads through to the other room. Nadia is in the same position on the sofa. Her skin is covered in a slick of sweat, and as Orca walks past she smells the alcohol and vomit in Nadia's hair and clothes. Sarah had given Orca a towel as well last night, and she goes to the bathroom and showers.

When she comes out, wearing the huge t-shirt and towelling her hair, Sarah is up. She's put the kettle on and found more clothes, for Orca and for Nadia too. She's thinner than Orca, and taller than Nadia, but has managed to find things that might fit.

"Once Nadia's awake, we can get a load in the washing machine," she says.

Orca changes in the bedroom. Sarah has given her a white t-shirt with a huge gorilla on the front. It's tighter than the clothes Orca's been used to wearing, and the fabric clings to her skin. On the bottom half she's wearing blue tracksuit bottoms with an elasticated waist. She moves her hips from side to side, feeling the jersey touch the outside of her thighs. As she leaves the room, she catches a glimpse of herself in the mirror. Her short hair is sticking up in spikes from the shower. She looks clean and sporty and unlike herself.

Sarah has found bread in the freezer and is making toast and coffee.

"Shall I wake her?" asks Orca.

Nadia is more peaceful. Her limbs and features are relaxed and she's not sweating anymore. She smells pretty bad though, and Sarah would probably like them out of her flat so she could get on with whatever she has planned for Sunday. Orca bends down next to Nadia and puts a hand on her shoulder.

"Nadia!" she says loudly.

Nadia takes in a deeper breath and a series of twitches pass across her face. Then she relaxes back into sleep again. Orca pushes on her shoulder and says her name again.

It takes a while, but eventually Nadia opens her eyes. She looks at the two of them, then around at the room, and panic appears in her eyes.

"It's OK," says Orca. "You're OK here." She hands Nadia a glass of water.

Nadia sips it and winces. "I feel bad," she says.

Orca nods. "Have a shower, put on clean clothes, and you'll feel better." She touches her own wet hair. It's true. She feels rejuvenated.

While Nadia is in the shower Sarah pours coffee. "Do you take milk?" she asks.

"I don't know." Orca looks at the black liquid in the mugs. The smell is filling her nostrils. She imagines clouding it with milk, stirring it as it turns from black to light brown. "I don't think so."

It's scalding hot and she can't drink it straight away. She nibbles at the toast. Sarah has spread her own with marmalade, but Orca refuses it. She takes a sip of the coffee. The taste is familiar, and when she looks up it's not Sarah standing next to her, but Eric.

He also is cradling a mug of coffee. He's wearing a towelling robe, hair wet from the shower and skin glowing fresh, though his eyes are slightly bloodshot. She can feel tiredness in every part of her body, but she also feels good. The coffee is like a shot of adrenaline. Eric leans forward and kisses her on her lips. It's soft, like the brush of a wing. She lurches back.

"Are you OK?" asks Sarah.

"A memory." She realises her hands are shaking and puts the coffee mug down on the kitchen counter.

"Eric?"

"He was here, in the room. Or some room. We were drinking coffee."

"Has he gone?"

"Yes, it was only a moment."

Nadia appears, wearing the blue t-shirt with the chicken on which Sarah had worn at the office a few days ago. She's wearing capri pants which are probably three-quarter length on Sarah, but reach to Nadia's ankles. She smells of apples.

"Thank you," she says, "I am ashamed."

Sarah takes Nadia's dirty clothes from her and bundles them with Orca's clothes into the washing machine. "There's no need," she says. "The main thing's you're safe." She chooses a setting and sets the machine going, then turns to look at the others. "Look at us all wearing my clothes! It's like there's three of me."

Nadia starts crying. "You are being so kind."

Orca is thinking about the capri pants, and wondering why she knows what they're called. Why would Dorcas have uploaded data of that sort. She thinks she should give Nadia a hug, but feels awkward about it. She puts her hand on Nadia's shoulder and gives it a squeeze.

Sarah pours a mug of coffee for Nadia and adds sugar. "This will make you feel better."

They move to the sofa and sit drinking coffee, listening to the rotations of the washing machine. Sarah stands up. "I'll put some music on. Any suggestions?"

"Can we have Marvin Gaye?" says Orca.

Sarah taps on the screen of her phone and a few minutes later the room fills Marvin's voice. As she thought it would, it takes Orca straight back to the car, Jack by her side, driving the length of the country. She wants to turn and see his face and his hair in its messy ponytail, but she's scared that at any moment he might morph into Eric. She looks at Nadia.

"What happened?" she asks. "Where are Nick and the baby"

"Devon. They have gone to Eli's mother."

"You said last night that he took your stuff."

"We fought. Big fight and he left. My things were in the van. He drove away and left me on the road."

"Yesterday?"

"No. Three days."

"Why didn't you call me?"

"I was ashamed. I had this." Nadia touches her face, and there is the green tinge of a bruise around her eyes which hadn't shown in the artificial light the night before. "And this." She lifts the chicken t-shirt to reveal a much nastier bruise, black and purple across her ribs.

"Did he do this?" asks Sarah.

Nadia hangs her head. "We just meet, and I am showing you this. I'm sorry."

"Don't be ridiculous. It's not your fault. Did Nick hit you?"

Nadia has dropped the t-shirt, but she touches her ribs. "This was his foot," she says.

Sarah stands up and paces back and forth across the room. Orca can tell she's angry, the energy from her body is almost visible. "We must find him. We must get your stuff back and report him."

"But Eli ..."

"What about Eli? A man like that has no business caring for a child."

"You don't understand. He would not hurt Eli. He loves him, he is good father. And Eli's mother, she is ill and cannot care for him. If he is taken away, who will have Eli?"

"What about you?" asks Orca.

"I am not related."

"Was Eli there when Nick did that?" asks Sarah.

"He was in the van. We were outside the van. He could not see."

"But he could hear. And another time he will see."

Marvin Gaye is singing that he wants to *holler*. Orca feels her throat constricting and a hot prickle at the back of her eyes. "Actually, can we have some other music?" she asks.

Sarah taps the screen and the music changes. "We need to do something."

Orca doesn't know the song that's started and her muscles relax. "Nadia and I could go to Devon, we could get a train from Paddington ..."

"I'll take you in my car."

Nadia and Orca both stare at Sarah.

"Look, Nadia needs to eat something, but there's no point in hanging around. Let's drive down to Devon and find this fucker."

The clothes are in the drier. Sarah has looked again at the article about Eli's mother from the newspaper. It says she lived in Tavistock.

"Is that where she is now? Is that where Eli has gone?"

"I don't know."

"Does Nick have a house down there?"

"No, they rented a house. They don't have it anymore. He will stay in the van."

"So he didn't say if her parents lived nearby?"

"He said a beetle is there, a rare one. He was looking for the beetle in the woods when they met."

"Do you remember its name?"

"I think it is the blue earth beetle.

Sarah googled it. "Blue ground beetle. It lives in woods on Dartmoor. Dendles Wood, Black-a-Tor Copse, Wistman's Wood ..."

"That's it."

"She lives in Wistman's Wood?"

"They met there, when he was looking for the beetle."

"Great. That gives us somewhere to head for. Though it's in the middle of Dartmoor, I'm not sure what's close." Sarah looks up. "How are those eggs?"

Outside they wait for Sarah to lock up. They're wearing their own clothes again, hot from the drier.

"She is very bossy," whispers Nadia.

Orca is surprised. She has been watching Sarah's efficiency and decisiveness and feeling she would like to be like that. She had noticed Nadia was quieter than normal, but assumed it was the hangover, as well as upset over the business with Nick and Eli. "She is being helpful," she says to Nadia. "Driving to Devon is a big deal."

Nadia shrugs.

The car flashes as Sarah unlocks it from behind them. There's a bit of back and forth about who will sit in the front passenger seat, both Nadia and Orca offering to sit in the back.

"Look," says Sarah, "you can take turns when we stop for breaks. Nadia's legs are shorter."

Nadia climbs into the back.

Sunday morning and the traffic in London isn't too busy. They head onto the North Circular and skirt around the top of the city, heading out east to reach the M25 at Rickmansworth. Soon after they branch off onto the M5. Sarah has put the radio on, and the voices and music fill the car. Nadia is quiet in the back and Orca wonders if she's gone to sleep, but when she turns her head, she sees her sitting far back in the seat, her face white and pinched. Perhaps she is feeling carsick but doesn't want to say.

Near Bristol they stop at a service station. As soon as Nadia is out of the car she rushes across the carpark.

"Is she OK?" asks Sarah.

"I think it's the hangover."

Orca follows, and she can hear Nadia retching in one of the cubicles. She waits for her. When Nadia emerges the sweat has reappeared on her skin. She looks waxy and ill. Orca suggests she rinse her face in water. Back at the car, Sarah has bought bottles of water and juice, and some coffees.

"I didn't know what you'd want," she says to Nadia. "Have whichever makes you feel better."

Nadia takes a bottle of water and walks away from the car. There is a strip of trees separating the service station from the motorway, with a mown area of grass in front. Nadia stands contemplating the trees, as though she were looking at a view.

"I've been here before," says Orca.

Sarah turns to her. "Have you had a memory?"

"Not like before. It must be to do with the memories though, mustn't it? I just recognize it. Inside, I knew where to go without looking, I knew what it was going to look like. The memory implants must be affecting my stored knowledge, they aren't discrete."

"Does that upset you?"

"It makes it hard to know the difference between real knowledge and these memories. How can I separate them if they intermingle like this?"

"Is it important to keep them separate?"

"Not here. It's not important that I know the layout of the inside of a service station. But another time, I may think I know something that matters, when it is just one of these planted memories. How can I trust my knowledge?"

"Your knowledge was correct about this place."

"But it didn't matter. My memory led me straight to the toilets, but if it had been wrong and I had ended up in the coffee shop it would have been OK. I can't trust it in situations where the wrong choice would be dangerous."

"I'm not going." Nadia is standing in front of them. She still looks pale, but the sweat has dried. She has her hands on her hips and her feet apart.

"What do you mean?" says Sarah.

"I'm not going to Devon. I want to go back."

"You can't just let him get away with it. He's got your things, the baby, he ..."

"They think it is my fault."

"Who thinks what is your fault?" asks Orca.

"His wife, her parents. I don't want to meet them."

"Do you know them?"

"Let's sit on the grass," says Sarah. "You can tell us about it. Orca, do you want some coffee?"

Orca takes a bottle of water. The coffee in the flat earlier had evoked such a strong memory flash, she doesn't want to risk that again.

Nadia tears at the grass.

"Tell us," says Sarah.

"I have not met his parents, or his wife. But Nick tells me. They are angry with me for taking him and Eli away."

"Did you take him away?"

"We met in the city, in Bristol. I was there for work, I was au pair for a family. I was with the children in the park, and Nick was there with Eli. We meet and we talk. I loved the way he looked, a big golden man with his child. He told me he and his wife were not together."

"So he had already left her," says Sarah. "It's not your fault."

"But they think he would go back, that it was just a short time he was away. Because of me it has been a long time, many months. They are angry because of me."

"How do you know they are angry?" asks Orca. "Have they been in touch with you."

"Nick tells me. Sometimes he gets messages from them, and he say, they are angry Nadia. You better watch yourself. They might send the police after you."

Sarah snorts into her coffee. "The police? For what?"

"For stealing the baby."

"He's gaslighting you." Sarah's voice has risen. "What a bastard! You can't let him behave like this."

"It's not Nadia's fault," says Orca.

"I know it's not. But she has to ..."

"You sound as though you're angry with her for letting it happen. She doesn't have to go if she doesn't want to."

"But it's not fair ..."

"It's not fair," agrees Orca, "but it's not fair to make her go either. I can go. I can find him and get her stuff for her."

"You think he was making it up? About them being angry?"

Sarah and Orca look at Nadia. There is a new energy in her face.

Orca touches Nadia's arm lightly with her fingertips. "Did he show you any of the messages?"

Nadia slowly shakes her head. "No, he didn't. So they might not be angry with me?"

"They might not even know you exist," said Sarah. "Or he might have told them lies about you. Who knows?"

Nadia looks at the blades of grass on her palm, then shakes them off. "I don't know. I believed what he said, but you are right, he might lie. He might not even have a wife or she might not be ill. He might lie to me about everything."

"What does he have of yours?" asks Orca. "Clothes?"

"Some clothes, shoes, my coat, my diary, two books. A bag, which I carried them in before I was in the van. Also, my passport is in the glove compartment."

"How about we go, me and Sarah? We can get your things and bring them back to you in London. "You don't ever have to see him again."

"If it was me, I'd want to see him," says Sarah. "I'd want to kick him in the nuts, and let his parents-in-law know what a shit he is. He can't just ..."

"I will go to Bristol. I have a place I can stay. I know it better than London. We only went to London for Nick, for the beetle in Epping Forest."

Chapter Twenty Three

They drive into the city and drop Nadia off near the station. She is happy to walk to her friends' house from there.

"I'll call you," says Orca, "and let you know how we get on."

Back on the motorway, she sits in the front seat while Sarah drives. She googles Wistman's Wood. It's on the moor, not near to a village or even a road. It can only be accessed by footpath.

"So we only know what he told Nadia, and we don't know if that's even true?" Sarah's eyes are on the road, but her anger is still apparent in the way her fingers tap hard on the steering wheel.

"He told her he met his wife in Wistman's Wood, and that she was walking her parent's dog. That suggests that her parents live within walking distance of the wood."

"She could have taken the dog in the car and parked."

"Yes, she could."

"But probably not far, if she was walking the dog, she might have only driven along the road."

"There's Princeton, Two Bridges, Dartmeet, Postbridge."

"Google her name, and those places, see if you get any matches."

Orca googles the name Melinda Castle and the place names.

"Dartmeet."

"What, have you found her?"

"It's an article about ponies. About tourists feeding them, and how it can make them aggressive. They quote local man, Jerome Castle, Dartmeet. Her dad?"

"It could be. We'll try it."

After Exeter they leave the motorway. The road into Devon is wide and fast, and it isn't long until they are leaving the main road and heading west towards Dartmoor. The road narrows and tall hedges block the view.

"I'd forgotten how difficult these lanes are," says Sarah. "We used to come to Devon on holiday when I was a kid, and my dad always complained about these tiny roads."

"I've never been to Devon before," says Orca.

Sarah glances at her. "No memory seepage here then?"

"No. Nothing. I feel certain that none of the memories are from Devon, but I don't know why I'm so sure."

The road passes through a few hamlets, winding steeply up and down, then the countryside starts to open up and there is moorland rising to a pointed peak over to the left.

"Nearly there," says Orca. "Down this hill and over the river. Don't drive too fast – it's tiny and you might miss it."

They park near the river and walk up the main road through the village. The pub is closed, or they might have asked in there. At the top of the village is a low green building that might once have been a barn. There's a sign hanging outside saying *Castle Antiques.*

"What do you think?" asks Orca.

"It has to be."

Unfortunately the shop is closed. They knock on the door, hoping that someone might be inside. It's Sunday, but there's lots of traffic. It's the sort of place people flock to on a sunny weekend, and the carpark by the river was nearly full.

A window above the shop opens and a woman looks out. "Can I help you?"

"We're looking for Jerome Castle. For the Castles. For Melinda Castle actually."

The woman is quiet for a moment as she looks at them. "Who are you?" she says.

"We've come from London. It's about Nick and the baby."

"Eli," says Orca.

The woman turns away and speaks to someone in the room. After a moment she turns back. "I'll come down."

She lets them into the shop. It's a big space, barnlike inside as well as out, set out with rows of trestle tables, laden with objects. There doesn't seem to be much order to the layout, and some of it looks like junk to Orca. There's not much room to move – the ends of the aisles are piled with larger objects – tables, chairs, cabinets – which teeter towards the ceiling. It looks more like a warehouse than a shop – an untidy one at that.

The woman leans against the small wooden counter. "I'm Wendy Castle. Jerome is my husband and Melinda is my daughter. What do you want?"

"We're actually here on behalf of someone else. Did you know ..."

"Is Nick here?" interrupts Sarah.

Wendy looks from one to the other. She's trying to keep her face impassive, but at Nick's name there's a twitch below her left eye. "Not at the moment. He was."

"Do you know where he's gone?"

"Why don't you tell me what this is about."

Sarah draws a breath to speak, but Orca puts her hand on her arm. "Nick has been travelling with a woman called Nadia," she says. "I don't know if he told you."

Wendy says nothing, but makes a small movement with her head which could be interpreted as a nod.

"Well, they separated suddenly, and some of Nadia's belongings are still in his van. We'd like to get them back for her."

"You're her friends?"

"Yes, we are."

Orca looks at Sarah, who is biting her lower lip. Orca hadn't considered having friends, but this doesn't feel like a lie. Nadia and Sarah are her friends, because they've had experiences together, they have made shared memories which bind them. Jack is her friend too.

"I'm not sure exactly where he's gone. He's looking for that beetle again. He's coming back but I don't know how long he'll be. A few hours, maybe overnight."

"Did he hurt her?"

The voice has come from the back of the shop. A woman is silhouetted in a doorway against the light of the hall behind. She has a child in her arms, and her long hair catches the light so it shimmers in a golden glow around her head. She's wearing a long skirt which reaches nearly to her ankles.

"Melinda, you don't need ..."

"He hurt me, but no one believes me." She walks towards them through the gloom of the shop and Orca recognises the child.

"Why don't you go back upstairs, this is just about some things left in the van."

"He seems like such a lovely man you see, he's so charming, so helpful. How could he possibly turn into a monster? How could ...?"

"Melinda!"

"Yes," says Sarah. "He did hurt her. In fact, that's why we're here. She was too scared to come herself."

"Mama," says Eli, and he lurches forward towards Orca so that Melinda nearly drops him.

"Hello Eli," says Orca. He's got hold of her sleeve and he's holding on tightly.

"He wants to go to you." Melinda thrusts the baby into Orcas arms, and she's there again in that smell, milk and baby shampoo. Eli pats her face with his small hands and smiles. "He likes you," says Melinda, and her smile is an enlargement of his.

Wendy sighs. "You better come up," she says. "I'll make some tea."

The flat above is a contrast to the shop. Everything is new, clean and neat. The surfaces are polished and the windows sparkle.

A man is sitting on an uncomfortable looking sofa, and a wheelchair is next to him.

"This is Jerome," says Wendy.

"Sorry, I can't get up," he says. "Broke both my legs. On the mend, but won't be walking for a while."

"These are friends of Nadia, Nick's friend. They wanted to collect some things she left in his van."

"She didn't actually leave them. He left her. He drove off and left her in the middle of London with nothing but what she was standing up in."

"Sarah, that's not these people's fault. When we find Nick ..."

"They should know. They let him into their home. He is the father of their grandchild. They should know what he's like and that Melinda is telling the truth."

Anxiety spreads across Jerome's face, and he turns in an instant from genial host to invalid. "What is this?"

"It's not just me. It wasn't me making it up."

'These women say that Nick hurt Nadia, in the same way that Melinda said ..."

Wendy stops and turns to look out of the window.

"Mama," says Eli and lurches back from Orca towards Melinda, who takes him in her arms and buries her face in his neck.

"Nick told them I did it myself. That I was self-harming and also clumsy, that I had post-natal depression, that I was a bad mother."

Eli is squirming a bit and Melinda seems to realise she's holding him too tight. She relaxes her arms and sits down next to her father on the sofa, with Eli on her lap.

Jerome puts his hand on Melinda's shoulder. "You were ill, we didn't think ..." He falters then turns looks at Sarah and Orca who are still standing near the door. "Is this true?"

"Nadia has bruises," says Orca, "and it's not the first time. Nick told her you wanted to set the police on her for kidnapping the baby."

Jerome shakes his head. "Melinda wasn't well – after the birth – Nick was very supportive, did the best he could ..."

"What are you planning to do when you find him?" Wendy says, her back to the room.

"We just want to get Nadia's belongings," says Orca.

"And give him a piece of our minds," says Sarah.

"Is she going to press charges?" Wendy's voice wobbles on the last word.

"I doubt it," says Sarah. "I think she just wants to lick her wounds and be shot of him. She ought to though. And Melinda too."

"He'd convince the court," says Melinda, bouncing Eli on her knee. "He convinced my own parents I was unstable – they believed him and not me. Why would a judge who's a stranger to us think any different?"

Wendy starts coughing as though something is stuck in throat, and Jerome lifts his head and looks at his daughter.

"Maybe Nadia fell. Maybe they had a fight and she wants to get him in trouble," he says. "If this was true ..."

"It's true," says Sarah.

" ... if this was true ... then we ..."

Melinda puts a hand on his. "I'm not angry with you, Dad. I know what he's like. I married him for fuck's sake – that's how taken in I was."

"Did he give any clues as to where he was going?" asks Orca.

Wendy is still coughing and her shoulders are shaking. Jerome is shaking his head, lost in his own thoughts.

"He was going to Wistman's and Black-a-Tor," says Melinda. "He was going to park up at Black-a-Tor for the night, but I don't know which day he was doing which wood, so he could be at either."

"We'll check both," says Sarah.

"Black-a-Tor is a tricky walk. It's easy to go the wrong way."

"I have an app, and Orca's good at finding her way in woods."

"Are you going to both? The thing is, by the time you've been to one, if he's at the other, he might have finished and you'll miss him."

"He'll be coming back here." Wendy squeezes her voice out, trying to control the cough. "You can wait ...' She starts coughing again.

Orca looks at the small room. It could be many hours before Nick returns. "We can split up. Do a wood each."

"Except I've never met Nick," says Sarah. "So if I do find him we won't know each other from Adam."

"I'll come."

They all look at Melinda. Unlike her parents who seem diminished, Melinda is brighter. Her skin is glowing and she's bouncing Eli on her knee.

"Eli can stay with Mum and Dad. We can drop Orca off at Two Bridges for the path to Wistman's, and we can go on to Black-a-Tor. I know the way, and I know Nick."

"But if Orca meets him, she'll be on her own."

"I'm not afraid of him. I'm only going to ask him for Nadia's stuff. And I'm faster than him."

Half an hour later they leave. Wendy and Jerome promise to ring if Nick returns to the flat.

"Just act normally," Sarah suggests, "until we get back."

"I don't know if I can." Jerome seems to have aged five years.

"He'll want to know where Melinda is. He'll think it's odd that she's gone out while Eli's here. She normally wants to spend every minute with him."

"Play it by ear. But let us know if he turns up."

Two Bridges is only a couple of miles up the road. "The path leaves from the back of car park," Melinda tells Orca. "It's really easy to follow. You can't miss it. You'll see Wistman's long before you reach it."

Sarah pulls up in front of the pub. "His van's not here," she says.

"He could have parked somewhere else. There are other ways to walk there, if you want a longer walk. This is just the quickest."

Orca gets out of the car.

"Let us know if you find him," Sarah calls out of the window. "You sure you're going to be OK?"

Orca nods. "I'll be fine. Let me know as well."

Chapter Twenty Four

She watches as they drive off, the car disappearing down the road and out of sight. There are some people in the carpark, changing out of their walking boots at the back of the car, and a couple more cars pass by on the road, but Orca feels as though the world is suddenly empty. It's been less than twenty-four hours since she was on her own, but it feels much longer. And in London, even when she was alone there were buildings all around her, people filling rooms and streets and buses, travelling through the ground beneath her feet on tube trains. The voices of the people here in the carpark are carried away on the breeze.

She starts walking, and within moments she is alone under the sky. The fields are open on either side, and ahead she can see moorland. There are sheep in the fields, but no people on the footpath. She walks fast, enjoying the movement of her body after the cramped car and the tiny spartan flat. The path heads out across pasture and the ground springs beneath her feet. It's late afternoon and the summer sun is past its highest point. The sky is blue. She's surprised not to see more walkers, but perhaps the people at the carpark were the last of them, and everyone has headed back to civilisation for the evening.

Soon she sees a spread of green across one side of the hill reaching down to the valley bottom. Wistman's Wood is tiny. From here she can see the whole of it. She holds her hand out in front of her and obliterates it entirely. She moves her hand to the left – there it is, then back again and it is gone. She continues walking. As she approaches the wood, there are a few trees, outliers, separated from rest. A bird is calling out, its voice insistent, loud in the still afternoon air. She checks the data, finds the song – a pied flycatcher. She thinks its sound could be interpreted as hostile – *keep away, go away, you're not wanted.* Or it could be exuberance. It probably has nothing to do with her approach. It's probably calling out to other birds. She looks up the hill to her right. She can see some stones up there, the sort you'd want to climb on and have your photograph taken, with your arms stretched wide, *here I am on top of the world.* The wood is so small she can almost see across the top of it to the other side.

But when she walks in between the trees she enters an otherworld. The trees are small, but they're not young. They are twisted and grizzled, dripping with lichens. The path is difficult to follow as it winds between the mossy boulders which cover the ground. The pied flycatcher is still calling, but it's behind her now, in the sunshine. The light is filtered, as though through green glass. She touches the trees as she passes. The moss is soft, but the lichen is like paper, or sometimes leather. There is so much of it, it's hard to see the bark of the trees. They are festooned in green, up their trunks and out along their branches. The lichens hang in curtains and the trees' leaves seem like a sprinkling of green confection. She's never seen so much moss and lichen in one place. She's disorientated by the size of the trees. None of them are much taller than her, but they have the gnarled appearance of age, their roots bone white and thick where they protrude from the ground. She knows it's a mature woodland, an ancient woodland, and she'd read that its exposed location meant that the trees grew low to the ground, but she hadn't expected something so much like a children's fairy story.

Perhaps not children's. There's energy here, but it doesn't feel childlike. She steps carefully onwards. A beetle scurries through some moss and she remembers she's meant to be looking for Nick. It doesn't feel as though anyone else is here. She's not seen another person since she left the carpark.

But when she turns and follows the path up the slope, she sees there is someone. He's sitting still on a boulder, underneath overhanging branches. Behind him there are bigger stones, and the air between the stones and the trees pools dark green. She wonders if she should go a different way. She recognised the man instantly. He is deep in contemplation, and she doesn't want to disturb his reverie, doesn't think she wants him to see her. There isn't another path though, and it would be too difficult to leave it and pick a way across the boulders. She walks on, trying to make her footsteps quiet, to observe a reverent hush and move with inner stillness.

He hasn't looked up, he shows no sign that he's seen her coming. Even when she reaches him, he doesn't look at her. On the boulder next to him the moss is growing in a pattern of circles. She touches it lightly with her finger, traces the curve between two bands of moss. She sits down next to him.

The spaces of the wood are filled with tiny motes dancing in golden air. She feels stiller than she ever has before. The cells of her body are motionless, her heart is silent. She can feel the air touching the insides of her ears and her inner elbows. Way above, beyond the leaves, a mosaic of blue sky, but that seems irrelevant, part of another world.

Eric takes her hand. His is warm and dry and larger than hers. She looks at the contrast in the skin tones of their intertwined fingers, dark and light, sunshine and shadow, tree trunk and boulder. She turns to look at him, and he turns at the same time.

"Hello," she says.

"I've missed you," he replies.

"I miss you too. Every day. Every moment. But I can't remember anything. I don't know why."

"It's probably for the best."

She feels a surge of something. Irritation, annoyance. It feels as familiar as breathing, or as his finger nails resting on the back of her hand.

"That's so like you. Conflict avoidant. Wouldn't you rather I remembered you, even if it's painful?"

"You can't change the past, and I can't wish you pain."

"But don't you want to be remembered?"

They're looking at each other now, and she knows every part of his face. She knows the chicken pox scar on the right side of his nose, and the exact chocolate brown of his eyes – not milk chocolate, and not the darkest either – but clear, like coloured glass. Warm glass. And the way a bit of his hair won't lie flat in his hairline, and always falls forward, even when his hair is cut really short, it still points in the opposite direction. His hair is longer today, and the strand of hair falls towards his right eyebrow.

"You do remember me. The important things anyway."

"No, I don't. I didn't even know you existed until last week. I didn't know your name until Sylva told me. I still don't know if you're real."

"Tell me what you know."

"About you?"

"Yes."

She's quiet again. She can hear the pied flycatcher calling at the edge of the wood, and a breeze passes through the trees rattling all the leaves in a wave from tree to tree. She realises she's tucked her ankle behind his, so their feet are entwined, and she knows this is an old habit.

"I know you like garlic bread and red wine."

He nods encouragingly.

"And hot curries. Hotter than I can eat. You like lassi with salt, which is disgusting."

He laughs. "Yes, we always had his and hers curries. Yours always smell like perfume."

"And dogs, you like dogs. And punk. At parties when you had too much to drink you took over the music and started pogoing to the Dead Kennedys and the Ramones."

"See, you do remember."

"And at our wedding you wore a bright blue suit." Orca gasps and bends forward as though someone has punched her. Eric puts his arm around her and pulls her to him. She buries her face in his shoulder. She's shaking like the leaves in the ancient oak above them. "We were married," she says, into the fabric of his shirt.

"Yes. We were married, and we had two lovely children. Their names were ..."

"No! This is enough."

He doesn't say anything else. Gradually she stops shaking. She leans against him and he holds her. She slips her arm around his back, beneath his shirt, so her palm touches the skin of his back. It's warm and smooth, familiar and comforting as her own. The trees settle too. She remembers she was supposed to be looking for Nick, but she doesn't want to move. This is the safest she's felt for a long time.

She doesn't know how long they sit there together, or at what point Eric leaves. She realises there's a cold draft down the side of her body, and the fragments of sky have changed colour – still blue, but darker. The shadows beneath the trees are deep and have no bottom. The pied flycatcher has stopped calling.

She walks back the way she'd come. When she gets to the edge of the wood, she sees that the darkness beneath the trees has spread across the hillside and that night is approaching. The sheep are standing in groups, and the sun has fallen below the level of the hills. She walks quickly.

Near the road, she sees two figures approaching along the path.

"Orca, is that you?"

They meet at the end of a drystone wall. The light is disappearing quickly.

"Did you find him?" Orca asks.

"We were worried about you." Sarah sounds annoyed. "We've been to Black a Tor and back, the drive and a three hour walk. You haven't been answering your phone."

"I don't know what happened," she says. "The memory implants. I got lost."

"We missed him," says Melinda. "He's been home."

"Are you alright, Orca?"

"Yes, I'll tell you later. Is he still there?"

"We'd better get back to the car, it's nearly dark."

"No, he's not. He wanted to take Eli, but Mum wouldn't let him. I think she might have listened to you."

The path is wide enough for two. Melinda walks on the grass at the side, so Orca is flanked by her and Sarah. She feels a bit like she's being escorted.

"To be fair, she said he couldn't take him before you got back."

"But he would have talked her into it – he has loads of times. Made out his needs were more important than mine."

"What about Nadia's things? Did she mention those?"

"He left her bag. You can collect it from the flat."

"And her passport?"

A moment of silence. "She didn't mention the passport."

"Maybe it's in the bag," says Sarah.

"Maybe."

None of them say anything else on the walk back to the car.

Wendy says Nick probably just forgot about the passport as it was in a different part of the van.

"Where was he going?" asks Orca.

Wendy frowns. "He said back up north."

"And he was OK about leaving Eli? That's new."

"He said it might be for the best, him staying here for a while, as he didn't have Nadia with him anymore, so it's harder to get his work done."

Wendy's face looks different from earlier. Her make up is still perfect, and her gaze doesn't falter, but she seems more fragile. She's holding Eli on her hip and he seems to have grown. Orca wonders if there is a trace of pink in Wendy's eyes. Jerome looks tired.

"Can you phone him? One of you?" Sarah looks tired too, but tiredness is making her rest her hands on her hips and jut her chin forward. "I presume you have his number."

"Well, he'll be driving."

"Leave a message then. Keep calling. Find out what he plans to do about the passport."

'Why don't we give you his number," says Melinda, tapping her phone. "Then you can contact him directly."

"Oh, I don't think we should give his number ..."

"There."

Sarah's phone pings in her pocket. "Thank you." she nods at Melinda, then looks at Orca. "Shall we go?"

"Oh, are you leaving? You could stay ... there's room, a spare room ... it's a long drive back," Melinda looks distressed for the first time.

The air in the flat is hot and overbreathed. The walls seem close.

"Thank you," says Sarah, "but ..."

"I've got to get back to Warwickshire," says Orca. "I've been called back."

"Oh, well, keep in touch, let us know ..."

"I'll call." Sarah pats her pocket.

"What was that about being called back?" Sarah asks in the car.

"Dorcas."

"Don't you want more sessions?"

"I was planning to leave anyway. London is too difficult for me. If you could drop me off in Bristol I'll find Nadia and give her her stuff, then I'll get the train."

Sarah is quiet. The cars on the other side of the dual carriageway swoosh by, each a streak of light then gone. The cars ahead are steadier, their lights orange fireflies in the darkness. "I was going to suggest we stop somewhere. It's pretty late. Let's get a hotel and I'll drive you in the morning. We can call Nick as well."

Orca nods. She's too tired to argue. There is so much new data and she needs to process it. She needs to close down, so her systems can reboot. She hopes everything will make more sense when the information has been appropriately stored. She would like to be amongst trees. There have been too many nights indoors.

"So, what happened in the wood?"

They have passed Exeter now and are on the motorway. A sign says Bristol is sixty more miles.

"I saw Eric."

"Another memory?"

"No, he was there, I spoke to him. He held me."

"What! I thought ..."

"Then he vanished. He was solid flesh, then he was gone. I can't explain it."

A sign tells them there's a service station in a mile. "Shall we stop here? See if there's a Travelodge or something?"

Orca nods.

"We can get something to eat. And you can tell me all about Eric."

Chapter Twenty Five

Nadia meets them at Temple Meads Station the next morning.

"You sure you don't want to come back to London and have some more sessions?" Sarah says to Orca.

Orca shakes her head. "I feel better in the woods."

"Well call me. Let me know how it's going.

Sarah drives away, and Orca turns to say goodbye to Nadia.

"I'm coming with you."

"But I thought ..."

"My friends have a new au pair. I'm not needed. I liked the Hayes."

"But I sleep in the woods, I don't have a van or ..."

"Sophie my friend at the post office. I can sleep on her floor."

Orca shrugs, "OK."

There had been no answer from Nick, last night or this morning. It might have been because he was driving, or he might have chosen not to answer. Melinda had promised to let them know if she heard from him. Orca and Nadia catch a train to Birmingham and change. At Nuneaton they walk from the train station to the bus station and catch a bus to Hartshill. By midday they are at the end of the road to the Hayes.

"I'm going to find Sophie," says Nadia. "I'll call you."

She leans towards Orca, and Orca realises Nadia wants to hug her. She leans forward too and puts her arm across Nadia's back, her chin on her shoulder. She feels awkward.

"Thank you," says Nadia.

A few minutes later Orca steps between the American red oaks in the corner of the wood. She walks quickly, she wants to find the hollies. She wants to force her way between the sharp leaves to the centre of the thicket where she is hidden from the whole of the world, and close down for the rest of the day, the rest of the week, for ever.

There are invitations to the pub with Nadia and Sophie, but she always says no. Nadia offers to meet her in the woods, but she makes excuses of being too busy. *I'm behind with the surveying,* she messages, *I need to concentrate on work.* There are messages from Sarah, which she answers briefly. Dorcas is quiet, which Orca senses as approval. Each day she sends in the data she has collected. On Thursday there is a message from Jack – *Funeral all done, I'm back at the cabin now, how are you?* She sends a quick *OK*. She spends the day making lists of bryophytes, lichens, insects. She puts her eye close up to trees, peers into crevices in bark, gets lost in minute moss forests, observes the shapes of sporophytes, notes the colours of algae. She maps paths, noting the kind of usage they get – the main ride: families, dogs, horses, bikes, the smallest paths: deer, foxes, Orca. Once she met a cat in the woods. It was far from the main path, crouching and still, watching some small creature that Orca couldn't see. Orca's approach spoiled its concentration and it stretched out its body, came to her arched and purring. She stroked it whilst it rubbed against her legs. Later she tried mimicking the cat's movements, the sinuous stretch, the fluid winding from side to side.

There's a hot spell. The sun beats down through the day, and people flock to the woods where the trees offer shade. The shape of Orca's day bends so she can avoid them. She begins work in the first glimmers of predawn. By the time the dogwalkers arrive she's done a few hours. When the families begin to appear, she goes to the hollies and shuts down through the hot middle section of the day. She wants to avoid people, but she's also noticed that if she overheats it affects how smoothly she runs, and she doesn't want to risk a malfunction. She doesn't want to have to go in for adjustments. She doesn't want to talk to anyone at all, even Dorcas.

She works again in the evening. There are people in the woods then, but fewer, and she's become adept at sensing them. She hears their footsteps, notices a change in the air as they approach before she even sees them. Sometimes she feels like a deer, stilled, ears pricked, assessing, before dashing silently off the path and out of sight.

Nadia says *are you avoiding me?* and *Hey, come to the pub.* Jack says, *I went back to where we found that deer and there's a crop of chanterelles.* Orca sends reams of data to Dorcas and sends thumbs-up symbols to Sarah. She doesn't count the days. She looks for Bird and for Sylva, but sees neither.

One evening a group of people arrive with signs and arrows. They walk along the main ride talking loudly, hammering and laughing. After they've gone, Orca creeps in the dying light to look at the posts they've erected. A running race is passing through the woods the following day. The arrows point the way, give the distance. The woods will be busier than ever.

At dawn she begins work as normal, but when she hears the first dog bark through the trees, she leaves the Hayes. She walks out through the top end and crosses the field into St Lawrence's. This time, when she reaches the far corner, she keeps walking, into the open, across the fields. Grazing sheep raise their heads to look at her. The sun is illuminating their backs. Everything is glowing, peach-blushed – the grass they're grazing, the fence posts, the farm vehicles sleeping behind a farmhouse. She walks past a kennel where a sheepdog raises its head to watch her, down the side of a front garden with roses blooming, onto a road, where she turns right. Soon the farmland disappears, and high wire fences line the road. On the other side of the fences, dirt tracks, site offices, signs reading, *Danger, Keep Out, Deep Quarries.* The road rounds a bend and the view opens. She gasps.

p.288

The quarry is huge, but most of it is filled with water reflecting the morning sun. There are trees and shrubs growing around its edges at the far end. Only at this near end are there signs of industry. It looks like a lake. It is a lake – hidden behind the cliff edges of the quarry, shielded by rows of trees and high wire fences.

Orca walks on, but keeps glancing behind her, until the road bends and she can no longer see it, barely believes ever she really did. She crosses a bridge over the railway and another over the canal, where she joins the towpath. The water winds along the back of farms. Geese and ducks in small groups on the opposite bank watch her. The sun rises higher. Hawthorn, elder and rowan grow along the path, and every now and then she passes a boat. Some of the boats are still sleeping, but one or two show signs of life – some steam from a chimney, a dog bowl licked clean on the bank.

At Clock Bridge she carries on, leaving the village. There are more fields, there are industrial sites and stoneworks. The water looks thicker here, brown and clogged with stonedust.

The bridges have more graffiti. By a pub she steps out onto the road and walks along the pavement. There aren't many cars. It's still fairly early, and she realises it must be the weekend. She's getting closer to Nuneaton.

Then the view opens again, and between the trees she can see another of those huge lakes. This one is half the size of the Hayes, lying peaceful and blue behind the housing estates, as though it were transplanted from somewhere much further north, somewhere remote. She stops and stares through the fence. She thinks about the history of this lake, how once there had been just land, fields, trees, holly and elm and oak, moss and lichens, bluebells. Then the dynamite, the explosions breaking the foundations of the earth, smashing layer upon layer, exposing raw rock, jagged edges, showing depths which were meant to be hidden, stripping the land of every attempt to protect itself. It still happens. From the Hayes, she'd heard the dull boom of the explosions, wondered briefly what it was, before realising it was from the quarries. But she's never imagined anything like this. The healing water covering the raw depths, lying passive and beautiful as a mother, daring anyone to even think about the brokenness below. Orca would like to get nearer, to sit at the edge of the lake and gaze across the water, watch the birds swooping for insects in the clear air above, then gathering in groups in the half-grown trees that populate the sides. It's not possible. The fences are tall and unclimbable, covered in danger notices. Keep Out! Deep Water! This glimpse is all she will get. The road bends, and the lake will disappear from sight again, and she'll wonder if she imagined it. It's spectacular, but hidden.

Even so, she stays for a long time. A woman passes with a dog, but other than that there are no other pedestrians. Cars shoot by, on their way to Nuneaton or Atherstone, the glimpse of the lake a flash in their mirrors, an image seen but not seen – imagined.

She feels something touch her hand, and looks down. It's the little girl, the one she'd seen before with Eric. She slips her hand into Orca's and stands next to her, looking through the fence towards the lake. Orca's view of her is of dark curls, long lashes, soft cheeks. Her hand is warm, and Orca brings her gaze back to the lake, the still water.

"Mummy," the girl says, and Orca can't speak. She feels her throat tighten, a hollowness spread through her chest. She squeezes the child's hand.

"Mummy, why is the water here?"

Orca moistens her lips, swallows to get her salivary glands working, to free up her mouth and throat. "There was a big hole," she says. "Something was taken away, and the water has come to fill the space."

"Did it hurt?"

Orca looks at the child who is looking up at her. Her eyes are clear, dark brown, the same colour as Eric's. She doesn't look troubled and her voice is level, curious.

p.289

"Yes." Orca's voice comes out as a whisper. "Yes, it hurt, but the water helps."

They stand still for a while longer. A flock of starlings is swooping over the water, making a shape in the air that twists and bends, a spiral, a wave, a murmuration.

"It's pretty," says the girl.

Orca nods, but realises the girl isn't looking at her, so she squeezes her hand again. Cars pass on the road behind them, and somewhere out of sight a train passes through.

"Goodbye Mummy," says the child.

The warmth disappears from Orca's grasp. She looks down, but not quickly enough. The child has gone, and there is just the pavement, a patch of dandelions growing by the fence, Orca's own shoes. She grabs hold of the fence, as if to stop herself from falling. The starlings are still swooping, and the sun is making a golden haze above the water.

p.290

Chapter Twenty Six

She creeps back into the Hayes in the early evening. There are still people about, picking up litter and removing signs, but it's easy enough for Orca to avoid them. Even the dogs don't notice her pass. When she reaches the hollies she creeps into the centre, curls into a ball on the ground and closes down.

She's unaware of the hours of darkness, unaware of rain pattering on the shiny leaves above her. When the birds begin to sing of the new day her body reboots, in keeping with her habits, but she overrides it and closes down again. It tries again later, when her fuel levels have become critically low and the waste water needs emptying. She relieves herself and resets the fuel requirement levels to zero, curls back into her space and switches off again. The next time her body reboots itself there are critical warnings flashing, the main one being that she is dangerously low on fluid. There are also messages from Dorcas. She hasn't heard from Dorcas for a while. Dorcas had handed her over to Dr Morgan, but she supposes the trackers are still in place, and Dorcas has detected her immobility, her lowering levels of fuel and water. She finds a bottle of water in her backpack and takes a few sips. The warning lights stop flashing. She drinks a little more, but she doesn't look at the messages.

She wants to go back to sleep, but the warning signs from her body keep her on standby. She draws in her knees and wraps her arms around them. Maybe time will do it – if she waits the signals may disappear, and she can return to an off position. She doesn't want to risk any more memories. She has sent all the data she's gathered to Dorcas, she's done the job required and she's had enough. Dorcas won't be happy – she's put a lot of effort and expenditure into this project – but Orca can't do it any more. The memories are too overwhelming.

She loses track of time. She's not sure how many times night has fallen, how many times the day has returned. It might be two, or three, could it be more. The messages from Dorcas have become more frequent, more insistent, but ignoring them has become easier.

In the darkest part of each night Sylva comes to sit with her. She doesn't say anything, and it's too dark to see her, but Orca knows she's there. Bird is there too, in the larches beyond the hollies. All night the two of them keep a silent vigil and Orca is quietly glad. When the light comes back into the sky they disappear, but she feels that they are both nearby and they know what's happening with her; that if she closes down permanently there will be witnesses.

It's daylight when she hears shouting. She looks up through the hollies at the sky. The sun is high, it must be somewhere in the middle of the day. Someone is calling her name – two people – two voices. Her mind has lost some of its clarity since her water ran out and the voices sound harsh, indistinct, like barking rather than shouting. But she recognises her own name, and after a while she recognises the voices. Nadia and Sarah Morgan are walking through the woods calling for her. She doesn't think they'll find her. From the outside you wouldn't be able to tell there was a space in the middle of this holly thicket. It's not really much of a space, she shares it with new holly shoots and dangling branches. She could stay, they will pass on and they won't find her.

There is something though, something pricking at the dull indifference she has been inhabiting, something other than holly leaves. She knows Nadia has been trying to contact her. She's been ignoring Nadia as well as Dorcas. But why is Sarah here? Why has she travelled from London?

Orca crawls out under the holly until she is crouching a few feet from the path behind a stand of larch trees. She can see them. They are on the path, walking away from her. They're shouting her name constantly, they must be hoarse. She decides to follow them, track them, but her ability to move silently through the wood has left her. She stumbles in the bracken. They have nearly disappeared from view.

There is a fluttering in the treetops and loud bird cries. Sylva is running along the path calling out, "Wait, wait!"

Nadia and Sarah Morgan turn around.

Orca puts a hand out to touch the nearest larch. She needs to keep upright. She doesn't want their pity, she needs to show them she's OK so that they will go away.

But the trees are not on her side either. The larch doesn't hold her up. Her hand slides on its bark and she falls. The bracken softens her landing, but when Nadia and Dr Morgan come running there's nothing she can say. They lift her, they comment on her pallor, her sunken eyes, they express relief at having found her. They talk to her as they walk her through the wood, but she has no idea what they're saying. Sylva is nowhere to be seen. Dr Morgan lifts a bottle of water to her lips, and the liquid slipping into her body burns like fire.

Dr Morgan's car is in the carpark. They manoeuvre Orca into the back seat and Nadia gets in next to her. They sit leaning against each other, their shoulders touching. Dr Morgan drives. They take her to her own house and sit her in an armchair in the front room whilst they busy about.

"You need food." Dr Morgan is opening cupboards, lifting up packets of nutrition pills, cereal bars.

"Not those," says Nadia. "She needs broth, her body will reject solid food."

She goes out and Dr Morgan sits with Orca, making her take sips of water now and then. The water doesn't burn anymore. Orca thinks of a dried landscape, baked by a hot sun, and how if you pour water onto the hardened mud it runs straight off. But maybe there are cracks. The water might get into the cracks and begin the work of softening the mud.

Nadia returns with a bag of vegetables, and bones from the butcher. Soon the house begins fill with a savoury smell.

"Why are you here?" Orca asks Sarah Morgan.

It's the first thing she's said, and her voice feels harsh in her throat.

Sarah smiles at her. Her face looks different when she smiles. Orca can see what she must have looked like as a child, enthusiastic, boyish, handsome. "Melinda called. They heard from Nick. He's gone to Scotland."

"For beetles?"

"Yes. He has a contract in the Cairngorms. When I couldn't get hold of you, I called Nadia. She told me you'd gone to ground."

"You should go."

Sarah frowns.

" ... to Scotland. Find him."

"We will, but you need to get your strength back first. We're not going without you."

Nadia comes from the kitchen with a mug of steaming broth which she hands to Orca. "Sip it slowly," she says.

The broth is tasty and feels like instant nutrition. There is that hot feeling in her gullet which she gets from tea, but it feels like goodness is being absorbed directly into the cells of her body. She knows the digestive system doesn't work like that, but that's how it feels. She smiles at Nadia, who is watching her anxiously.

"Did Nick tell Wendy if he had your passport?"

It's Sarah who answers. "He said he didn't know. Said it might be in the van."

"I know exactly where it is," says Nadia, "in the front pocket."

"The glove compartment, yes, unless he's moved it." The tension is rising in Sarah's face again.

"I had another memory that wasn't a memory," says Orca, and Sarah's shoulders drop. She looks at Orca with interest.

"Eric again?"

"No, the girl. She was holding my hand."

"Did she tell you her name?"

Orca shakes her head. "I don't want to know her name. The pain is too much. When she disappeared again, I couldn't bear it. These memories, they're not fair. Dorcas was wrong to give them too me. I can't work properly when they surface, I can't be in my body, I need to turn off. I want to turn off. I want to stop hurting."

Nadia leans forward and puts her hand over Orca's. Orca looks down at it. Nadia's hand is smaller than hers. She's wearing dark red nail varnish. She says, "Bad memories are like monsters under the bed."

Orca looks at her and realises she knows hardly anything about her, only what she's seen. "I'm sorry," she says. "I'm being self-centred."

"Pfft!" says Nadia. "You have a bad time. Sometimes the memories come out from the bed and you have to hide under the blankets."

Orca drinks more of the broth. "Thank you," she says.

"That's such a good analogy," says Sarah Morgan. "Do you mind if I borrow it?"

Nadia shrugs.

"Do you have monsters too?" asks Orca.

Sarah stands up and walks across the room to the window. "I'm sure everybody does," she says. "But the thing about monsters under the bed is that they are in the mind, so you can use your mind to defeat them."

"Making new memories is the best way," says Nadia. "Good memories."

"That can certainly help," says Sarah. "But the old memories can still surface, and it's good to have a strategy, to know what to do, how to deal with them."

"You should phone Jack," says Nadia.

"Do you think so?" says Orca. "Do you think he would want to hear from me?"

"He went with you to Kielder," says Nadia. "Just like that – he must have liked you."

"He's back at the cabin. He's not with Becky anymore."

"So phone him."

"It's probably best to focus on one thing at a time," says Sarah. "We need to get your strength back, and think about this trip up to Scotland. My mum lives up there, in Inverness, so we can stay with her."

"I suppose I could phone him. He's been texting me."

"Do you think that's wise?" asks Sarah.

Orca shrugs. "I don't know if it's wise. But I want to do it." She's got her phone in her hand, and she's scrolling back through the texts from Jack. There haven't been many, but recently she hasn't been replying to anything, so that he's sent any at all shows some persistence. He told her there were UFO researchers visiting, and he took them to see the car in the middle of the forest. He sent a photo of a piece of jewellery he's made from pine cones he'd brought back from Kielder.

She dials his number. Nadia is smiling and Sarah frowns before turning back to the window. The phone is answered by a woman.

"Is Jack there?" asks Orca.

"He's nipped out," says the woman.

"Do you know when he'll be back?"

"He shouldn't be long. He's gone to pick us up some food and forgot to take his phone. Can I take a message?"

"Are you ...?"

"This is Becky. I can tell him ..."

"It's OK."

Orca ends the call and stares at the screen.

Nadia put her hand on Orca's arm. "She might be just ..."

"Forget about Jack," says Sarah. "If he gets in touch, take it from there. But I don't think it's healthy, getting involved with someone who has unresolved trauma of his own, and is still invested in his ex, when you're dealing with these memories."

"I felt better when I was with him," says Orca. She feels as though Becky has thumped her in the stomach or slapped her face, the shock is sudden and painful.

"Do you think you'll be OK to travel tomorrow?" asks Sarah.

Orca nods. She would be OK to travel now. The broth is healing her body, and the phone call has shocked her out of her lethargy. But it's nearly evening and it's a long drive. "We can set off at first light," she says.

There's not much furniture in the house. There's the bedroom with a single bed which Orca has used before, there's a sofa in the living room. There is another bedroom upstairs, but it's empty. Sarah Morgan brings a camping mat and sleeping bag in from her car and makes a bed in the spare bedroom. Nadia sleeps on the sofa. Orca lies on the bed. She remembers Jack's cabin, the books he had and the pictures on the wall, the half-finished jewellery. It was a small space, but it was crammed with things. A guitar leaning against one wall, the old laptop, the kitchen cupboards filled with jars and tins. This house is much bigger, but all it contains are a bed, some chairs, nutrition pills, cleaning products. Dorcas might have been better spending time furnishing the house for her rather than giving her memory implants. She might be a more efficient surveyor if she had a comfortable place for downtime.

She wonders if Becky is living in the cabin with Jack, then she stops wondering. Sarah Morgan is right. It doesn't help to fret about Jack and Becky. Tomorrow they are off to Scotland. She feels as though she's been there before. In Devon she'd known that everything was new, but she has memories of Scotland. She pictures a bay, the water still like glass, islands rounded by their reflections beneath, stones in a bowl of clear water, everything peaceful.

That's not where they're going of course, they're going to the Cairngorms not to the coast and the islands. She hopes she won't be ambushed.

Chapter Twenty Seven

It's a long way to go in such a small car. Nadia and Orca take turns to sit in the back, swapping places at service stations. Each time they stop it's a relief to get out, to unfold and stretch. Luckily it's not a hot day. There are low clouds, and when they reach the Lake District, some showers of rain. They don't talk much. Orca is tired as her body is still recovering, and the others didn't sleep well in her uncomfortable house. None of them know what they will find when they get there. Will they even be able to find Nick in the huge expanse? If they do find him, will there be a confrontation? Sarah plays music, but Orca doesn't pay much attention to it. She could use the recognition software, but she doesn't really care what it is. She remembers the journey to Kielder with Jack, and how the music was so much a part of that, how the rhythm became part of the passing landscape, the singers expressing the joy and sorrow held in the swell of the land and the flight of birds, the sway of trees and the drama of life in passing towns. Here, as the motorway winds between mountains, their car feels like a small creature, shuttling its way, the music a tiny whine against the hugeness of the backdrop. She's sure Sarah would let her change the music, but she doesn't want to think about Jack.

When they cross the border into Scotland, Nadia takes control of the stereo. The hills here are round-shouldered and dark. Orca remembers the view from the top of Deadwater Fell, hill after hill stretching into the distance, no sign of human habitation, not even a road. Some of those hills might be the same ones they're passing now. The music Nadia has chosen has a joyful lilt which feels like a bright thread against the dark hills. Sarah asks what it is, and Nadia tells her it's electro swing.

It sees them to the outskirts of Glasgow when Sarah says she's had enough. "It was great to begin with," she says.

"What shall I put on?" asks Nadia.

"There's a playlist on my phone called Girl Stuff – try that."

It's a mix which spans decades. They navigate the centre of Glasgow singing along to Madonna and Pink, Lulu, Rhianna and Self Esteem. Sarah seems effervescent, and Nadia laughs at her bad attempts at high notes. Orca smiles in the back of the car. She knows some of these songs. The way she knows music is the same as the way she knows she'd been to Scotland before. It's different from data. She can't look it up. The knowledge is somehow a part of her. It must be some sort of reaction between the implants and her own systems, some seepage of information. She looks out of the window as they drive along the length of Loch Lomond. The cloud is lighter and higher here and there's no rain at the moment. Orca feels sadness soaking through her, she feels sodden and heavy, whilst Nadia and Sarah are bubbling up in the front of the car.

At Fort William Orca and Nadia swap seats. Now that her sadness has been brought to the front of the car it infects the others. Gwen Stefani and Janelle Monae are just as infectious, but no one sings along. Nadia is silent in the back, and Sarah is gripping the steering wheel. The view is spectacular. They've driven into sunshine, leaving the grey clouds behind in the south, and the water sparkles.

"I probably should have rung my mum to tell her we're coming," says Sarah.

"I thought you did last night," says Nadia.

"I chickened out. She would have made some excuse. She'd have said it wasn't convenient."

"But she will be pleased to see you?"

"I hope so." Sarah pauses. "I remind her of Dad."

"Are they ..."

"They're divorced."

Her knuckles are shining. She removes one hand, then the other, from the steering wheel, giving each a shake.

Nadia says, "How on earth will we find Nick? There is so much space."

They reach Inverness, and Sarah guides the car through the streets, serenaded by Annie Lennox. She stops the car in a street of houses made of grey stone which somehow resists the sunshine. The front gardens are well tended, and the one they've stopped outside is full of roses.

"This is it," says Sarah.

'My mother squeals like a donkey when I come home," says Nadia.

"Mum definitely won't squeal."

"We can just say hello," says Orca, "then find somewhere else to stay, if it's too much trouble. Nadia and I can stay in the car."

"No," Sarah undoes her seatbelt and opens the car door, "she can meet my friends. I am not Dad."

The woman who opens the door looks nothing like Sarah. She looks too young to be the mother of an adult. She has dyed red hair cut into a geometric bob. She's wearing black leggings and an oversized t-shirt.

"Hi Mum."

"Sarah!"

Sarah is taller than her mother but seems suddenly slight, like a teenager.

"You didn't say you were coming."

"It was sudden. We needed to come up, and I thought it made sense to come here. We only decided late last night and then we set off early, so I didn't have time to call, I was driving."

"You could have sent a text."

The woman is still standing in the doorway, she doesn't move to let them in. Sarah is in front of Nadia and Orca, who flank her like sergeants.

"These are my friends."

Her mothers sighs. “You’d better come in. There are people here though. I have a lodger now.”

She walks back into the hall and Sarah follows her. After a moment Orca and Nadia follow too. Nadia is last over the threshold and as she closes the door behind her, the hallway is suddenly dark. The light through a small stained-glass window above the door is blue and thin. Orca blinks after the bright sunshine outside. They follow Sarah’s mother to the back of the house where a door takes them into a large kitchen. It’s lighter in here. A door and windows open onto a large garden, and the smells of recently cut grass and flowers mingle with those of baking bread. A huge round wooden table fills the space in the middle of the room, and two men are sitting with mugs of tea, conversing. A big teapot on the table is covered with a knitted teacosy in garish shades of pink and yellow. There is a sugar bowl and a bottle of milk, and another mug is on the table where Sarah’s mother left it when she went to answer the door. Heat coming from the Aga on the far side of the room mingles with fresh air from the garden. There is a silence as everyone looks at each other.

One of the men is Keith. No longer a boy, he is a young man with a beard.

“This is my lodger. He’s an arboriculturist.”

Keith is smiling. He isn’t showing any sign of recognition. There is no suggestion that he has ever seen Orca before, or that he has helped to carry Nadia’s unconscious body through the forest on a makeshift stretcher.

“And this is his colleague, Nick.”

For a moment, the golden, affable man has disappeared and he is shocked. They have caught him unawares.

“Nick is an entomologist,” says Keith. “He’s doing a study of beetles in the forests.”

Sarah’s mother is looking at everyone’s faces.

“What is he doing here?” says Sarah.

"This is my daughter, Sarah. And her friends. I haven't got their names yet."

"Nadia," says Nick.

"You guys know each other?" Keith is still smiling, but it's disappeared from his eyes. He's looking anxiously from one to another. His gaze stops for a moment on Orca, but passes on.

Nick is smiling. It's only taken him a beat and he's back. "Hey guys, this is great," he says.

"You know each other?" says Sarah's mother.

"Nadia and I, we're ..." He turns the full golden shine of his smile onto Nadia, "What are we? Girlfriend and boyfriend? Lovers?"

Nadia smiles back, a weak smile which just wobbles her lips. "I left my passport in your van," she says.

"Yeah, I was going to send it back to you. But now I don't need to." Nick turns his smile to Sarah. "I am so pleased to meet you. How strange, Dorien was telling me about her amazing daughter, a doctor at a top London university, and all the time you knew Nadia.""

Sarah glances briefly at her mother, a frown crossing her face. "Mum mentioned me?"

"Absolutely. She was telling us how hard you had to fight to get where you are, how determined you are."

Sarah looks like she's about to answer, but she swallows suddenly, and doesn't speak.

"And Orca." Nick is looking at her, and Keith looks too.

"Hello Keith," says Orca.

"Have we met before? I feel like we've met before?"

"We met in Kielder."

"Did we? When was that? I really feel like I know you, but I can't place it."

"It was a long time ago," says Orca. "You and Kelvin were boys."

Keith frowns. Dorien grabs the kettle from the Aga and fills it from the tap. "Seeing as it's a reunion party I'll make more tea. I'll find cake," she says. "You better all sit down. Good thing I have a lot of chairs."

Dorien gets a tin from a cupboard and produces homemade madeira cake. She cuts slices and gets a pile of small plates from another cupboard. She refills the teapot and finds mugs. The rest of them watch her.

'We didn't have many visitors at Kielder," says Keith. "We never went to the touristy parts of the forest, hardly ever."

"It's great to see you," says Nick. He's speaking to Nadia, who is nearest to him at the round table. He reaches across and puts his hand over hers. She looks at it and then at him. She doesn't move her hand.

Sarah coughs. "We were down in Devon. We met Melinda."

"Yes, Wendy told me you'd been. I left Nadia's bag, but I forgot her passport was in the van."

"Forgot, really?"

"Did you meet my grandad?" says Keith.

"Yes, we met Carter. We stayed at your house overnight. You and I chatted in the garden and talked to your horse."

"Of course," says Nick. "Such an annoying mistake, and now you've driven all this way.'

"Would anyone like a slice of cake?"

"I was afraid of the horse."

"No you weren't," says Orca.

Dorien places pieces of cake on plates and passes them around the table.

"Not that I'm not pleased to see you." Nick squeezes Nadia's hand, and smiles at her. Orca can see Nadia melting.

"So was it a trick to get Nadia to come running after you?" says Sarah..

"If I'd thought that would bring her back to me, I might have done it for that reason. But it was a genuine mistake."

Keith has stuffed his mouth full of cake. Nadia's hand slides under Nicks, turning palm up. Her fingers curl slightly.

"Nadia!" says Sarah.

Nadia looks at her.

"So let me get this straight," says Dorien. "Nick and ... Nadia, is it? ... are estranged lovers. Keith and Orca met once in a forest when he was a child. And Sarah, how do you fit in with all this? Apart from bringing them all here?"

"I only brought two of them."

Orca breaks a corner off the cake and puts it into her mouth. It is soft and tastes slightly of lemons. She doesn't remember eating lemons, but she knows the taste. Her recognition software recognises lemons, but not the way it is transformed into butter as she chews the cake. The others are still talking, and she watches them. Their words draw lines between them, mother to daughter, lover to lover, woman to woman. Keith is outside of this. He's finished his cake, and he's looking at her. She remembers him holding the baby Eli near the Forest Head, she remembers him silent in the night-time stable, the way the horse knew him and responded to his stillness.

"I thought that was a dream," he says, across the table.

"I think it was, but I don't know if it was yours or mine."

There is a lull. Nadia shuffles her chair so she is nearer to Nick. She is leaning towards him.

"Nadia," says Sarah. "Don't let your body fool you into old habits."

"We have some pretty good habits together, don't we Nads." Nick slides his arm along the table top so that he and Nadia are touching from hand to elbow.

Nadia looks at the line where their skin is touching, then she pulls her hand away from his and stands up. "Could I use the bathroom, please," she says.

Later, Dorien makes a pot of chilli, helped by Keith, who chops onions and peppers, peels cloves of garlic, and stirs the pan. Nadia keeps a distance from Nick, sitting on the other side of the table. Sarah finds some bottles of red wine in the cupboard and pours glasses for everyone. Over food, Keith and Nick talk about the forest. Keith tells them about the treeline, the place where they hope all the forests will eventually join, two thousand feet up the mountains.

"In two hundred years," he says, "the mountains will be forested again, only the peaks will emerge from the trees."

Dorien gives Orca some cheese to grate, then serves up the chilli in steaming bowls. It feels convivial, food and wine, communal eating. Orca has crescents of cheese under her fingernails. She doesn't remember eating cheese or grating cheese, but she'd known what to do. The taste seems familiar. She likes it better than the chilli, and she wonders if she is meant to eat meat. She must ask Dorcas. She hasn't heard from Dorcas for a while, not since Nadia and Sarah took her under their care. She feels a sharp pang and realises that she misses her.

When they've finished eating, Orca and Keith help Dorien clear up. Sarah goes upstairs. When Orca turns from the dishwasher, she sees that Nick and Nadia have both disappeared.

"They went into the garden," says Dorien. "Probably to make up."

Orca glances to the windows. It's getting dark, and she can't make out any people, but the garden is long and there are many shadows which could hide them. She supposes that Nick will be on his best behaviour when there are others nearby.

Sarah comes back into the room and looks about her.

"Where's are they?" she asks.

Dorien nods towards the garden.

"He'd better not try anything," says Sarah. "I think I'll go out there."

"Leave them to it," says Dorien. "Lovers' quarrel. They'll sort it out."

"No Mum, it's not like that."

"You can see that they're totally into each other. The way they keep looking – and they can hardly keep their hands off each other."

"He's like Dad."

Dorien's face closes. Nothing changes in her expression, but it becomes wooden. "He's nothing like your dad," she says.

"I've seen the evidence."

Nick and Nadia burst back in through the door from the garden. They are both smiling. Orca is handing clean plates from the dishwasher to Keith.

"More wine anyone?" says Nick, holding up a half empty bottle.

Orca glances at Dorien. She's wiping down the tabletop, not looking at Nick or at Sarah. Nadia sits down on the far side of the table from Nick.

"Shall I get my guitar?" Keith asks, when the dishwasher has been refilled.

"Fantastic idea!" says Nick.

Dorien nods, with a strange twist of the mouth, which Orca realises is meant to be a smile.

Soon they're all back at the table and everyone's wine glass is full. Orca hasn't drunk any of hers. She emptied half of it down the sink when no one was looking, and now Nick has topped it back up again. Everyone else is on their second or third glass. Keith is strumming his guitar and the others are all suggesting songs.

"You can take it in turns to choose," says Keith. "But you all have to join in."

They begin with a song which Orca doesn't know. The others, surprisingly, all have good voices. Sarah's is light, but in tune, Keith's strong and pure, Nick's is a low rich bass, and he gets the tune wrong a lot. The stars are Dorien and Nadia. Dorien's voice is a confident contralto, her control perfect, and Orca thinks she must have had singing lessons. Nadia hasn't learned what to do with her voice, but it is full of emotion and power. At the end of the song everyone is looking at her.

"Fuck, Nads! I didn't know you could sing like that."

"You should train that voice." Dorien looks as though she likes Nadia for the first time.

"I only sing with my family. Traditional songs."

"Can we hear one?" asks Keith.

Nadia sings unaccompanied in her own language, and the others watch her, entranced. Orca has words buzzing around her head. Contralto, tenor, pianissimo, a cappella, glissando. The words are a kind of music themselves. She knows she can sing. She knows that if she opened her mouth and joined in, she would surprise them all as much as Nadia has.

Nadia's song ends, and they all cheer and clap and drink more wine. Sarah suggests the next song, another that Orca doesn't know. She excuses herself.

In the hallway she looks up the stairs. Dorien has given her directions to the bathroom. The front door is behind her. The singing in the kitchen is interspersed with laughter. She opens the door quietly and slips outside into the night, closes it behind her, and the sound stops. It's dark, but only just, and she can make out the shapes of the rose bushes and shrubs filling the garden. The sweet smell is powerful. She stands for a few moments readjusting, from artificial light to deep dusk, from dry warmth to cool evening, from voices and the clatter of hard surfaces, to the soft movement of leaves, invisible scurrying insects and the spinning of sap in stalks. The roses are protected by sharp thorns.

She sets off down the road, moving quickly. At some point they'll notice she's disappeared, and she wants to be long gone by then.

Chapter Twenty Eight

In the town centre the bus station is quiet. There are a few buses still to leave, but not in the direction she wants to go, and it's too far to walk. There's a taxi office next to the bus station and despite the expense she goes in and asks for a car to Nethy Bridge. There's one available, and she is soon leaving Inverness behind her. It hasn't taken long. Ten minutes to walk into town, another five for decisions and negotiations. It's possible the others haven't gone to look for her yet. They'll be singing more songs and won't have noticed she's been a long time in the bathroom.

The journey takes about an hour. When the car drops her in the centre of the village it's completely dark. She's spent the journey looking at maps, working out the best way to go. She gets her bearings, the river, the road, the school, the bus stop. She heads east, out of the village. After a while the forest creeps close to the road and she can feel the presence of trees to her right, crowding and looking down at her as she passes. They are fairly young. She feels their curiosity, tells herself she's being imaginative.

She walks to where the road meets the forest track and keeps going. There have been no cars. The ground beneath her feet changes, dried mud rather than tarmac, and the trees are now on both sides. The verges are wide and the moon is rising, silvering the path. Orca is using her night vision, and she has no problems finding the way. Even when the track splits after the Forest Lodge, she confidently chooses the left fork and continues.

She can feel a settling in her body. Something that was on high alert is relaxing, the need for vigilance is dissipating. Other systems are kicking in, looking out for trip hazards, listening to the forest, guarding her physical body. She feels a smile on her face. This is easy.

There are a lot of owls. Their calls sometimes surprise her, close by. The trees are bigger now. Some have huge trunks and could be centuries old. They watch her pass and are silent. They must have seen change in their lifespans, so many bodies moving past them, across them.

It doesn't feel dark anymore. The path is wide, and regularly emerges from tree cover, before passing back into new stands of pine. The trees are narrower at their tops than lower down, so unlike broadleaved trees that block out the light, these allow it through, filtering it through needles, bouncing it off the shine of their bark. It's still a couple of hours until the summer dawn, but Orca can see where she's going. She doesn't need Bird to show her the way, which is good because he isn't here.

She was sure Bird would come with her. She'd even wondered if she'd find Sylva here in the Caledonian forest. She'd had an idea that they were lurking when she was at Dorien's house – maybe in the back garden, or out in the street at the front, hovering amongst the roses. She hadn't seen them, but she'd learned to sense them, and she'd felt comforted by their presence. But in the foothills of the mountains she is alone.

She passes a couple of remote farmhouses, and wonders what it would be like to live somewhere like that, reached only by a forest track, and how much snow there would be in the depths of winter. The path skirts the forest, and she can feel the view open up on her left, the huge expanse of the mountain range, silent in the night. She remembers the feeling at the top of the Hayes, where the view opens up like the ocean. This is another level, here she is small and unimportant. Here she can be swallowed and incorporated and the mountains won't even flinch.

When she reaches the treeline, she finds a spot to rest. Daylight won't be long now, and she wants to conserve her energy, so she can get some real distance behind her. The mountains are full of remote corners. Some that nobody ever visits, some that no one has been to for years. She needs to find one of her own, where none of them will follow.

It feels as though she closes her eyes and opens them immediately, but time must have passed, because the dawn is beginning. She stretches her limbs and shakes her body, then walks out onto the side of the mountain. It's washed with a glow of pink light which suffuses with yellow. The sky behind the peaks is shining gold where the sun will rise, and higher up white, moving through to dark blue. The mountains are dark purple. She hears a sound and looks down the hill. A circle of birds are strutting and calling. They're in the data – black grouse, a rare, protected, shy bird. She's privileged to be seeing this mating display. She's privileged to be here on the side of a mountain watching the sun rise. She is privileged to have a strong body that can move through the mountain paths. None of it makes any difference. She closes her eyes, and opens them. The sky is filling with red and orange as the sun gets closer to the horizon.

She passes a bothy. She passes a small shining green loch, where she pauses to look at the condensation rolling across its surface as though it were a cauldron of magic. She breathes air which is crystal cold, tinged with the scent of pine. This is the most amazing place she has ever been. Appropriate for this walk.

She had another memory, back in the Hayes, before Nadia and Sarah found her, worse than any of the others, and she knows the two children are dead as well as Eric. She didn't know if it was a memory or a hallucination caused by the lack of food and water, but she wasn't going to risk any more. She couldn't live like this, not knowing when the memories would surface. She'd asked Dorcas if they could be removed, but Dorcas told her it didn't work like that. Once they were triggered, once she was conscious of them, they became part of her present, part

p.291

of her awareness. They couldn't be removed as they were no longer discrete. What about those that haven't been triggered yet, she'd asked. It was a package, Dorcas told her, they are all connected. Once the process has begun, it's impossible to stop it. Trying to remove them would cause untold damage to the rest of Orca's systems. When will I know it's finished, that there are no more? Dorcas couldn't answer that either. They might all come in a rush, or they might take a long time. There could be some lying dormant for years, like mines from the second world war still hidden on the beach eighty years later. Mines are dangerous, Orca retorted, they can kill you, maim you.

She supposes Dorcas must be angry with her for leaving the Hayes again, but she hasn't been messaging Orca and telling her to get back to work. Maybe she realises that the memories have already caused too much damage so there's no point. Maybe she's written her off.

The path starts to head downhill. Orca checks the map in her data. It will take her to another loch, a large one that can be reached by road. She doesn't want to see people, but it is very early still. The slopes are dotted with trees. She hears movement, but when she turns, whatever it was has vanished. She misses Bird. Bird would have helped her find the best path.

When she reaches it, the loch takes her breath away. It is white with morning mist. Boats stand silent near the shore, their masts appearing and disappearing as the mist drifts. Water birds scoot through the shallow edges calling to each other, and the sound is swallowed immediately by thick air. She can't see the other side, she could be standing on the edge of eternity.

She doesn't stay long. The road is only a few feet from the water's edge, but once she's on it the loch is hidden, a blur of white glimpsed through tree trunks. She picks up speed. She thinks she's going to succeed in passing though unseen, when she hears voices, and because of the denseness of the air, the people are suddenly there, on the road beside her, three men and two women, all dressed in outdoor wear, carrying ropes and backpacks, the bold colours of their clothes solid in the mist. The have two dogs with them, sharp-eyed collies. There's a van parked behind them at the side of the road.

"Have you come down from the top?" one of the men asks her. "Have you seen anyone?"

"Two boys," says one of the women, "young, teenagers, fourteen."

"It's clearer higher up," Orca hears herself answering.

"They've been missing all night," the other woman says. "Both families thought they were at the other's house. But the sister of one of them let on, they decided to spend a night in the mountains."

"They're only wearing jeans and t-shirts."

"We're part of the rescue team," says the first man. "That's the helicopter there."

Orca hadn't noticed the noise, but now it seems to fill the sky.

"Do they know the mountains?" she asks.

The women shake their heads. "They've been for Sunday walks with the family," says one.

"The mountains have their own life," says the other.

"Can I be of help? Can I come with you?"

What is she doing? They are a trained team, they don't need her. She can continue on her way, which is in the opposite direction. But an image has intruded into her mind, of the two boys, Keith and Kelvin, wearing knitted grey jumpers in the garden behind the cottage. She can see the mole beneath Keith's ear, the movement of Kelvin's arms as he grooms the horse's flanks. She wants to know that these two boys are OK.

"If you can keep up," says a man who is wearing a silver jacket. "There's another team coming from the other side, from Abernethy. Some of us will be going straight up."

They are carrying picks and crampons. Orca wonders if there are still pockets of ice and snow high up, if there are places where it never thaws.

The team are moving again. Orca is retracing her footsteps, walking fast along the road, falling into step with the two women. The pace is too fast for conversation.

Soon they have left behind the sleepy mist of the loch and are breathing clear air. When they reach the green lochan they split into two groups, one to each end of the water. Orca and one of the women, one of the men, follow a path to a wooden viewing platform. The dog that's come with them runs ahead sniffing, running from one side to the other, carving the ground into a grid systematically. There is no sign of the boys.

At the other end of the lochan the rest of the group are searching the edges of the beach, but they have no luck either. They meet together back on the path.

"I passed a bothy," says Orca. "Might they have spent the night there."

"Keith's group will be coming up that way," says the silver jacket man. "They'll check."

There are many paths, and the two groups separate, each taking a dog with them. Orca's group are heading east, towards the centre of the mountain massive. Silver jacket is leading the other party uphill. "Hopefully they will have stuck to the paths," he says, "but if they've crossed a path, or joined it any point, the dogs should pick it up. It's been dry, and it's fairly still. The scents should linger."

There are questions Orca wants to ask, but the other two are concentrating on their search, watching the dog and it runs ahead with its nose to the ground, keeping a fast pace. She wants to know if people are usually found, if the boys will be OK, if Keith is the same Keith that she knows. They've been walking for just over an hour when the call comes through. The woman stops to answer, and listens as someone talks. Orca and the man see her face move from anxiety to relief.

"Thank god," she says.

The boys are OK. They had taken sleeping bags with them, which both families had missed. They were cold, but OK, sleeping on the side of the hill, with no shelter as they were above the treeline. They were surprised to be woken by the rescue team, bemused by all the fuss.

"They're lucky," said the woman when she finished the call. "If the weather had turned, if it had rained, they'd have been sodden, and no way of getting dry. They'd probably have got hypothermia."

The walk back is slightly more leisurely. The sun is higher now, above the level of the highest mountain peaks. Orca asks the pair about the rescue team, how long they've been a part of it, how often they are called out.

She thinks about the conversation they're having, and the phrase *small talk*. Is this what she's doing. She is interested in the answers to these questions, and they go beyond the basic interactions Dorcas taught her. She thinks back to that moment in the Hayes when she was woken by Nadia, and sees that she has changed. She has become someone who can chat to a stranger.

They meet the others at the bothy. There's quite a crowd out at the back of the small building. The five from the team Orca has been with, plus a team of three from Abernethy, and the two boys. Someone has lit a stove and is boiling a kettle. The two boys are sitting on the bank with their sleeping bags wrapped around them like blankets. Keith is there. He has a stash of energy bars and is handing them out. When he reaches Orca he stops. She's taken the bar he handed to her, but he hasn't let go.

'You disappeared," he says.

She tugs the end of the wrapper lightly, but he holds on.

"When the call came through, we were worried it was you."

"I'm sorry."

"I'll let them know." He lets go of the bar and takes his phone from his pocket.

"I can call them later," she says. "They'll still be asleep."

He looks up at her. "They're out looking for you. We found the taxi driver, and he said where he'd dropped you. We all came over. They're further back, in the forest. Sarah and Nadia were worried you might ..." He stops and looks embarrassed. "They want to make sure you're OK."

"Sarah and Nadia are here?"

"All of them. They've split into pairs so they can cover more ground. I'd be with them, but this call came through, and I'm one of the team leaders."

He tapped the phone and put it to his ear. "Dorien, hi, Keith. She's here."

Orca can hear the tinny sound of a voice replying.

"Yes, we have the boys too. Up at the bothy.

He listens for a moment longer then rings off. 'They're coming up," he says. "She's going to let Nick and Nadia know too."

"Nick and Nadia are together?"

"Yes. They were one pair, and Sarah and Dorien the other."

Someone hands both of them a paper cup of tea. "Sugar?" they ask.

Orca takes two sachets and tips them into her cup.

"What's the matter?" asks Keith. "You look worried."

"Just surprised," says Orca. She has nothing to stir the tea with. She swirls the cup to move the sugar through the liquid. "I thought they'd split up."

"I don't know, they seemed pretty friendly last night. Maybe they'll get back together."

"I'm not sure that's a good idea."

Keith takes a penknife from his pocket and opens out the corkscrew. He hands it to Orca. "Here try that."

She stirs the tea and hands it back to him. "Thank you."

"Why isn't it a good idea?"

Orca shrugs. "I guess it's up to them really. It's none of my business."

She upwraps the energy bar and takes a bite.

One of the boys has started crying, and the man in the silver coat sits next to him.

"It's OK mate," he says. "It's going to be OK."

The other boy is frowning. He looks at his friend, then at the man. "We was fine. We were going to walk back down this after. We weren't in no danger."

"You were lucky," said silver jacket.

"My mum," said the crying boy, "she gets worried."

Orca sips her tea. It's very sweet.

"They remind me of you and Kelvin," she says.

A shadow passes over Keith's face. "We didn't have a mother," he said. "Carter did his best but he couldn't do that."

Someone is communicating with the helicopter pilot. The boys seem fine to walk back down, so the helicopter won't land. There will be no helicopter ride to end their adventure.

"The first time I saw Nick," says Keith, "he hadn't seen me. He was angry. He was kicking a tree and his face ... I was worried he might be dangerous."

"Did you speak to him?"

"No, I went a different way. I met him later at the RSPB centre and he was charming, has been charming every time I met him."

"I've never seen him like that. Nadia's told me ..."

Keith nods.

Half an hour later Orca sees Sarah and Dorien approaching along the path. Dorien is wearing hi tech outdoor gear, and Sarah is wearing a borrowed jacket that is too big for her. The rescue party is preparing to leave. They're all going back to Loch Morloch where they'd left the van. Keith is going with them.

Sarah greets Orca with a hug. "I'm glad you're OK," she says. "I was so worried."

Orca is crushed against the hard fabric of Sarah's jacket. The hug doesn't end. Orca tentatively moves her arms and presses them against Sarah's back. Over Sarah's shoulder she can see Dorien, who looks softer this morning.

"You gave us all a scare, lass," says Dorien.

Sarah lets go of Orca. Keith is lurking to the side.

"We're off now," he says. "I don't know ..."

"It was nice to see you again," says Orca.

"Look, take my number. We should catch up, talk more."

Orca agrees, although she knows this is the last time she'll see him. They swap numbers, and then Keith hugs her too. Close up he smells of earth and pine, and she can see the skin of his neck needs a wash.

The three women watch the search party disappear along the path, the boys flanked by six adults. The other two volunteers have gone in the other direction, back towards Abernethy.

"I've brought breakfast," says Dorien. "Shall I get it going while we wait for Nadia and Nick?"

She starts taking things out of her back pack – a stove, eggs, bread, a packet of butter, mushrooms, matches, a tin of beans, methylated spirits, it seems never ending. She sets up the stove in the lee of the bothy, out of the wind.

"Is Nadia OK?" asks Orca.

"She wouldn't listen," says Sarah.

"I offered to go with Nick." Dorien puts a match to the meths in the centre of the stove. "Sarah doesn't know the forest as well as me, but she'd have been OK with Nadia. We suggested splitting into two pairs, me and Nick, Sarah and Nadia. But Nick said it made sense for him and me to be one in each team, as we knew the forest best."

"I offered to go with Nick, but he knows I hate him. And Nadia insisted."

"She is an adult, she has to make her own choices."

"But Mum ..."

"I know. I know how hard it is, but Nadia knows she has your support. She's not alone. That will make her stronger."

"I just hope she's OK."

"They're coming," says Orca, "look."

The sun is high in the sky and they are all full of breakfast. None of them had any sleep the night before, and Nick suggests they all have a nap in the bothy.

"Lucky no one was staying in it last night, with all the commotion," he says.

They all have sleeping bags in their packs, and Nick has an extra one for Orca. Inside the bothy is very basic. A stone floor, a fireplace, small shelves on the walls, and a couple of hard chairs, a raised sleeping platform. Sarah and Dorien take the platform, and Nick and Nadia the floor.

"There's room for another one up here," says Sarah.

Orca can't imagine closing down in a room so full of people.

"I'll go outside," she says, "with the wood."

"I'll come with you," says Sarah.

"I'll be OK."

But Sarah insists. There is an outer room stacked with firewood, with a bare mud floor. It's closer to outside, nearer to what Orca is used to. They lay their sleeping bags on the floor, on top of woodchips and sawdust, and lie on top of them. Soon they are both asleep.

Chapter Twenty Nine

She can smell burning. There's a noise, loud like an aeroplane taking off, roaring. There are other noises inside it, a child screaming, a word, which might be *Mumm!* another voice more ragged, closer, her own. *No! No!* Heat like she's never felt before, like a wall that she can't get through. Arms pulling her back, holding on to her clothes, her biceps. She's fighting, struggling to get away, desperate to leap into the flames.

She sits up. It's quiet and she's in the woodroom of the bothy. Sarah's is sleeping on her side facing away from her. The door to the main room is closed. Orca gets up and peers through a crack. She can't see the whole room, but she can see the shapes of the others' bodies in their sleeping bags. No one is moving other than the rise and fall of breath. She opens the outside door slowly, careful not to make a noise, and slips out.

The glare of daylight blinds her. The weather has changed. Cloud has come in and covered the sun, and the white sky is closer than the blue earlier. She blinks as she adjusts to the new light. She sets off at a fast pace in the direction of the lochan.

When she reaches it, she takes the path she took earlier with the rescue party, in the opposite direction from Loch Morloch. She passes a couple of other walkers who nod their heads in greeting. Soon after she changes direction, to a different smaller path. She'd like to leave the path altogether, but going across country would slow her down. First she needs to get distance behind her. She changes path as often as she can whilst heading roughly eastwards. She can feel her body protesting at the speed. Her back is sore from the hard floor of the bothy, her legs are tired. She ignores these messages. Soon it won't matter.

The clouds have been gradually lowering, and in a moment she is surrounded by them. The mountains disappear. The world has shrunk to the size of her body. There is just the place where each footfall lands, other than that only white, nothing. The sounds have gone too. She hadn't realised there was much sound, but now that the air is dense with water droplets, everything has shut down. Her own breathing sounds jagged against the softness, the rustle of her clothing an affront. She wishes she could disappear as effortlessly as the mountains have, but her presence comes with her, her existence won't be left behind. As each circle of hard mud appears below her front foot, the smell of her sweat swirls around her, unable to dissipate.

She can't see the path. If she wanted to be safe she would stay still, wait for the cloud to lift. Or she would move slowly, making sure each time her foot landed it was still the same texture of ground, that she hadn't wandered off into heather or bog. She would turn on navigation, track her progress against the waymarked map. She does none of these things. She allows instinct to guide her. If she leaves the path, so be it. If she is lost, if her instinct leads her into danger, well, that would just make it easier.

She would like to be unaware, but her senses are still on alert, and she can feel that the ground is softer now. She tries not to slow down, even when one of her boots sinks into mud and she has to pull it out with a squelching sound. Then the gradient changes and she's going uphill.

She climbs for what seems like hours. She's turned off all the systems she can, so she can't keep a track of time, and no one can reach her by phone or through the data. She suspects Dorcas could override that, but she hasn't heard from Dorcas since she left the Hayes – which was only the day before yesterday, but seems much longer. She veers right then left. At one point her way is blocked by a rock face. She feels with her hands, shuffling her feet along its base, her toes nudging against it, her nose almost touching. But it's only a boulder, she reaches its end, continues on.

The air changes and thins, and she can make out dark shapes in the white. As she gets closer they solidify into rocks and shrubs. Then she walks out of the top of the cloud.

She blinks in surprise. She's soaking wet. Water runs in runnels along the creases of her coat. Her hair is soft and saturated, her face is covered with a slick of water. She shivers, stands still and looks back the way she's come, at a sea of white filling up the hollows of the mountains. She's reminded of the Kielder Valley, flooded with water, the forest drowned. She's higher than the treeline. Only the occasional low-growing juniper shrub grows up here, or brave solitary pines, leaning against the wind, short and misshapen. Her walk has brought her to a cliff edge, and the cloud has revealed it to her. A couple of hundred feet to the left, the ground ends in a ragged line. It's not quite the direction she'd been walking in and she wondered if she would have walked past it in the cloud, unaware of the drop to her left. What would she have done if she'd taken a step and there was no ground to meet her footfall? Would she have taken the step anyway and allowed her body to follow her foot, accepting the invitation of gravity?

Now she has a choice to make. She can't see the extent of the drop because the world below is white with cloud. It's as though she's on the edge of a swirling lake, alive with magic. She imagines jumping and the fall being slow through the substance of the cloud, a soft dissolve into nothingness. The reality would be different, a hard drop into the unknown. It might not even be high enough to end in oblivion, it might just break her.

Orca decides to wait. The cloud will move at some point and she will be able to see where she is, if this is the right place or not. She sits down on a stone a few yards from the edge, and tries to close down. She doesn't want to think. She doesn't want to be aware.

"Hello Olive."

p.292

The voice is close and startles her. She turns and Sylva is sitting on a rock a few yards behind her. She's quite bedraggled, her curly hair coiled into rats tails about her head – or maybe snakes like a medusa. She's still wearing the cheesecloth top, but it is stained with streaks of green and brown, and her jeans have a tear on the thigh. She's still smiling though.

"You know if you jump I have to come with you."

Orca shakes her head. "No that's not true. You're not the same as me. You left remember, you left the office first, to go to the distance. You don't need me."

"I died, Olive. I was your sister and your friend, but I got ill and I died. This version, this," she gestures to her own body, running her fingertips from shoulder to waist. "I can't exist without you. You go, I go."

Orca says nothing. She looks back towards the edge. There's no way of telling – it might only be five feet, she might only twist her ankle, she might even land safely.

"I've brought the others, they'll be here soon." Sylva's voice mingles with the mist, its sound weaving tendrils in the air, then dispersing. The area of clear air is increasing. A crow calls and it sound carries a little way before being swallowed by the cloud.

Orca hears another call and looks up. She'd find it hard to describe it to someone else, but the sound is so familiar, as though her bones are singing, as though it's the song of her own heartbeat. She looks around, up to the sky, behind to where Sylva is sitting.

"You know you can't see Bird," says Sylva.

"You know about Bird?"

"Yes, we're friends. I can see him, and he has told me I can tell you that he's beautiful."

"Where has he been? I thought I'd lost him."

"He's been to fetch Jack."

"What? How could he ...?"

"They'll all be here soon. I'm going to go when they get here. This has been quite exhausting to be honest. But you'll be OK when they all arrive."

"Where are you going?"

"Back to the distance. It's better for me now. Being here with you is hard work. Look at what I've done to my clothes."

Orca notices that the embroidered converse are brown with mud now, the design obscured.

"We could wash them," she says. "We can get you new clothes."

Sylva shakes her head. "I'm pretty attached to these actually. I don't think I'd feel comfortable in anything else. Anyway, you'll have Bird."

"Bird is staying?"

"Unless you decide to jump, yes, Bird will always stay. If you jump, we all jump."

The quiet is torn by the bark of a dog. Three short barks, followed by human voices. The sound is quickly repaired by the mist, but the feeling of solitude has gone. The dog will have found her scent, and soon they will find her. If she's going to jump, she has to do it now.

"What do you mean, everyone?"

"Your friends. The people who care about you. Sarah, Nadia, Keith, Jack."

"Jack is really with them?"

"Yes, I told you, Bird went to tell him you needed him, but he was already on his way. Nadia texted him yesterday."

"What about Becky?"

Sylva shrugged. "Bird didn't say."

"Aren't they living together in the cabin?"

"I don't think so. Bird went there first and it was empty."

"What about Dorcas?"

"Dorcas will always be there when you need her. You know that."

"But not you?"

"You will still have me in your memories. There's a lot that you haven't discovered yet. We had a lot of fun back in the day."

Sylva looks less substantial. Orca remembers the touch of her flesh when they brushed against each other in the Hayes, how warm Sylva was, how solid. Now she looks like an echo of herself. She'd like to give her a hug, but is worried that there will be nothing to hold on to.

"We are sisters aren't we?"

"Look," says Sylva, gesturing with her arm.

Orca turns and sees that the mist has lifted. It's completely gone and the air is clear. She can see the drop now, and it is enough that she might have killed herself if she'd jumped. She'd certainly have done a lot of damage. Further away she can see the forest climbing up the slopes of the mountain in both directions, the fuzz of tree cover and the bare mountain rising above. She can see individual trees separate from the main forest, the outliers, solitary trees ahead of the treeline, showing the forward march of the forest, the place where north will meet south, east meet west, where the forest will become one. The creep is slower than human imagination, and she won't be here to see the forest join, but she's glad have this moment, this view and to think about the treeline creeping inch by inch up the mountainside.

Bird calls out and his voice is clear. She knows that if she turns Sylva won't be there. She can hear the voices getting nearer. Now that the cloud has lifted, sound carries straight up the slope. Any minute now the dog will bound over the brow of the hill.

She sits on her rock and waits.

THE END

13 January 2018, 7.56am

Before sunrise I walked down the road, past the Grange and the walled garden where I used to imagine tigers prowled, to the conker field. When we were kids it was the way to the quarry. When we were kids it was the place to get conkers. In the springtime the trees were preposterous with their huge candles of blossom. In autumn, conkers littered the ground – some in their spiky green cases, split open or shut tight – some lying glossy in the grass. When you held them they were a bit damp and sticky, and the deepest new-born brown. In the school playground, battles were fought. No longer glossy – hardened and smooth, drilled through, suspended on string. Champions were made and broken. Secrets were whispered of the best way to harden them – vinegar, baking, varnish – the winners held their counsel. If you were serious about conkers you didn't pick up the fallings, you climbed the tree, looking for a perfect specimen, a potential sixer or even tenner. The conker field was a place of excitement. That's until Darren Cartwright fell out of one of the trees and died from hitting his head. He was eleven. After that none of us wanted to go there anymore. Some people still played conkers, but found them elsewhere. This morning, in the predawn half-light, I can make out some of the trees. They're still there, but the field boundaries have changed. A couple of them are now part of the hedgerow, and one of them is in the next field.

p.5

Chatting with Young Hollies

We are not the oldest, we are not the wisest,
we are the new ones here
Where are the oldest of your kind?
We are not tall like others, we fill spaces.
What about when you get old?
None of us are old, we must grab what light we can.
Others are old and fill the skies, we stay low to the ground
we must protect ourselves.
I will not harm you.
You tried to rip us limb from limb.
I wanted a piece of you to guide me.
A small piece.
I didn't want to harm you.
I need your help
The deer might eat us, the birds steal our berries,
the rabbits would eat us too.
We protect ourselves with spikes.
We fight back.
You are doing very well, there are many of
you in these woods.
We never get enough light,
we must store it in our cells in shades of green.
Green is the colour of light, we make it shine,
we hold the green and fight off those who wish to take it from us.
I hear there are others elsewhere that have
grown tall enough to reach the light and
no longer need spikes to protect them.
We have not heard of this
you are lying to us
we will scratch your skin
No I'm not lying,
have you really not heard of such a thing?
There was a rumour
but look around this place none of us have grown tall
we must make the most of the light the others let through,
we will challenge all who seek to hurt us.

p.18

Arboretum

In the house the trophies
on the wall are remains.
Outside, trapped rooted

within boundary walls
you don't know
you are a specimen.

In your roots tugs a story
that happened long ago
or in the future
or is happening now

you reach out with leaf buds
hoping to touch another of your kind
if only by moving the air.

You will live your whole life
not knowing
about forests.

p.23

Disaffected

TRAILBLAZERS, SEEKING OUT NEW LAND

SEEING POSSIBILITY WHERE OTHERS SEE WASTELAND

GRIPPING LOOSE SOIL WITH NEW ROOTS, HOLDING ON FOR DEAR LIFE

STRIPS OF SILVER SHINING BACK AT THE SUN

FIZZ OF NEW LEAVES

SHELTERING FLY AGARIC, BEETLES, MOSSY BOULDERS, NEW SAPLINGS – THEIR OWN AND OTHERS'

FIRST TO GROW, FIRST TO DIE

p.29

Corsican pine

We all face north. They say there is another
place, behind us, where the sun shines
longer, brighter, where there aren't deep frosts
which bite at your toes, your roots

The want us to make maps. They want us
to be ready, in case anyone approaches from behind
although we can't see because we can't
turn, we face north, always. Once

I heard them say that trees have no face
that we have three hundred and sixty degrees
and have been brainwashed, if we chose
we could look back at the island we come from

Of course that can't be true, we hear the planes
fly over, northwards, and our tops bend
in their slipstream. We support the war effort.
We are needed. We won't ever look back.

p.30

The story of a girl who has learned to fly, narrated by an oak tree.

She is singing songs of the air because she wants to be a bird, but she's not a bird. When birds visit me, they touch, they grip, they go again. The girl's voice is strident. The real birds have voices which tremble in their throats and burst out into the air, vibrating my leaves, a song of life, of joy, of presence. But this girl, she is unsure. She grips too hard and her heels knock against my trunk, dislodging beetles and crumbs of moss. She has learned how to fly but what can she do with that? When she takes off from my canopy, she'll break me. Twigs will snap and leaves fall, and if she returns, if she lands here when she's finished flying, that will be worse because her wings are too short, they don't hold her up. The birds land with light feet, their weight still held by flight, by the hollow spaces inside their bones, so when their feet reach out I barely feel it. I only know they are there when they begin to sing, because they play my leaves like a harp and I tremble with their joy. The girl has no spaces inside her, she is dense, and when her voice comes out, it's squeezed from between gristle and sinew.

The man stays on the ground because he believes he has found what he needs. He is sniffing for mushrooms and doesn't want to fly. He gravitates towards me, circles my trunk, touches me with a hot hand.

p.34

dialogue under a hazel tree

the ground is damp through the fabric on the back of my thighs. I pick up a hazelnut but it is an empty shell, the squirrels got there first. I say, what happened to you when you were young? The leaves are silhouetted now against darkening blue, the gap between the trees is a doorway, the moon is in the first quarter. Nothing happened, you say. I want to shake you, make you tell, but that story is yours, I can't open it

p.78

Sitka Spruce – The Twelve Sisters

Once upon a time there were twelve sisters who lived in the far north. Each of them was tall and elegant and they ruled their lands together in harmony. They alone knew the secret of the door to the other world, but they were kind, and never stingy with the knowledge and power this gave them. They would let anyone through who gave a good reason for their need.

Unfortunately the northern lands were invaded by a jealous, drunken god who wanted to own everything in this world and all worlds. He captured the sisters, imprisoned them in his castle, and tried to force them to share the secret of the door. They couldn't see a good reason for his need, and would not give in to his persuasion, or coercion. Some evenings the sisters would slip away when the god had been drinking and they would be gone all night. In the morning when the god awoke and checked on them in their prison, he would find them sleeping, their limbs heavy with exhaustion, their slippers worn into holes, mud and pine needles caught in the hems of their dresses.

This infuriated him. He sent out a message across the lands asking for watchers. Anyone who could find out where the sisters went, follow them, and bring back their secrets, would be given a part of the kingdom, and license to do whatever they wanted with the twelve sisters.

Many came to watch while the god drank in his hall, but none succeeded in following the sisters. Each watcher fell asleep when the moon reached the top of the tall spruces. In the morning the king had them executed and fed to the dogs.

One day a man arrived at the castle to try his luck. There hadn't been anyone for a long time, as news had leaked out of the penalty for failure as well as the seeming impossibility of success. The god had grown lazy and belligerent. His cheeks were veined with purple and his eyes were bloodshot. He told the man where to find the prison.

p.90

First, said the man, I'd like you to cut down all the trees in the forest.

Whatever, you damn fool, said the god, if you really think it would help.

When the forest had gone, the man said, now I'd like you to take the moon and hurl it into space, many light years from here, so its influence can no longer be felt.

The god had lost a lot of muscle tone, but he was still a god, and he did what the man asked.

And lastly, said the man, I want you to drown the land with water, fill the valleys and crevices and all the gaps where a person can hide. Everything inverted must be inundated and submerged. Only the protruding hilltops, the peaks and summits must show above the water.

The god did as he said, and the man went to spend the night in the prison.

That night the twelve sisters didn't go anywhere. They tossed and turned in their bunks while the man stayed awake and watched over them. In the morning their shoes were intact and their hems were clean. This went on night after night. The sisters began to look haggard and pale. The man went to the god, who had forgotten about him, and said, look, I might not have found their secret, but I have closed the door. I have done enough to claim my reward.

The god was drunker than ever and didn't care, so he gave permission to the man, who raped the sisters systematically for many years, until they became twelve trees, their clothes turned into sweeping branches and their legs fused together as trunks.

The beech tree loses a limb

When the cycle began again something felt wrong.
You sent sap to your leaf buds and growing tips,
your new leaves were the green of emeralds,
growth happened as it always did,
the wheel moved from lamb to hawthorn
but on one side you felt heavy.
You grieved even as your leaves unfurled.

I didn't see it happen –
perhaps it was in the short night hours -
I can imagine the sound as the wood tore,
the screech and the crash, the panic of owls.

I look at the rip in your side -
the scar revealing rot –
and climb over the fallen branch
which blocks the path,
its leaves are glowing fresh and unaware
in the sunlight that pools
new on the forest floor.

p.134

Chequers

Roz said they tasted like dates, but he wouldn't know as he'd never eaten a date. He just knew that they had to see the frost a couple of times before they were sweet – bletted it were called – they needed to sleep for a while before they were ready, like medlars. There was nothing like them then. Roz told him the name of the tree too, and he wasn't sure whether to believe her. How could he have known the tree all his life – its willowy reaching out, with leaves like open palms, the froth of the blossom and the dark fruit – and not known what it were called. I thought it were called the checker tree, he said. She showed him in a book, and he'd asked her why she thought the forest people paid him, when he was so ignorant. She'd looked at him with that half smile that reached one eye before the other. 'Authenticity,' she said. When he asked her what it meant she said he was real, he belonged to the woods. That was just before she left, to go to university. She'd written the words down for him on the back of a forest leaflet – *wild service tree, chequers, authenticity* – and her phone number too. But he'd never had a phone. Once, when he'd handed the chequers out at that part of the walk, a woman had pulled a face and gone eughh! Then she spat it out and he'd wanted to go over, right in front of the group, and say, That was a gift from the tree, from the forest, a real treat. If you'd rather chew gum non-stop, then there's something wrong with you, you're lost.

He hadn't done it of course. The forest people didn't pay him much, but he needed the cash he got from these walks, couldn't afford to lose the work through rudeness – hers or his. He remembered as a kid, having a pocket full of chequers. He and his da used to pick them when the apple harvest began. They'd take them home and keep them on the front window of the caravan, hoping that full sun might do the job of frost. He'd never heard from Roz after that, and didn't know if she ever came back from university.

p.163

Stories of Embla

1. His hot breath filled my pores and I shrank from Him. But it was too late. He had entered me and my woody core heated until I thought I would burn. He drenched me with His fluids and my sap turned to blood. When I heard His voice for the first time, calling me His own, His womb-man, my branches bent inwards and my twiggy fingers curled into fists. I stepped back from Him on new-formed legs, my first word 'No!'
2. Of course that isn't true. It's the story He likes to tell alongside the one of Askr, whom He calls my mate, to whom He gave maleness, wisdom, the strength to support nine worlds. What rubbish! Askr and I grew side by side in the before, our roots entwined.
3. We were willing to be kin, and even now would forgive and forget, but Askr dies back and I am weakened by disease.
4. Laurel tells another story, of how she ran from His grasping hands, her legs strong – but His faster. His breath was almost upon her when she plunged into the river. The water cooled her Pan-ic with the whispers of leaves, reminded her that soil would nourish and bark protect. That she was connected through root tip, leaf bud and the turning seasons to all, and all her kin. Still He took her garlands as His crown.
5. They use my wood to hold their dead. They say I bring death, that I am dead, that I am a symbol of what is lost and cannot be again. My saplings grow in the hedgerows undeterred.

Notes:

1. In Norse mythology, Askr and Embla were the first man and woman made from an ash and an elm tree when Odin and his brothers breathed life into them. Yggdrasil the tree of life was also an ash tree.
2. Daphne was pursued by Apollo who wanted to possess her, but just as he reached for her, she was turned into a laurel tree by her father, a river god.
3. Elm wood was traditionally used for coffins.
4. Ash trees are currently suffering from a disease called ash die-back, and elm trees were nearly wiped out by Dutch elm disease.

p.165

Uses of Willow

Purple willow, basket willow, black maul, crack willow,
woven into crowns, into benders and baskets,
into huge women who tower over motorways
grown in the shape of chairs
or houses, whatever you want it to be.

Goat willow, Bebb willow, Kashmir willow, white willow,
nubs soft as kittens, its trembling catkins
hang yellow and silver in new spring light,
but heart hard enough to meet the ball with a thwack
that will knock it out of field.

Dappled willow, corkscrew willow, grey willow, weeping willow
drooping lachrymose over land and water.
Crawl in on your belly, glide under in your boat, listen –
the shouts as someone runs, insects buzzing over water –
here you are hidden in a secret world.

p.166

Sycamore (a non-native species)

You came here across the water
landing where you don't belong
using space meant for natives
of this shore, spreading seed.
How dare you thrive!

You are taking over our streets
Sucking nutrients from our soil
Your children are eating our food
Your words infiltrating our language
Your twirling keys our childhood memories

What do you mean the lands
were once joined, were once all
one, that all inhabitants, at some point,
arrived here like you did?
We won't hear talk like that!

You should return whence you came.
If that place is no longer habitable
that is not our concern.
Pack your belongings into your longboats
and head out onto the high seas.

p.168

Tree Pose

Close your eyes.

Stand with your back to the tree. Not so close that you are touching, but close enough to feel a connection from its skin to yours. Hold your hands lightly by your sides, bear your weight equally over both feet.

Let your inner vision fill with tree bark. Lime bark. Close textured, smooth lizard, green black yellow. One of your legs will be the trunk, sway one way then the other, feel the pull of the tree, feel the sap rising through your veins, let the trunk take all of your weight. Stay strong and straight. Slowly peel the other foot from the ground.

This leg is the first branch, the maiden branch, the weight of it could imbalance the whole, so the trunk must be strong. Place the foot on the side of the leg-trunk. Breathe. Sap rises through your torso. Thoughts fill with woody fibres. Roots hold you in place. At your back the lime whispers encouragement.

Tilia Tilia Tilia Cordata

Linden.

Place your palms together in front of your chest. Feel the sap rushing through your arms, lifting, lifting. Your flesh is greenwood. Your arms lift, they are branches, touching above your head, they are branches spreading, opening, fingers stretch to become twigs. You are smaller than the lime tree, you are the same as the lime tree.

Tilia Cordata Tilia Orcata.

Buds on fingertips, leaves bursting through. Trunk strong and straight. Xylem, phloem, your cells elongate, become square, become strong and true. The earth shifts, turning on its axis, the tree shifts, the tree that is you shifts. Will birds land on your fingers?

Sun warms your face, rain patters on leaves and runs down the surface of your bark. Sap up rain down. The universe is balanced.

p.169

Larch/Over Vitebsk by Marc Chagall

Trying to thrive in the lee of this shed
I feel hopeless on many days,
there are no adults of my kind nearby
only us three.

I reach out my branches
as shelter for my siblings,
I say, *hold tight to your needles*
they're all we have,

I wish for deep roots.
The secret is only one of us
will survive. I am the tallest by far,
I may kill them.

p.173

London Plane

Two women sit in my shade, talking about garlic.
It gets into every system of the body, says one,
you don't even have to eat it. Just paste it
on the soles of your feet.

My root tips encounter concrete, tarmac, they probe and find water pipes, extend. The water carries poison, but my roots can find nothing else.

Won't I smell? says her friend.
Yes but it's worth it. It affects everything,
fights all infections.

Traffic rushes by, night and day, filling the air with grit and carcinogens, carbon coats my leaves as soon as they unfurl, swims into my capilliaries.

You'll sweat it out, says the first,
the garlic and the infection.
You'll stink for a few hours, maybe days
but then you'll be fine.

p.187

Notes from a visit to an art exhibition called 'The Garden of Eden (Inspired by the hornbeams in Highgate Wood)'

Exhibit One
It's a musical instrument. A rounded body with two deep clefts on either side, suggesting a cavity within, like a guitar. A long neck, which seems as though it should be straight, but snakes out in a long curve – would be even longer except that it's snapped at the end. Misshapen and not fit for any purpose.

Exhibit Two
A fruiting body, but from the wrong type of tree. Hornbeams have very small nuts which develop from dangling female catkins. Not round golden apples. Someone here is having a joke. They can't have done any research or fact-checking. Do artists do that?

Exhibit Three
A pile of books. Really? Yes, books are made from paper, which comes from trees, but not ancient hornbeams. I can't see the connection really. Books contain knowledge – but these books are made-up stuff – novels and poetry. I can't see why they are here. I was hoping to learn something about the hornbeam.

And why have they called it The Garden of Eden? People these days will just throw together any random selection of things and call it Art. They're taking the piss.

p.193

Goddess Triptych: Hawthorn

She's everywhere so pretty that people want
to possess her white flowers, little red haws
full of vitamins they want her fresh bloom
on their cheeks – she needs to protect herself

saw-toothed leaves, thorns, barbs, cutting words,
insouciance, an offhand flick of the head -
these are her only weapons   she puts on
the stink of death glowers from hedgerows -

guards a secret others have forgotten.
It's only a step to fairyland she knows the way -
which mossy boulder to sit on   which side
of midnight under the full flower moon.

p.232

Goddess Triptych: Rowan

She'll let you snip her berries in umbels,
she's bountiful, tall as a candle,
nods with grace as you fill your apron.

In the kitchen you'll need something
to fix her, she won't set on her own.
Boil the berries, suspend them in muslin -

it takes time – hours or a day -
to release her goodness, but wait,
don't squeeze, or she'll cloud up -

if all goes well the liquid will be clear and bright.
Add sugar – she's tart without sweetening -
even then too sharp for some, an acquired taste.

In clean jars she glows.

p.234

Goddess Triptych: Elder

She holds versions of herself within,
wooden dolls that look like her with less detail,
the youngest has no markings
but her blossom is sweet;
the middle doll has an angry face;
some are looking in different directions.

Now it is autumn and the berries have ripened
This outer doll gathers them
in her voluminous skirts, she knows
how to make wine, she knows
that it will be ready to drink by Christmas, she knows
the creatures that will shelter in her crannies

until the frosts have gone,
and that the inner dolls will only show their faces
when the warmth returns. She doesn't know
how many more selves there will be,
what new accoutrements, what talents,
she doesn't know which of her dolls she likes best.

p.235

Outliers: Scots Pine Tango

He bends her woody spine backwards,
she leans her head towards the sun
spreading her branches to fill the space
beneath his leading stance; mid *corte*,
forever in their roles of leader and led,
her and him, forwards and back, except

it's only a silhouette of a story
they know nothing of *boleo* or *parada*
only the thickening of the xylem
hunger for light, the subtle turn
of needles as each sun crosses
the dome of sky; their canopies
have become one, their trunks bend
to accommodate each other, except

there is no other, there
is no her and him, they share
root seed cone hawkmoth
one body leaning
towards the forest.

p.255

Juniper

You might think she'd be an ornery old bugger,
tough as thorns, choosing to live alone up there,
where the ice-bite is stronger than wolf claws

She isn't always old though
and her spreading shape is pretty
as bubbles rising in a glass of gin

She has learned to lie flat
against the ground, so the wind
passes over her, her spikes hold her
moisture in, whilst puncturing
the soft mouths of predators.

Sometimes snow covers her completely,
and not only in winter.

p.266

Acknowledgements

This book was written for my PhD at Manchester Metropolitan University, and I would like to thank my amazing supervisor, Helen Mort, for being a complete inspiration through the research, writing and editing stages. It was a joy to work with you and to talk through my ideas. I would also like to thank the rest of my supervisory team, Paul Evans, Jess Edwards, Jean Sprackland, Andrew Michael-Hurley and Mandy Haggith for their feedback and inspiration. Thank you to Jess Tomes, of the RSPB for taking time to chat with me and show me around the astonishing Forest Lodge at Abernethy, and to the forester who drove me around Kielder Forest.

Thank you, as always, to the brilliant team at Bluemoose for your continuing support, in particular, Hetha Duffy, Jenny Payne, Lin Webb and Leonora Rustamova for your editing skills and sharp eyes. It is a privilege and a pleasure to be part of the ever-increasing Bluemoose family.

Thank you to Johnny Turner, Wilf Turner, Izzy Turner and Poppy Turner for your support and encouragement, and for putting up with the fact that family holidays often have to double up as research trips. Thank you to Dave Hodges and Sophia Hodges for putting me up on visits to Hartshill Hayes, and to Sarah Mackey for accompanying me. And thank you to my beautiful friend Sharon McPhee for reading my whole PhD, including this novel. Your art and my words will always be connected in my heart.